Punishment for the Crime

Punishment for the Crime

TAMMY JO ECKHART

RHINOCEROS

First Rhinoceros Edition 1996

First Printing June 1996

ISBN 1-56333-427-5

Manufactured in the United States of America
Published by Masquerade Books, Inc.
801 Second Avenue
New York, N.Y. 10017

To Tom, my husband, my lover, my best friend, often my inspiration, and always my favorite editor.

Punishment for the Crime

Best Friends

"Did I ever tell you that I hate men?" I suddenly say, then take another drag on my cigarette.

Beth sets her cola down and shrugs. "Maybe that's why you haven't gotten laid lately." .

"Yeah, like I'm really looking for that," I reply. I watch the smoke drift up from the cigarette as I hold it over the ashtray. My stomach tightens, so I crush out the cigarette. I feel Beth's eyes on me now. I never waste my fix like this. "I haven't scened in months," I tell her.

She nods as she pushes her tuna sandwich around list-lessly on her plate. "Yeah, me too. It's been dry around here since the summer started."

"I thought that club was a good place to pick up women." I push my own salad back.

Beth just shrugs.

Several minutes pass in silence as we wait for the bill.

Around us, I swear I hear the mundanes whispering. Sure we look odd in our black leather jackets, black shorts, and white T-shirts in this heat wave. Beth is certainly drawing a few glances at her collar. I wonder why she wears it in this heat, but then I'm not quite as flashy as she is. I mean, she is the one with bright yellow hair, not me.

"I'll take care of it," I say, snatching up the bill.

Beth frowns, then leans across the table. "Then you gotta go out with me tonight."

"I don't know," I begin, but she interrupts.

"It's a fucking Friday night, Nicky! You gotta go," she whines, and I can feel several pairs of eyes swinging our way. "There's an auction tonight," she adds.

Now I roll my eyes and stand up. Ignoring her, I take the bill to the cashier and pay it. I'm taller than her, and I walk faster, so it takes her half a block to catch up with me.

"Nicky!" She grabs my jacket, so I stop. "Come on, I'll pay the entrance fee and buy anything you want to drink," she offers.

I just roll my eyes. An auction will not get me what I need.

"We can go dancing afterwards," she adds hopefully.

Beth is beautiful, or would be if she stopped trying so hard to look different. Under that dye job there is light brown hair that matches her light brown eyes. Most men would classify her as gorgeous, but then that's one of the reasons she dresses like this. The other is because her ex-lover Gina was a punk, and Beth still isn't over her.

"That is the new love of your life?" Nicky whispered to her roommate as they got more snacks for their guests.

"Yeah," Beth replied with a sigh. "Isn't that hair cool?"

Nicky shrugged as she emptied more ice cubes into the serving container.

"I, uh," Beth lowered her eyes as she spoke, "she asked me to move in with her and I said yes."

"What?" Nicky whispered back harshly. "We've only lived here for two months. This is our first party in our first real house," Nicky reminded her.

"I know," Beth repeated, tapping one foot anxiously. "Gina says I don't have to pay rent, so I can still keep up my half of the mortgage."

Nicky pursed her lips in disapproval and turned to refill the ice trays.

"God, now you're angry with me." Beth pouted as she stared at the tray of veggies and dip.

"Our guests are hungry," Nicky replied. She looked over her shoulder after her housemate left. A growl escaped from her throat as she watched her best friend kneel at the punk's feet and gaze up at her worshipfully.

"Come on," she whines, stomping her foot. "I'll even buy you a pack of those cancer sticks."

I smile finally. "Okay. But we get the cigarettes first," I insist as we continue walking down the street.

We pause and enter every kinky store on our trek back to the train. Everyone knows us in these stores. Most of them offer us hugs, question Beth about the club she is manager of for the summer—a new lesbian SM club downtown which is scheduled to open next month—or ask me when the new book is coming out. Both still in graduate school, we are doing very well in the careers we came here to pursue in the first place. Who would have thought that a business major and an English major would have so much in common?

The two roommates glared at each other as the confused young man left their dorm room. The redhead placed her hands on her hips. "What gives you the right to yell at my boyfriend?"

"Boyfriend?" Beth replied with indignation. "Why didn't you tell me you had a boyfriend?"

"You didn't ask," Nicky retorted.

"I have to ask that?" Beth asked in surprise.

"It's something most people assume," Nicky stated matter-of-factly.

"Not people like me," Beth replied.

Nicky sighed and threw her hands up in the air. "Well, now you know," she said, walking to her bedroom.

"Don't walk away from me!" Beth ordered as she followed her and slammed the door behind her.

"Don't do that!" Nicky yelled, clenching her fists tightly and pounding them into her legs, counting to ten to calm herself.

Beth smiled slightly and moved closer. "Are you angry?" she asked softly.

"Of course, I'm angry!" Nicky screamed. "You insult my boyfriend of two years and expect me not to be angry?"

The other freshman frowned again. "See, you have to go and bring him up and ruin everything."

"Ruin everything?" Nicky looked at her roommate and remembered her boyfriend's earlier comments. "You have a crush on me?" she asked in shock.

"Well, why not?" Beth replied, unsure how to answer. She knelt next to the bed and quickly pulled out the hidden stash of books and magazines.

"Get away from there!" Nicky ordered as softly as she could, as she collapsed onto the floor and grabbed the box.

"We like the same music, the same food, the same clothes," Beth nodded at the collection, "the same kinky sex."

The two roommates stared at each other in silence.

Finally the redhead stood up. "Kinky stuff? This is just some research I'm doing," she lied.

"I know those magazines; I've heard of John Preston," Beth stated. "Why would a straight woman read this stuff?"

Nicky blinked a few times and looked at the box, then back at her roommate. "But this is gay guys' stuff," she said, as though it explained everything.

"Yeah, so you're a lesbian who can't find the good stuff," Beth replied with a smile as she stood up. "I know some places. Remember, I'm from around here."

"But, Beth," Nicky interrupted. "I read this stuff and imagine that I'm the top. There are so few things about women tops and men bottoms."

Beth's smile fell as she listened to her roommate explaining why she read the books and what she pictured when she read them. "So, you really are straight?" she finally asked.

"Last time I checked," Nicky replied. She sat on her bed next to her roommate. "I mean, if it doesn't bother me if you're gay, I don't see why my being straight should ruin our new friendship."

"Well," Beth sighed as the other placed one arm around her shoulders. "I can try to be nicer to James if you don't mind me having a little crush on you," she suggested, a twinkle in her eyes.

Nicky sighed and nodded. "Only if you read my writing. I write down some of my fantasies about that stuff," she said with a nod toward the box sitting on the end of the bed. "I could use some feedback."

"Is it all straight?" Beth asked with a half-grin.

"Mostly," Nicky replied with a slight blush. "I hint at some bi stuff, but I don't know what to write."

Beth smiled. "Asking the business major to help the full-ride English major?" she mused out loud. "Sounds fun.

Hey," she said, standing up, "can I get a date and the four of us go out tonight?"

Nicky sat for a moment, then nodded. Her boyfriend would break up with her a month later when she refused to change roommates.

Beth nudges my arm as she tries to look under it and into the bathroom mirror. "I'll be ready in just a minute," I tell her with a chuckle of frustration.

"This is fine," she says as she puts two more earrings into each lobe. Then she stands up straight as I move out of the way. "You think I shouldn't go like this?" she half states and half asks me.

I sigh, then nod. "I think it would help you forget if you changed the way you look. Don't you want to move on?"

"Get back here, slave!" the blue-haired punk screamed as she stood in the doorway of the split-level brownstone. The upstairs neighbors leaned out of their windows to stare at the commotion below.

Nicky pushed her former roommate behind her. "Get out of here, Gina, before I call the cops!"

"You get out of my way!" the older woman ordered. "That is my property, and I'm taking her home!"

"I'm calling the cops!" one of the neighbors yelled down.

Nicky pushed the punk back as she drove toward the crying Beth. "Get out of here! I am not repeating that again!" Nicky kicked open her apartment door with one foot. "Get inside, Beth!"

"Stay right where you are, Beth!" Gina countered.

The frightened young woman stood where she was, one arm cradling her stomach and the other covering the growing bruise on her face.

"She isn't yours anymore, Gina." Nicky softened her

tone, trying to reason with the punk. "Beth called me, and I came and picked her and her suitcases up. You saw me there...."

"I saw you stealing my stuff!" Gina yelled.

"We didn't take anything that's yours," Nicky replied, her voice losing its reasoning edge.

"She's mine!" Gina stated as she made another lunge.

Nicky responded as two years of self-defense and martial arts had taught her. Blocking the punk's attack, she used the energy to throw the woman onto her back. When the woman advanced again, Nicky threw one punch that knocked her out cold.

"The police are on their way!" the neighbor yelled down again.

"Great!" Nicky yelled back as she placed one arm around her best friend, preventing her from rushing to her abuser's side.

"We have time before things really get going at the club," I tell her. "I'll help."

Beth is tapping her foot again, a sure sign of nervousness. "Okay," she agrees softly. "But I don't know what I'm going to do about my hair."

I point to the linen closet and walk to it. Opening it, I find what I bought the day after I brought her back to our place. I turn around and hand her the bottle the beautician promised would get rid of that sickening color. "I thought you'd never ask."

The club is dark and warm, already crowded in anticipation of the auction. Beth is wearing her plain chain collar, a simple crop top, and short shorts. It's obvious that she is looking: what for I'm not sure, because this is the het hours at this club. I hope my outfit sends out less inviting signals.

To make sure, I gather my jacket tighter around me.

"Come on," Beth hisses as she grabs my hand and hurries me to a table, the only available one left. She presses her club dollars into my hand. "You'll have more options than me."

I look around the club and realize that it's true. All around me there are scores of bottom men, many of whom will humiliate themselves up on the block tonight just for the shot at a five-minute scene. I've bought a few. I was always disappointed, very disappointed. They couldn't take a heavy scene and often, if they saw you at another club or another event, they would follow you around, expecting you to pay attention to them. Fuck relationships; I just want someone to pound on every now and then.

Poor Beth; every relationship she's had has failed. First because she didn't tell them about her kink until well into the courting. All of them dumped her, calling her terrible names. Then she focused on the leather dykes, but found a lot of them wanted that lifestyle shit the old guard preaches.

Those new-age prophets aren't great either, with all their talk about emotions and safe sex. Hell, sometimes I just want to beat someone, then go home and get off. Why look for a relationship that will only bring you down? I wonder what Beth wants, after her last attempt ended so miserably.

"I gotta go for a moment," Beth whispers, then slinks off into the crowd.

I pull my jacket tighter around me and glare at this man who makes a move toward the table. I move the empty chair and place my feet firmly on it.

The lights dim down in the club so that the main focus is the platform in the middle of the room. I sigh and look around for Beth. No sign of her anywhere.

The people up for sale are the usual collection. Mostly men, claiming to be bottoms or sub, but really interested in only one or two activities; most shudder whenever a gay man bids. Almost all are snatched up by the pros that cruise these places for potential clients. A few of these pros go up themselves. The bids for them far outweigh those for the men.

I look around again for Beth, cursing her for leaving me here alone. Then I see her, and my mouth drops open.

She walks up onto the platform and poses. The crowd goes wild when they hear she's a bottom, a heavy bottom just looking for a rough time. I get worried very quickly when the bidders turn out to be men. In contrast to the men who were up for sale earlier, the crowd has blatantly ignored Beth's sexual orientation statement. Not that that is a surprise.

"What the fuck!" Nicky exclaimed as she walked into the middle of her dorm room to find her boyfriend and her roommate lip to lip.

"Get him off of me!" Beth yelled as the young man backed up, his hands raised. She pulled her torn shirt closer to her body and ran to her own room.

Nicky just stared at her boyfriend as he muttered an explanation.

"Come on, it wasn't anything. Just testing her out, you know, seeing if she really is gay," he said casually. "You know, I'd have thought you'd be happy that I was trying to set her straight."

"What?" Nicky asked as she moved to the end table by their brightly colored sofa.

"Hey, it's not like we're going steady," he added. "But if you don't like it, I know lots of my friends would be willing to help us. Ouch!" he yelled as the book from the end table struck his arm. "What are you doing?"

"Get out!" Nicky yelled as she picked up another book from the stack, conveniently left there from studying last night.

"Hey, this jealousy thing won't fly with me, doll," the guy replied, the look on his face showing how full of himself he was.

"Get out!" Nicky screamed as the next book struck his head.

With a curse the jock ran from the room.

Nicky shut and locked the door after him. When she looked up, her roommate was watching her from her open bedroom door. "I'm sorry," they both said as they crossed the distance between them to hug each other and reassure each other that they were all right.

Fucking chudwahs! I sit up, then stand, to try to get a clearer look at her face. She hadn't been expecting this. She brought me to a mostly straight club tonight, not one of the ones she usually cruises. I look down at the wad of club cash she handed me and quickly add it up. Each bill is worth twenty-five points—you get five when you enter—but Beth somehow had at least four times that amount.

"Three hundred!" I yell out. The crowd turns around and stares at me, as does Beth. Soon the bid rises to six hundred, and I growl as I make my final bid. The last man bidding against me grins as he waves his hand of cash at me and ups the bid.

Beth's eyes are locked onto mine, and I hit the table with my hand. Suddenly several piles of club cash land on the table. It's the pros, offering their saved dollars. One of them sits down and counts it out quickly. With muttered thank-yous I start bidding again.

The crowd loves it, and soon it becomes a war, half of them siding with me and the other half with him. Beth is leaning into the arm of the auctioneer as the bids spiral out of control. Finally I bid the entire amount I have.

Everything goes silent as the other side counts. Then the

man who had been bidding against me slams his fist into the table with a curse about those fucking bitches. I go forward to collect my prize, hands pat me as the crowd parts, and I feel dizzy from the excitement.

Beth smiles as she hops off the stage and wraps her arms around me.

"You bitch," I snap, but she only giggles and leads us toward the St. Andrew's Cross.

"You want me to take off my shirt, Ma'am?" she asks with a mock curtsey.

"Stop it," I tell her in a low voice.

"Good," Beth replies with a grin. "I was afraid you would take this seriously," she says, but I sense she is disappointed. She motions to a member of the crowd standing nearest us, and one of the men up earlier in the auction hurries over and kneels at her feet.

"You bought someone?" I ask, suddenly very confused.

"For you, Ma'am," she says, her arms making an elaborate model's move as she points down at the man.

He looks like every other guy in this place. Leather jock pouch, chain collar, a desperate look in his eyes. Not what I need. I look at Beth and see the sincerity in her eyes. "I'm a sadist," I state. "Hey," I poke his knee with the toe of my boot, "I said I'm a sadist."

"That's what she told me, Mistress," the man replies.

"Don't call me that," I snap back and turn to walk away.

"Oh, you think I got him for you to top," Beth suddenly says. I stop in my tracks, wondering how she'll cover this. "No, I want you to teach me how to top him," she says slowly.

I turn around with a chuckle. "So you want to learn to top?"

"Sure," she says, her foot tapping slightly as she speaks, "switches seem to have more luck in the lesbian scene."

"Lesbians!" the man exclaims as he scrambles to his feet. Somehow he seems more excited at the thought.

"Yeah," I say as I pull Beth close to me, "this is my girl-friend and together we're going to give you the ride of your life." I roll my eyes and remove my arm. Both of them just stare at me. "Okay, come on," I say as I shift the weight of my toy bag on my arm.

"Why not here?" Beth says, placing one hand on the cross.

"Nah, you need more privacy for your first scene," I tell her.

I motion her ahead of me and take the opportunity to fuck with the man's head. "You know, it's her first time. Things might get out of hand," I tell him. He looks at me with wide, frightened eyes. "But don't worry," I continue, "I know first aid, and the hospital isn't far from here."

By the time Beth has the man securely fastened to the spanking horse, he is definitely sweating. I feel a tingle of excitement as he looks at us in fear. Maybe this will be an okay night after all.

"They don't wear much clothes, do they?" Beth says as she takes out my paddle.

"We don't have to do this if you're not comfortable," I point out to her, holding my hand out for the toy.

Beth shakes her head, the one set of earrings in her ears jingling slightly. "No, I want to learn," she insists with a quiver in her voice.

I lean down and look at the man. "You sure you want to do this?"

"Yes, Miss…" he replies and bites back the title.

I move to his rear and place a hand over his tailbone. He shudders beneath me. "Don't hit here; don't ever hit here," I instruct Beth as I take her hand and place it where mine has just been. "The best place is right here." I take a little swat, which lands right in the middle of both cheeks, right where the ass curves down, right over the anus.

"Like this," Beth says as she swings back with the paddle.

"No," I say, taking her hand. "Start with your hand. It will help you get a feel for where to aim. And keep your other hand over the tailbone until you learn," I tell her.

I step back and watch as she takes a few tentative swings. As she seems to get more confident, I encourage her to strike harder.

"It hurts," she whines, shaking her hand.

I tilt my head and lean down toward the man. "You got a safeword?"

He nods. His face is already covered with sweat and glowing from pleasure.

"You want to share it with me?" I ask.

"Red," he replies.

I sigh. At least this one seems to understand what a safeword is; most of these losers don't have a real clue about the scene. "Make sure you say it if this gets too intense for you," I remind him.

Beth has stopped and is listening and watching. "Double-checking safewords," I inform her as I hand her the paddle.

There is another bench nearby, so I sit on it to watch. In a place like this, it doesn't take long for another man to walk over and ask me to spank him. Politely I turn him away, but he refuses to leave. Big surprise. I tell him that I'm busy, and he purposely steps between me and Beth's first topping scene. I stand up, and he walks away, muttering something about lesbians that it is probably best I can't fully hear.

Beth has stopped briefly and is wiping the sweat from her eyes. She glances at me and smiles. She swats the man's ass as he pushes it back, eager for more. With a set smile, she lays into him hard with the paddle until he can be heard grunting.

Actually, he isn't that bad. He looks to be in his thirties but has a full head of hair. His stomach looks leaner than most around here. He thrusts back and begs for another slap when Beth pauses again.

"What else do you like?" I ask him as I crouch down next to his head. Suddenly I'm feeling dizzy with hunger. He arches his back and moans as I drag my long fingernails down his back, leaving faint red lines. "Do you like that?"

"Yes," he whispers hoarsely. "Yes, please, more," he pleads.

I stand up and look at my housemate. "He wants more."

"I need a break," Beth tells me as she hands me the paddle. "This is hard work," she adds.

I just chuckle softly as I place the paddle back into my bag. "You have a problem with my doing you now?" I ask him in a husky voice.

"Please, yes," he responds.

I trace over the lines already on his back with my fingernails again. The heat from the tiny welts travels up my fingertips and down to my groin. I move my hand to his ass, bare except for the tiny leather strap holding on his pouch. I note how taut it is pulled and weave my other hand into his hair.

"Tell me you like this," I demand as I pull his head back by his hair. He swears he does, so I release him, causing him to moan in disappointment.

"This one might actually be worth something," I tell Beth as she stands over me, watching.

"Do you mind?" she asks, her chest heaving as my other hand adds another set of ridges to his back.

"Watch all you want," I tell her, "just don't get in my way." I place my hands on the reddened areas of his ass.

The heat there is less pleasing to me, because I didn't cause it. I stand up only to move behind him, and lean over him, our legs resting on top of each other.

I reach around and drag my nails harshly along his sides. He moans and bucks back into me. I feel his ass press against my mound, and I feel the wetness begin.

"Hey!" the dungeon master says as he looks directly at me. I step back to show him that my jeans are on and that I'm not wearing a strap-on. "Make sure it stays that way," he warns me.

As I settle back down, I glance out of the corner of my eye to find Beth sitting wide-legged on the other bench, one of her hands resting on an inner thigh.

"You want to see how a lesbian gets off?" Beth asked Nicky as she shoved the manuscript back into her hands.

The other roommate glanced around their suite for a few minutes.

"Well, do you? Because this isn't it," Beth stated flatly.

"I based it on what I do," Nicky began to explain.

"And it ain't quite right. At least, not for a bottom," Beth replied. She stood up and walked to her open bedroom door. "Remember, I'm an exhibitionist." She reminded her roommate of the conversation on that topic they just had last week.

Nicky looked at her writing, then sighed and stood up. Her professors told her over and over to write what you know and research what you don't. When she walked into her roommate's room, she just repeated that over and over to herself.

Nicky sat down in her best friend's desk chair. She felt her face flush as the other young woman removed her clothes.

"I like to get completely naked," Beth explained as she removed her panties. She stood for a moment, then lay on her bed. Slowly she let her fingers brush over her skin. Her nails left red lines along her stomach and breasts. Her breath quickened as she pinched each nipple, first one at a time, then together. She reached out over the side of the bed. "Can you hand me my toys?" she asked.

Nicky stood up slowly and went to the trunk at the foot of the bed, where all of Beth's kinky items were hidden. Nicky glanced up and hurried to the bed when she saw her roommate's hand disappear between her legs.

Beth took the box and laid it next to her on the bed. She reached inside and took out two nipple clips.

Nicky glanced around her nervously as Beth placed the first one on, moaned, and thrust up into her hand. When the other was finally in place, Nicky felt her stomach tighten. She closed her eyes and tried to calm the empathy pains in her own body. Only a few minutes more passed before the redhead had to leave the room. Outside the door, away from the visual image, she enjoyed the sounds of tortured pleasure.

Suddenly the man isn't there; he's just an object, a means to push Beth. I keep my eyes on her as I continue to scratch the belly and sides and even legs of the body under me. Soon Beth is rubbing herself through her shorts, her head nodding back and forth in time to the man's attempts to escape my fingernails.

I lie down on top of the body and reach all the way underneath it. The nipples are firm and eager. I take each between two of my nails and pull down on them until a cry of pain escapes from its throat. One of Beth's hands has reached inside her crop top and she repeats the actions I'm doing. As I pull harder on the nipples, Beth's head tosses back and forth, and her moans join in with the many cries from around the room.

"Red!" That one word snaps me from my half-dream state. I stop touching the body, which is once again a man, and get off him. I push my hair back from my face with both hands, take a deep breath, and crouch down to unfasten his ankle cuffs. When I move to the front, I notice that Beth has collapsed onto the floor and is watching me like a lost puppy.

"Sorry about that," I mumble to the man as I unfasten his hands.

"It was great," he replies as he stands up, the proof of his statement jutting forth, threatening to break his posing pouch. I let him kiss the back of my hand, then pick up my bag.

I stand in front of my roommate for a moment, then motion toward the exit with my head.

Beth just stands up, straightens her shorts a bit, and follows me out of the club. Once outside we begin walking toward the main streets.

"Ice cream?" Beth guesses correctly as we walk.

I simply nod. I feel like I want to say something, but I'm not sure what.

When I take out a cigarette she tells me that I'm going to die. I chuckle and stuff my hands into my jacket pockets, letting it hang on my lips.

Beth moves closer and crooks her arm inside mine. I don't pull away as I normally would at this time of night. No mundanes around to freak, yet I don't seem to mind such an intimate touch so much. In fact, I loosen my arm so she can get closer. It feels right for Beth to be this close.

I immediately realize that the next time she asks me to scene, I'll say yes. I don't feel frightened or pressured anymore. But I'll be damned if I ever admit just how wet this evening has made me.

"So," Beth breaks the silence as she stops in front of an

open ice cream store. "If I buy you a double scoop of anything you want in a waffle cone, will you go to the club's opening next month?"

I pause just a second. "Make it a large sundae and you have a deal," I tell her.

"Yes, Ma'am," Beth says as she opens the door for me.

As I step inside, I realize that I might be too limited. Maybe it isn't all one-night stands or heartbreaking relationships. Maybe there is something in between. I point to three flavors of ice cream, and Beth reads their names to the saleslady. Contented, I nod my head. A best friend, a hot scene, and a triple chocolate sundae. What more could a woman want?

One Chance

#12906 tried to wipe the dirt from his eyes but only succeeded in moving it to his already filthy forehead. The break bell rang again. He straightened his back slowly and laid the pick across the mine walls. He trudged into line and headed for the water trough.

It was hard to tell what any of the mine slaves looked like under years of dirt and filth, but the new guard kept her eyes peeled for the bright neon green tag marked #12906. She threw her staff in front of him as he was about to pass and waved those behind him on.

#12906 waited with downcast eyes as the other slaves passed. He only glanced up when she struck his shoulder lightly with her staff.

"I hear you give good foot massages, boy," the guard said, her voice holding a challenge for him.

#12906 waited for the guard to sit on her post chair, then

23

knelt in front of her black shiny boots. He carefully removed one boot, setting it on the rocks. He gently rubbed her foot, starting at the heel and working up to the toes. At her word, he replaced the boot and turned his attention to the other foot.

Through trial and error, he had learned to perform this task perfectly in the three years he had been in the mines. It was a chance at better rations, a chance to work in a better area, a chance for a kind word or two. Slowly he had earned these small benefits, but none of them made up for the harsh reality of mining. Every day he served one of the guards and prayed that their superiors would hear something about him and give him a chance to get out of this living grave.

"Stand up, boy!" the guard ordered when the massage was done. She handed him a cup of water. "You do that real good for a scum bucket like yourself."

"Thank you, ma'am," he whispered, handing back the empty cup.

#12906 fell back into line as the slaves returned from break. As he picked up his pick, he glanced at the new guard. "Please," he mouthed softly as he struck the mine wall with the pick.

As the work day dragged on, his mind returned, as it did every day, to his old life on the farm of his former owners. At the break of sunrise, all the farmhands would be herded from their barracks to the mess hall, where they ate a meal rich in grains and whole milk. Then they would be sent out in groups to do the various work. These groups rotated their job assignments every week so the work was never boring. In the fifteen years of his life on the farm, he had helped deliver newborn livestock, plant crops and care for them, harvest crops, mend buildings and machinery, and fight off insects and flood waters. For all the muscle aches and sunburns and frozen bones, the memories once more caused him to cry.

Hitting the wall in anger, he cursed the day his old master had his heart attack—the day everything started going downhill on the farm. At least as a home-born slave he had been one of the last sold off. He didn't know how he could have survived more than the three years he figured he had been in the mines. As he coughed again, he felt the terror inside that told him he could not survive for much longer in the coal dust and damp cold air.

#12906 glanced up as something struck his shoulder. He lowered his eyes in the presence of the new guard and another, obviously higher ranking, guard.

"This is the one?" the superior asked. "Look up, boy!" he ordered.

#12906 looked up, keeping his eyes straight ahead. He only moved when the man's hands pushed or pulled him in a direction.

"What do you think, sir?" the guard asked.

"I'll take him to show the captain. You may have gotten yourself a bonus, private," the man answered. "Follow me, boy!"

#12906 followed the guard out through the maze of tunnels. At the mouth of the mine, he threw up his arms to shield his eyes from the sunlight he had not seen in three years. The guard took his arm and steered him across the plain to a wooden building.

They entered an office where a man in a more decorated uniform sat behind a desk. "Bring it forward," the captain motioned.

The guard pushed #12906 toward the desk.

The captain stood up slowly. "It's hard to tell under all that dirt, but I think we might have a winner, lieutenant."

"Yes, sir." The lieutenant took a piece of paper from his jacket. "Here is the report, sir."

The captain took the paper and looked it over. "Boy, tell me why you are in the mines. What crime did you commit?"

"I did not commit a crime, sir," #12906 answered softly.

"Then why are you a slave?"

"I was born a slave, sir."

"Why are you in the mines?"

"My masters had to file for bankruptcy, so we were all sold," the slave answered as truthfully but as briefly as possible. He had learned that was the best way to survive in his lifetime.

The captain sat on the edge of his desk. "Clean my boots off, then give me that massage you're famous for."

#12906 looked down at the boots, just slightly dusty. He knelt and glanced up at the captain. "Sir, I am filthy."

"Then use your tongue, boy." The captain lifted one boot so it touched the slave's lips.

The slave swallowed once as he looked at the dirt. It didn't look like coal dust, and he had certainly been made to eat that in his years in the mine. He took a deep breath and began to lick each boot so clean it shone. The captain handed him a wet towel and ordered him to wipe off his hands after he inspected his boot. Then #12906 removed the boots, careful not to get them dirty again. He slowly massaged the captain's feet until they were pulled from his hands.

"That's enough." The captain picked up his boots and returned to his chair. "Get him cleaned up, lieutenant. I'll call her."

"Yes, sir." The guard tapped #12906 on the shoulder and led him back outside.

#12906 looked in the mirror. He touched his reflection gingerly, marveling at just how much dirt he had been covered by. His skin was slightly red from the scrubbing he had been given by a couple of silent slaves. His body had matured, and his muscles were firm from the hard labor. Not an inch of fat was visible, nor were his cheeks rosy from the sun as they had been when he lived on the farm. Even though he was naked, he did not look over the rest of his body. That prohibition from his farm days remained.

"My God! You're Caucasian!" the lieutenant exclaimed as he entered the bath chamber.

#12906 turned with lowered eyes to the guard. His hands remained at his sides, where he had learned they should be since being in the mine. They still clenched with embarrassment, though, as the guard took a few minutes to look him over carefully.

"Follow me," the guard said simply and turned on his heel.

#12906 hurried after the guard. He stood on the line the man motioned to. He glanced around the room under his eyes. It was white and bare. Mirrors lined the wall facing him.

The voice of the captain floated out into the room. "Have him turn around slowly."

When #12906 was facing away from the mirrors, he heard the captain's voice again. "Bend down, hands on your knees. Spread your legs. Stand up and face the mirrors."

The slave obeyed stiffly, as though it took great willpower to make his body display itself as commanded. Tears welled up in his eyes as he bent and moved at order.

The captain turned to the cloaked woman standing next to him. "What do you think, Your Majesty?"

"Have him trained completely," said a low, seductive feminine voice.

"You don't want a closer look?" the captain asked carefully.

"No." A tanned, long-nailed hand reached out from the cloak, commanding silence. "Train him completely, then bring him to me."

"As you wish, Your Majesty," the captain replied. He pressed a button and spoke to the lieutenant, "Get him ready."

#12906 found himself in a black room. He tried to move his arms but felt straps around his upper arms and wrists. Similar restraints were on his legs. Light suddenly flooded the room, causing him to close his eyes from the sudden pain. He heard two figures approach him. When they stood over him, his eyes had adjusted enough that he was able to recognize their faces from the branding and piercing he had suffered right after his display in the mirrored room.

The woman smiled and ran her fingers through his hair. "You passed out when the first nipple was done. Don't worry, we did the other while you were unconscious."

The man stood on the other side of #12906. "Do you remember why you are here, boy?"

"Yes, sir. To be trained," #12906 whispered.

"We should use his name," the woman pointed out.

"Do you remember your name, boy?" the man asked.

#12906 thought for a moment before answering. "Yes, sir. My former masters called me Les."

"How very quaint," the man mused. "If you learn well, perhaps your new master will give you a new name."

"We should begin now," the woman said. She unbuckled the straps that held Les down. The man helped the slave to his feet and led him to a mirror. The woman had a thin stick, with which she pointed to his body. "These are the nipple piercings. High gauge to hold a lot of pressure. Your nipples will become used to them, and to much more. Spread your legs. These are the PA and the guiche. These too will become comfortable to considerable pressures."

Les's face reddened in embarrassment as he watched his body in the mirror. The odd sensations these rings produced made his wince in shame more than pain.

"The purpose of this training," the man began speaking as they led the slave to a low couch, "is to prepare you for use by any master in any sexual manner they see fit. We will begin with the simplest things."

The woman removed her robe to reveal an ample form. She sat on the couch and spread her legs wide. Les swallowed as he saw a woman's entire body for the first time in his life. He felt strange stirrings in his body that caused the rings to hurt him more.

"Use your fingers to bring her to orgasm." The man smiled when the slave simply looked at him with a frightened expression. "We will direct you in what to do."

Les knelt and slowly, carefully, followed the man's instructions until the woman started giving her own. A few times, the man struck his hand with the thin stick for making a mistake. Just when Les thought his fingers would fall off, his efforts were rewarded by the woman's shuddering and a loud, tired gasp. The man pulled Les back from the couch.

"Well?" the man asked as he helped the woman to her feet.

"You're a total virgin, aren't you?" she asked the kneeling slave.

"Yes, ma'am," Les replied.

"Can he learn?" the man asked.

The woman rolled her eyes. "Of course. His fingers are probably exhausted, so I think we should work on his mouth."

The man removed his clothes. "I'll sit down for the first time."

The woman motioned for Les to resume his place in front of the couch, this time between the man's legs. "He's limp. Use your mouth to arouse, then make him come. Follow our instructions."

Les started licking the balls, then worked his way up the now-firmer shaft. He followed their instructions, only earning one box on the ears from the man when his teeth scraped the shaft. His lips remained firm as the warm liquid squirted into his mouth and slid down his throat, but his eyes filled with tears from the flood of despair that accompanied it.

"Well?" the woman asked as she helped the man to his feet. "How long do you think?"

"A couple of months will have to do it," the man answered, picking up his cloak. "She doesn't like to be kept waiting, you know."

As he was led back to his cell, Les placed one hand on his stomach and tried to control the retching need that filled him. When he was alone in his cell, he sat down slowly. He looked at his food and picked up the spoon. With effort he scratched one mark in the wall next to his cot. The food made his stomach turn just looking at it.

He thought about the activities that had been demanded of him since he had been taken out of the mines. Sex was something he had been taught back on the farm was for reproduction only. He thought he knew what sex was, having seen it between livestock on the farm, but these things that his trainers demanded were completely unexpected. His hand wandered down to his piercings and gingerly touched them. The burning pain returned, but it was accompanied by that strange yearning he had felt on occasion in the training room. He bit his lip and prayed that he would succeed, because he knew that this was better than the mines and it surely couldn't get any worse.

Les breathed through his nose as instructed as the cock rammed against the back of his throat. The woman had released his arms, but he kept them behind his back. Finally, the now-familiar liquid shot into his throat. As the man released his head and backed away, Les swallowed and gasped for breath.

"He passes that," the man announced.

"Good, then we agree he is ready for the next step." The woman handed the slave a cup of water to rinse out his mouth and throat.

The man went to the table where the slave had originally been restrained. "Get up here, boy!"

Les hurried to the table; the intense week of training had impressed upon him the need to obey quickly and silently. He knelt on the table, then lowered himself to his hands and knees at the man's command.

"The way your mouth has been used is the way your ass will be used," the man stated.

Les started to sit up but found the man's hands firmly on his shoulders.

"If you can't stay in that position, we will strap you down," the man told him. "Just like before, this will go slowly."

"He's a virgin, so this may take several weeks," the woman said as she joined them at the table. "I brought all the equipment."

The man nodded. "We'll use the smallest."

Les moved his legs apart at the man's command. He felt the man's finger spread something cold and wet around his anus. Then he felt something thin press against it. He panicked and tried to pull away.

The woman stood in front of him and grabbed his hands. "Relax. That is the key. We must be as harsh as possible so you won't be caught off-guard with your master, but remember that you are a thing for pleasure. Relax and it will be easier for you. Relax and you may even enjoy it yourself."

Les took a deep breath and relaxed his muscles. He felt the object slide into his anus, further and further. His eyes rolled back in his head as a sudden wave of pleasure swept over him.

The woman glanced between the slave's arms to look closely at his face. "You found it," she told her partner with a grin.

"Don't come unless you are given permission," the man ordered, adding a slap to the slave's ass in emphasis. He slid the tiny buttplug in and out slowly. After a few minutes, he removed it and gently patted the slave's butt. "Good job, boy."

The woman released his hands. "Go eat and rest, Les. You're learning well."

Back in his cell, Les released his shame in a violent wave of vomit into his toilet. He sank to the floor and cried in fear and guilt. His mind screamed scriptures at him, condemning him as the slave preacher had instructed them all once a week back on the farm. His body cramped with these thoughts. His body, however, also still tingled from the invasion and he cried harder from his frustration.

Les couldn't help letting a moan escape as the buttplug was inflated more. Even two weeks of training couldn't silence his pain and pleasure as he was stretched further than ever before. The straps held him firmly to the table so all he could do was wiggle his ass, thus earning a hard smack on the cheeks.

"Shut him up!" the man ordered.

The woman held a ball up to his lips, and when he didn't open, held his nose shut until he gasped for air. She shoved the ball behind his teeth and fastened the straps behind his head.

Les's eyes watered as the plug was inflated once more. His ass felt as if it were going to burst, but he tried to relax as the woman instructed him in her low, soft voice. When he could relax, he knew the pain would lessen but it took him a few minutes to override his fear and shame enough to start relaxing his muscles.

"We'll be back," the woman whispered.

Les watched helplessly as the man and woman left the room. The silence of the room closed around him. He turned his mind once more to the past, remembering his childhood and youth on the farm. A few stories had circulated among the slaves that the masters required sexual service from a select group of slaves. But those had been just rumors, bred in the boredom and helplessness of slavery. Surely his former masters had not done such things as he was being taught now to their farmhands.

As the minutes passed, the slave's mind turned from his memories to the feelings of his body. His limbs were used to such confinement now and it would take hours before they began to ache. He swallowed the saliva that gathered around the ball gag. A tear escaped his eye at the shame having such an object in him triggered. He was supposed to be voice-trained and he had disappointed himself and his trainers. His back tingled as it anticipated the whipping he would receive later for his lack of control.

Now he turned his mind to his ass and in a few minutes he felt his muscles loosen and the plug slowly move in deeper as if it were being sucked inside. He moaned low and hungrily as his body now responded to the plug's presence. The pressure inside him caused his cock to harden and the weight on the ring to swing slightly. He moved as much as he could and the weights on his nipples swung and pulled another moan from his throat.

He tried to relax and wait patiently. Minutes that seemed like hours passed and his mind was filled with a frenzied need. He thrust his ass as far as the straps would allow him, desperately trying to be fucked by a master who was not there. His years of conditioning on the farm in the proper way a slave behaved had evaporated in the month he had been there. His trainers told him that he responded almost naturally to them and that he had been meant for sexual service. Bending his head and thrusting his ass, his body surrendered completely to their words. In his mind, too, his memories of the farm faded and were replaced with his physical desires.

The sound of heels clicking as they approached made him freeze and breathe deeply in an attempt to regain control over his body. He blinked helplessly at the woman as she returned. "You are doing very well," she whispered.

"You have taken the biggest one we have and in just less than two weeks," the man added. "We'll release you so you can eat and rest. Tomorrow you start training with the real thing," he added, patting his own groin.

Les knelt on all fours on the floor. The man knelt behind him. "Now, I'm not nearly as big as what you have taken, but I'll be moving. You have to learn to move with me, read my body's signals, and then finally to do the work all by yourself. We'll go through the whole thing today and for however many days it takes for you to get it right. Turn around."

Les turned around on all fours and found the already-erect penis in front of him. He took it into his mouth as he had the plugs and made it wet. As his tongue and mouth caressed the cock, he felt his own respond in hope as his anus loosened and opened eagerly. Before he really wanted to, the trainer told him to turn back around and present his ass.

The man grabbed his hips and forced his cock into Les's hole with one push. After several strokes, the man spoke. "Push back when I push forward, boy." After a few attempts, the men were moving together. "Stop," the man ordered as he stopped thrusting. The trainers exchanged looks of pride as their student responded so naturally and quickly. "Now you do all the motion, at my commands."

Les pushed back, then pulled forward, at each order from the trainer. He quickened his pace and slowed it at the man's word. He felt drops of sweat fall from his body. "Please, sir," he whispered as his own cocked swelled up. "Please, sir."

"No!" the man yelled, grabbing the slave's ass and thrusting into it so his come filled the hole. The man moved back and ordered the slave to turn. "Clean me up!"

Les licked the cock clean. As the man rose, he lay on the floor and started thrusting. The man grabbed his very short hair and yanked him off the floor, pinning his arms behind his back.

The woman was suddenly in front of the slave. "No, no," she told him as she struck his face twice with the back of her hand. "That is something that you must earn from your master." She took a device from under her cloak and strapped it around his cock and waist and through his legs to lock in back.

The man released him and held his hand out to the woman to help her to her feet. "We'll have to work very hard on your control. It is your greatest weakness."

The control training was the most difficult. Even with all of the religious prohibitions against sexuality, all the slaves on the farm had masturbated in silence when they could find a moment alone. In the mines, even when exhausted from the day's labor, the slaves could be heard humping their hands and floors in desperate need. But a sex slave's sole purpose was to serve his master, so his pleasure must be under careful control—ready to burst forth at a word, yet making him yearn and beg pitifully or wait silently for his owner's use.

As the weeks rolled by, Les learned to control these responses and to cater to his trainers' whims. In a real sense, he was learning to be a master himself and not simply a slave to his body. He could stand for hours, holding a fragile and expensive object in his hands, while the trainers touched, probed, and abused his body. Or at their pleasure he could writhe wildly on the ground, fucking unseen forces as he begged for release. At other times he could fuck one of them for hours and give them many orgasms as he held back his own, sometimes kissing their feet in gratitude for the experience though no release was allowed for himself.

One morning, after practice in meal serving, the woman looked at Les and mouthed one word silently: "Come." The empty tray fell from the slave's hands as his back arched and his cock spurted forth violently. Several spasms racked his body and drove him to his knees, where he gasped for breath. The trainers nodded to each other. "You're ready," the man announced. "Go to your room and wait for the doctors to prepare you."

Les sat on the mattress on the floor of his tiny cell. He rolled over to his side so he could get the old spoon he had snatched that first day to scratch another mark into the wall. "Fifty-one days," he said to himself. He tried to relax in the body harness that he had been wearing for the past three days as he waited as patiently as he could for his trainers to return.

He closed his eyes and concentrated on the feelings of his body. He felt the three-inch collar that held his neck straight. Attached to that was the posture strap that ran to the belt around his waist. His wrists were fastened to the sides of the belt, but his fingers only touched the leather covering them. He leaned forward and felt the weights on his nipples swing. He moaned behind the penis gag. Then, leaning back and relaxing, he moved the buttplug deeper inside. The spreader bar on his thighs kept him from moving the plug much more. Finally, his mind focused on the cuffs around his ankles that further limited his step.

His body felt tense as he remembered the mines. His skin felt gritty as it slowly tricked him into thinking he was covered with coal ash and dirt. A drop of sweat formed on his forehead as he remembered the wretched rations that could be cut for the slightest infraction of the rules. His joints began to ache as they felt old wounds from the hard floor where he had knelt to scoop up the products of his labor.

A creak outside his cell snapped him from his reflection. Les lowered his eyes to the floor as the door opened. "It's time," the woman's voice told him.

The man helped him walk out of the cell and down the hall. "This is the big demonstration that determines where you go—back to the mines or to the master. Do everything exactly as you've been taught," the man reminded him.

Les found himself in the first room he had been in after he was cleaned up from the mines, the white one with one mirrored wall. He stood silently as each part of his harness was removed. Then he followed the man to the pole and grabbed the rings hanging from the top. He counted each lash out loud as his trainers beat him with several different items. At the end of the session, he sipped the water the woman held up to his lips.

Now he turned around, and the pair placed clips of various sizes all over his body. He counted each one out loud as it was removed by a single-tailed whip. In his mind, he focused on how desperately he needed to escape the mines forever.

The captain of the guard turned to the cloaked woman next to him. "Your Majesty, are you pleased?"

"It is impressive for a bred slave," the woman admitted. "My decision will be based on the entire display, Captain. Don't try to rush me. Just enjoy it," she ordered as one hand's nails traced down his arm.

Les hungrily serviced the woman's clit with his tongue as the man rammed his ass. As he felt the man near climax, he quickened his pace on the woman so that both shuddered together.

Les now found himself on the floor alone. The woman returned and emptied a bucket of ice water over him. Les knelt as the water dripped from his skin.

An oddly familiar voice floated out over the room. "Prepare him and bring to the room."

Les followed his trainers to the table. "The master will inform you of the decision," the woman told him.

"Did I make it, sir, ma'am?" Les softly ventured to ask.

"The master will tell you," the man replied as he replaced the plug in Les's anus.

Les was placed in the full harness once again. This time a leather hood was placed over his head so that only his nose was free. He followed his trainers as best he could. His bare feet felt carpet beneath them, and he heard a door shut.

The hood was removed, and the light made him squint. As his eyes adjusted, he saw a beautiful woman covered in green jewels sitting on a long couch. His female trainer whispered in his ear, "Your master, the queen of our land."

The woman smiled and held out her hand. "Welcome to my palace, slave."

Les knelt as best he could to kiss the offered hand. He thanked any gods that existed that he had escaped the mines.

Punishment for the Crime

"Are you sure you want to see him? He hasn't been tamed yet," General Corriger pointed out to her liege as they walked through the slave barracks.

"I feel like a challenge, Valerie." She stopped at one of the cells and snapped her fingers in front of the bars. The man inside hurried to her, kneeling and licking her fingers. "I believe you have broken all of the slaves. I think I deserve a little fun, too."

"I agree, though I thought the raid we're planning would provide that."

"It's fun, but it's almost too easy."

The two continued through the barracks to the palace in silence. When they reached the princess's second suite, the general opened the door, saying, "He's a drug dealer, Yvonne."

"I know," She crossed to her desk, where she removed her helmet.

"He's gone through three owners since the sentencing five years ago."

"I know." Yvonne ran her fingers through her shoulder-length bright red hair.

"He has a record that's pages long."

"I know." She sat down in the plain oak chair in the center of the room. "He is the best challenge since the system was put into effect fifty years ago. I read the reports. Experts say he can't be broken. I don't believe it. The right methods haven't been used."

"And you know the right methods?"

"I think I do." She raised her hand as footsteps and curses approached. "I think that's him now."

The general nodded and stood slightly behind the chair.

"Enter!" Yvonne yelled before the knock came.

Two guards entered with a struggling man. His clothes, which had been new for the auction, were torn and bloody from his resistance. He blinked and cursed when the blindfold was removed. "Fuck! Turn down the goddamn lights!"

Yvonne sat silently as the guards forced him to his knees. Each guard placed her foot on his calves. "He's been like this the entire transport, Your Highness," one explained.

General Corriger stepped up to him, grabbing his long black hair to force him to face the princess. "This is your new mistress. You will obey her every command."

He slowly looked over the beautiful young woman sitting in front of him. "I know what you need, Your Highness," he said with a sneer.

"You son of a bitch!" The general raised her fist to strike him, but was stopped by a shake of her liege's head.

Yvonne waved her hand.

"Are you sure?" the general asked. After another wave of the princess's hand, the general turned to the guards. "We're dismissed."

The guard released the man, who jumped to his feet and watched them leave. He turned to the woman seated on the chair. "They didn't lock the door. What's to stop me from leaving?"

When the woman didn't answer, he reached for the door. Immediately his body was struck with electricity that made him scream. He released the doorknob and staggered away. The woman was now reading from a folder and didn't even glance at him. He hurried to the windows only to find them barred and a guard smiling back at him from a balcony.

"We are five stories up," the woman replied calmly.

After examining the entire room, he started to approach her from behind. Suddenly, his shirt was pinned to the bedpost by a dagger.

"Such a pity to have to ruin that lovely shirt," the woman replied as she came and pulled it out. She returned to the chair. "Do you know who I am?"

"You mean besides a bitch?" he replied, walking to where he could see her face clearly. "No, I don't, and I don't really care."

"Look at this." She threw him her helmet with the royal crest. "My parents named me Yvonne."

He caught the helmet and recognized the crest and the name. "You're the Butcher?" He shook his head to clear his mind of the images of slaughter he had seen on the streets for years: the prostitutes, druggies, and dealers dead in the street every night in the big cities. "You can't be; that was years ago."

"Call them my reckless teenage years." She picked up the folder and opened it. "You are called Jake."

"That's my name; don't wear it out."

"Convicted on several accounts of petty crime since the age of ten until your sentencing for drug dealing five years ago. That would make you twenty-five now. Do you enjoy being a slave, Jake?"

"Oh, sure. It's a blast. What the fuck kind of question is that?"

"You desire to be a slave, Jake. The laws have been quite clear since before you were born."

He remained silent for a moment. "Hey, why you'd have the collar and tattoos removed?"

"You have to earn those symbols of slavery."

"Oh, and I suppose I'm gonna beg you for them, right?"

"Yes. Right now, in fact." She sat up straight in the chair. "On your knees, now."

He approached slowly and bent down so they were face-to-face. "Fuck you!"

She stood up and he backed up a few steps. She picked up her helmet. "I will be on campaign a few days. This is your room. Do what you want. You will be taken care of as you deserve." Without further words, she opened the door and left.

Jake hurried after her, but the door closed in his face. Electricity shot through him as he grabbed the doorknob again. He backed off and nodded his head. "It's no big deal, lady! You can torture me all you want, but it won't work!"

Yvonne entered her second suite after four days on campaign. She had showered and changed into her dress uniform for the supper she would be attending shortly. The man walked up to her angrily as she closed the door.

"What the fuck is going on here?"

"Is something wrong? You look clean, new clothes, hair cut, face smooth. What's the problem?"

"They haven't brought me any food since you left!"

"Oh, I'm so sorry."

He glanced at her shiny uniform and her calm, even somewhat concerned, face. "So, you'll tell them to feed me?"

"I don't have any control over who gets fed here."

"What do you fucking mean you don't have control? You're heir to the throne, aren't you?"

"Only four types of people are fed around here. The family, the guests, the staff, and the slaves," she stated flatly.

Jake ran his hand through his spiky hair. "I see what you're trying to do. But it's not going to work, see?"

Yvonne nodded. "I'm off to a dinner now. Good evening," she added, closing the door behind her.

Jake threw himself against the door and was shocked once more. He sat where the electricity had thrown him and stared at the door in anger.

Jake stood looking out the bars of the double doors to the balcony. The guard there didn't interfere with his looking out over the main entrance and road. He had gotten up early every day since he'd last seen her to shave and try to look his best. Since anger didn't work, maybe a little charm would.

"It's been a hell of a week, otherwise I would have been here sooner."

He turned at the sound of her voice. She was dressed in a black negligee and robe, black slippers on her feet. He checked his voice and manner before approaching her. "I was hoping you would come."

"Really?" she folded her arms.

"Yes, of course." He stopped a few feet from her. "Has anyone ever told you how beautiful you are?"

"Many people."

Jake paused to reconsider this approach. He started to unbutton his shirt. "You've had a busy week. I bet I can help you relax, Your Highness."

She laughed out loud at him for a moment before shaking her head. "I'm leaving tomorrow morning to tour some prison camps. I may be gone several weeks." She glanced at the ground directly in front of her feet, then into his eyes. "Is there anything you need before I go?"

His eyes darkened in hate. "No."

Yvonne left without a word.

"It isn't working, is it?" the general asked after her liege had closed the door behind her.

Yvonne put her arm around the other woman. "It's working quite well. Just as I planned, in fact." She unclasped one of the buckles on the general's breastplate. "We don't need to sleep for a few hours. Come with me."

The general took the hand that had moved to her neck. She passionately kissed it. "It would be my pleasure."

Jake dragged himself from the bed. He looked in the bathroom mirror at his cheekbones, clearly visible now. He took off the shirt he had fallen asleep in and counted his ribs. He drank a glass of water and brushed his teeth. He sank to the floor, unable once again to step into the shower. He crawled from habit and turned the water on cold. This woke him up enough to shave. He crawled to the double doors and opened them slightly. "Please. How long?"

The guard shook her head. "You should be branded and collared."

"Please?" For the first time his voice really sounded pitiful.

"Twenty-one days since she was last here."

Jake crawled from the balcony and managed to lift his head up to the bed to rest there. *Thirty-two days without food. Oh, God. Why didn't she just stab me that first day?* He heard the door opening and waited for the guards to come in. For the past week they had come, and the last six days he hadn't been strong enough to fight them off. "Please?" he whispered as they picked him up and threw him onto the bed on his stomach.

They laughed as they pulled his pants from him and forced his legs apart. "You're nothing. Only family, guest, staff, and slaves don't get raped around here. You're nothing."

After the guards had finished, he managed to pull up his pants. *No blood again.* He was trying to turn himself over when the door opened again.

Yvonne walked in and over to the bed. She had come straight from reporting to her father, so she was still dusty from the ride. "You look like shit."

Jake reached for her hand. "Please?" His eyes begged.

Yvonne cocked one eye and stepped back a little. She waited for a full minute. "I've just come to tell you I've been called away on political business up north, so I'll not see you for a week or more...."

"Please..." He hurled himself from the bed to her feet. He groveled at her feet. "Mistress, please," he whispered.

She stepped back a few paces. "What did you say?"

He crawled until his head rested in front of her boots, his body flat against the floor. "Mistress, please."

"Only my slaves are allowed to use that title for me."

Jake swallowed his last shreds of pride. "Please allow me to wear your collar and your mark."

"I thought you were dead set against being a slave." She walked to the chair and sat down.

Jake crawled to her feet and prostrated himself there. "Please. You were right...."

"Right about what?" she said, leaning closer to him.

"You said I must want to be a slave, otherwise I wouldn't have dealt drugs. You're right, Mistress. Please allow me the honor to be your slave. I'll do anything, no matter the job," he added.

"You're not worth the honor of shoveling shit in the barn around here."

He started to weep softly. "Please, please, then just kill me."

Yvonne bent and ran her fingers through his hair, then gripped it tightly in her fist and yanked his head up. He didn't struggle at all as she placed the dagger to his throat. "Being my slave means complete obedience to me and me alone. Obedience without question or hesitation. Obedience to any and everything that I command. Obedience to my unspoken commands and desires. Nothing will exist for you but me."

"I don't exist except for you, Mistress," he managed to yell in his terror.

"Who doesn't exist?"

He swallowed and ventured again. "Jake doesn't exist except for you, Mistress. Please."

She removed her knife and released his hair. "Lick the dust off my boots and make them shine."

Jake slowly started to lick the right boot. The dust almost made him sneeze, but he continued. By the time the first boot was shining, he moved with eagerness to the next boot. He recalled her words and burned them into his mind: "Being my slave means complete obedience to me and me alone." *To you alone, to you alone.*

When the other boot was finished, Yvonne pushed him aside and went to the door. He scrambled to his knees in fear, but dared not speak. "Guards!" The guards entered and stood at attention. "Take him and follow me!"

Jake tried to walk between the guards so their grip on his arms wasn't so painful. He was taken to a dank, dark room several stories down. He was thrust into a chair while the guards held him.

Yvonne disappeared while a man in a dirty apron approached him. He measured his neck. "He's emaciated. I'll add a little for him to grow." The man looked at the metal strips hanging along the wall. "Type?"

"Gold-plated," Yvonne's voice called from the other room.

The smith placed a two-inch strip around his neck. "Don't move, or you could die." He fired his blowtorch on low and soldered the two ends of the metal together. Jake would have flinched when the flame grazed him, but he didn't have the energy. He suspected the smith had done it on purpose.

The guards then lifted him from the chair and carried him to the other room. One held his arms as the other loosened his pants and stripped him to the waist. They bent him over a table and strapped his arms and legs to it before leaving the room.

Yvonne stepped into his sight. She held a smoking branding iron in her hand. "We don't tattoo. We brand our property. This is your last chance."

He felt the sweat drip down his forehead into one of his eyes. He lowered his head to the table. "Jake doesn't exist except for you, Mistress," he stated again. He couldn't hold back his scream as the iron burned into his buttocks.

"Guards!" Yvonne replaced the iron and gripped her slave by the hair. He was barely conscious from the pain. "Take him to the steward. I want him fed, cleaned, clothed, and shown the palace and grounds. After a night of sleep, I want him brought to my office by nine sharp."

The guards nodded, unstrapped the slave, and carried him away.

Jake followed the steward through the palace. He had to keep reminding himself that there was no way out now, so he would stop looking for one. "Let's rest a minute. Okay?"

The steward paused with distaste. "You have no stamina."

"You try not eating for a month and see how much stamina you have." The cockiness was returning to Jake's voice.

"You brought that upon yourself. Perhaps you need to be reminded of that," the steward threatened as he stepped closer to the drug dealer.

Jake stood up slowly, wincing at the pain in his buttocks. "I'm not going to punch you out, because my mistress ordered me to follow you. So lead the way."

Jake was escorted to her office, which he remembered from his tour was near the throne room. "Hey," he started before they reached the door, "any advice for me?"

The guards' laughter sent chills through him as he recognized them as the rapists. They opened the door and pushed him in.

He stood there in front of her desk, unsure what to do. She didn't glance at him but only at the computer screen. He looked at the clock on the wall. *One minute to nine. Nine o'clock. Why isn't she noticing me?* He knelt on one knee, then the other. After another minute he prostrated himself flat on the floor in front of her desk. He held his breath as her boots moved from under her desk and reappeared in front of his face.

She didn't speak but simply tapped one toe once. He swallowed quickly and moved to that boot. He licked it slowly until it shone, then moved to the other boot. "Stand up."

He rose to his feet and looked her straight in the eyes. He was knocked to the floor by her blow.

"Stand up."

He rose to his feet but focused his eyes on the second button of her shirt. He was knocked to the floor by her blow. He touched his lips and tasted blood.

"Stand up."

He rose again to his feet. He stood straight and focused his eyes over her shoulder. He felt her walk slowly around him. He didn't fight as she moved his hands, arms, legs.

When she squeezed his raw buttcheek, he sucked his breath in through his teeth.

Yvonne sat on the edge of her desk and admired him for a moment. "You lost some weight, but you'll get it back. I see he burned your neck. Do you think he meant to?"

"Perhaps." He saw her start to stand up. "Perhaps, Mistress," he added quickly. He saw her smile and nod.

"You will follow me today and every day until I tire of your presence. We don't sell our property. When that time comes you will be given away as a gift or killed."

He followed her out of the office and into the throne room. *She is very straight with me, at least.* He stayed about three paces behind her. She stood, glancing at her watch until an older gentleman and lady entered. On their heads were the crowns of the realm. He recognized them from all the money he had handled from his years on the streets.

"Father, Mother." Yvonne embraced them both warmly. She turned to the slave behind her. "I told you I could tame him."

Their majesties glanced at each other and their daughter. The queen approached the slave, who stood his ground but did not look her in the eye. "He seems a lovely lad. A little thin."

"That was necessary, Mother."

"If you say so, my dear." The queen held out her hand.

"Kiss her ring," Yvonne whispered.

He bowed low and barely touched the queen's ring with his lips. He remained bowed until told to rise by the queen. "Jake, Your Majesty," he replied softly to her inquiry.

"He seems quite fine to me," the queen stated as she moved aside for her husband.

"Looks can be deceiving. But you know that." His speech was obviously directed toward his daughter.

"I don't trust him at all, Father. He hasn't earned that

yet," Yvonne walked up behind her father and glared at the slave. "Tell my father who you are."

Jake avoided both their eyes as he repeated the words. "Jake doesn't exist except for you, Mistress."

The king held out his ring hand and nodded as the slave bowed and kissed it. "Watch him, my dear. Now," the king turned to his daughter with a smile, "it's about time for petitions. Shall we go, my girls?"

Yvonne followed their majesties to the three thrones and sat at her father's right hand. Jake stationed himself behind and to the right of the throne.

Jake tried to listen with interest to the cases brought before the royal court. He hadn't been fed that morning; the steward's excuse had been that she hadn't specifically ordered him to. His stomach growled softly. He saw her fist clench and feared she had heard. His interest was piqued when a man was dragged into court by some cops. *Eddy? Oh, shit, dude.*

The man was defending himself against his drug use and dealing conviction. The punishment for this was death, because the theory went that enslaving someone who was already a slave to drugs wasn't a deterrent. Yvonne motioned to Jake, who knelt by her side, and moved his head close to hers. "Know him?"

"Unfortunately." After a second, she had her hand around his throat. "Yes, Mistress," he croaked. His throat was released. He remained by her side.

"I have a question." Yvonne stood to speak. She walked toward the defendant. "Mr. Nole, do you recognize that man?" she asked, pointing to her slave.

The druggy shook his head quickly.

"Jake, come stand before the defendant so he can get a closer look at you." She waited until the slave stood directly before the other man. "Look at him closely, Mr. Nole."

The man glared at the slave and mouthed something to him.

"What did that man say to you?" Yvonne asked.

"He said 'traitor,' Mistress."

"You fucking bastard!" The defendant tried to beat the slave, but was pulled off him by the cops.

Jake took a deep breath and glanced at his mistress. She returned to her throne, saying, "Feel free to ask him any questions, counselors."

"Yes." The prosecution stepped forward. "May he stay on the floor for the questioning, Your Highness?"

"As long as you need him," she replied as she seated herself.

"What is your name?"

"Jake Monroe."

"Social security number?"

Jake paused to think, then rattled off the nine numbers.

After a moment both attorneys had copies of his record on their mini-computers. "You were sentenced to open-market slavery five years ago for drug dealing. Is that correct?"

"Yes," Jake folded his arms angrily, remembering his own trial.

"Do you know the defendant?"

"Yes, unfortunately."

"Why unfortunately?"

"We had the same supplier, but he used to do more dope than he sold, so they cut him off. He started coming around begging me for some. He even stole a kilo from me once," Jake added with a glare at the druggy.

"Would you consider Mr. Nole to be an honest person just needing medical attention?"

"No. He's the type of guy that would sell his birth mother for a capsule of speed."

The prosecution turned to the defense lawyer. "Your witness."

"You were sent to reform school several times, weren't you?"

"Yes."

The lawyer smiled icily. "You've been sold four times since your conviction for drug dealing, haven't you?"

"Yes."

"You are a liar, a thief, and a scam artist, aren't you?"

Jake brought his hands down to his sides in fists. Out of the corner of his eye he saw his mistress lean forward in her seat. "Yes," he whispered angrily.

The lawyer smiled and nodded. "No further questions."

The prosecution lawyer nodded and dismissed the slave. Jake returned to his place behind his mistress's throne.

"Hey, yo! What's to eat around here?" Jake walked into the main kitchen through the slaves' entrance.

A young woman approached him. Her slave collar was thin and made of iron. "Why didn't you report at feeding time?"

"I get time to eat when the princess tells me it's time to eat. I have thirty minutes tops."

"I'll make you a sandwich then. The milk is in the fridge over there, and the glasses are in the cupboard next to it." The girl opened another refrigerator and got out bread, meat, cheese, and butter.

"Aren't you a little young to be sentenced to slavery?" he asked, sitting down at the table to watch her make the sandwich.

"My mother was convicted of giving AIDS to three of her johns. She was in the hospital at the time of the sentence, so I took her place so she could get health care."

"Your mother gave AIDS to royalty?"

The girl handed him the sandwich. "No, the royal family heard about our case and interceded on my behalf. I would probably be dead by now if they hadn't."

Jake nodded as he chewed. *Victims' families can be bitches.* "How long you been here?"

"Four years."

"How old are you?"

"Eighteen. How old are you?"

"Twenty-five."

"Why are you a slave?"

Jake paused to finish his sandwich before replying. "Drug dealing." He excepted the girl to yell at him or even physically attack him. Most slaves did when they found out what he had done, the exception being other drug dealers. Instead she just walked quietly away from him. Jake finished his milk, rinsed it out in the sink, and drank a glass of water to clear his throat. "Where's the toilet?"

The girl pointed to a small door, then ran from the room in tears.

Jake hurried from the kitchen through the corridors. He slowed down when he spotted a clock. *Ten minutes. I can stroll back.* He stopped by one of the windows to get an unobstructed view of the main entrance. *This place is huge.* He slowly continued through the corridors until he reached the main dining room. He slid in through the slaves' entrance and took his position three paces behind his mistress's chair. *Two minutes early.*

He stood there listening to the dull conversation until she set her napkin aside. He moved to her chair and pulled it back as she stood.

"I think I'll be dining alone tonight, if you don't mind?" Yvonne asked her parents.

"Of course, darling," the queen said as the king merely nodded. "You need some vacation time."

"Thank you both." Yvonne turned on her heel and left the room. She walked quickly down the hall and to the elevator that took them to the ground floor.

She entered a different room from any he had seen yesterday. He followed her to a bench and recognized the gear stored there as riding gear. When she sat down, he knelt before her.

"Boots," she stated simply.

He got the boots by the bench. After removing the others she wore, he placed these on her feet. Next, he helped her into her jacket and handed her the riding crop that she promptly struck his cheek with. He stood there a moment, then fell to his knees at her feet. "Mistress?" He stopped before saying anything further.

"The horses need exercise, and so do you. While I am riding, you will run along the racetrack four times. That's two miles."

Jake looked up at her in shock and received another lash from the riding crop. "Yes, Mistress." He followed her out of the building to the early spring air. He shivered in his simple shirt, pants, and shoes.

"You'll warm up." She left him at the track and took her horse from the groom who came out.

After she was out of earshot, he spoke to the groom, "Can you believe that she wants me to run two miles on that track?"

"That's four laps," the groom replied. "You don't look like you're in very good shape. You'd better get started. She only rides for half an hour."

"Thanks for the sympathy," Jake replied as the groom returned to the stables. He headed to the track.

He saw her returning as he finishing vomiting from the four laps. He wiped his mouth on his hand, which he then wiped on the grass. He walked as quickly as he could back to her.

Yvonne glanced at him. "That's what you get for not eating for a month," she told him bluntly. "Show him the bathroom, Mike," she ordered the groom.

Jake followed the man to a small bathroom, where he was able to vomit again. Afterwards he rinsed out his mouth, drank a little water, and used the toilet. The groom showed him where his mistress's ready room was. She was standing there in her riding gear waiting for him. He removed her jacket when she turned her back to him and changed her boots when she sat.

"Time for a snack," she announced.

They went back through the corridors of the palace to the main kitchen. The girl was there and bowed low when they entered. "What do you have that's good for a snack, Betty?"

"My lady, baking was done yesterday so there are many types of breads, cookies, and pies." The girl wiped off the table and pulled out a chair for the princess.

"Bring an assortment of cookies and two glasses of milk." After the girl had bowed and left, Yvonne kicked a chair out from the table. "Use that as your table, Jake. You look like you need some food, too."

"Thank you, Mistress," he said, kneeling by it.

"Sit down and join me, Betty," Yvonne said when the girl returned with a platter of cookies and two mugs of milk. "Let's talk."

The girl giggled and sat down opposite the princess. She waited until Yvonne had handed her slave several cookies and bitten into one herself before taking one. "I made the sugar cookies and the peanut butter ones," Betty whispered.

"You are a great cook," Yvonne said with a smile. "You're going to make someone a good spouse someday."

The girl set the cookie down and sadly looked at the table.

"You'll be eighteen in less than two years. I'll convince my father to let you marry and live out on the land. Don't you believe me?"

The girl looked up with tears in her eyes. "Oh, yes, my lady. It just seems so far away at times."

Yvonne nodded slowly. "You should start looking around for a mate. Let me know if you're interested in anyone and I'll arrange some meetings." She leaned across the table. "Anyone caught your eye yet?"

Betty blushed. "Well, there's the groom, the younger one. Sometimes when he comes to get their meals I see him smiling at me," she whispered.

"Mike?" Yvonne nodded and finished her milk. "I'll arrange for you to take a few evening meals out at the stables so you can visit with each other."

Jake stood quickly and pulled her chair back so she could stand. *She is so weird. One minute yelling and hitting and the next arranging nice things. Maybe I should have just starved to death.* He shook his head slightly to clear his mind.

"You've met this character?" Yvonne asked the girl, with a nod at her slave.

The girl frowned. "Yes. He ate lunch in here."

"You don't like him." Yvonne suddenly turned to him and grabbed him by the hair, forcing his head on the table. "Drug dealers are the scum of world. Tell him why your mother was a hooker."

"This bastard laced her drink at a restaurant. He got her hooked on it and made her turn tricks to get the stuff." The girl's voice dripped venom with each word.

Jake stood up when his hair was released. "I'm sorry, but I didn't do that type of stuff." He waited in silence as the girl gathered the platter and mugs and walked away. When he felt his mistress turn to go, he followed three paces behind her.

They went to the fourth floor and stopped in front of elaborate double doors. "This is the lower level of my suite. You know the way through the slaves' entrance, but just in case you have to escort a guest to me you should know what it looks like from out here." She opened the door and entered.

Jake followed. He looked around the room, then stopped himself and just stood at attention after she shut the door.

"Go ahead. Look around," she said, then disappeared down a small hallway.

The room was surprisingly elegant, not militaristic as he had imagined. There was a spiral staircase in one corner. An embroidered divan and chairs sat before a low table. Full bookcases lined the walls. He walked down the hallway after her. She stepped aside to let him look in the restroom. He followed her back out to the main room.

"This is where I receive guests. If you have to bring someone to see me, you bring them here." She climbed the stairs. "This is where I live when I'm home."

Jake looked at the much darker room decorated in blacks and reds. He was at first startled by the weapons that lined the walls. *This is more like it.* He waited at the foot of the stairs for her to wave her hand for him to look around. He found a full bathroom, also dark and foreboding. Three huge sliding doors displayed her clothes. Another smaller unit held clothing she said would be his. *I've never seen stuff like this.* He closed the door and returned to the main room to find her sitting on the four-poster bed. It was enormous and covered with a blood red quilt. He knelt at her feet and removed her boots, which he carried back to her closet where all the shoes were.

Yvonne reclined on the bed, staring at him as he stood silently at attention. She sat up at the sound of a bell. "You will exit through the slave corridors, get our dinner, and return with it the same way. When I am not eating with my family or guests, you will get every meal. Unless you are otherwise occupied," she added with a half smile.

"Yes, Mistress," Jake bowed and hurried through the

slaves' entrance. He paused after the door closed behind him to stare at it. *Handcuffs?* He hurried through the narrow corridors to the kitchen. *Thank God for the signs.* He hurried into the hall and first met the girl Betty. "I'm here to get the princess's dinner."

"It's over there on the table."

"Thank you." Jake took the large gold tray that held three covered plates, two goblets, and a bottle of wine. "I'll bring it back when she's finished."

One of the cooks shook his head. "No. You just leave it outside the slaves' entrance and I'll send someone to pick it up."

Jake nodded. "Sure." He hurried as quickly as he could through the corridors. *Wonder if I'll get to eat.* His stomach growled as the tasty fumes rose from the platter. He realized gratefully that the door to her suite swung inwards, so he backed his way in.

"Set it on that small table and bring the table here," her voice ordered him.

The room was darker now because the sun was setting. He brought the table to her. He stepped back when he saw she was dressed in the same negligee she had worn weeks earlier when he had attempted to seduce her.

"Pour two glasses of wine. You'll be eating with me."

He knelt on the floor by the bed and filled both goblets. He handed one to her and sipped his own. As she ate, she would hand him various bits of food that he quickly licked from her fingers. He noticed she was careful to give him only the bland foods and not pieces dipped in the rich cream sauce that rested in a bowl next to the meat dish. When she finished the main meal, she uncovered the dessert—a small chocolate torte covered with chocolate curls.

"Sit up and face me."

He turned and knelt so his face was directly in her view but carefully focused his eyes over her shoulder.

"Close your eyes. Are you afraid of me?"

He paused for a second, then whispered, "Yes, Mistress."

"Good. Open your mouth."

He opened it wide and felt something enter it.

"Close your mouth."

He felt metal, then felt it sliding from his mouth. *Chocolate*. He started to bite, but felt a cold metal prick right above his collar. He waited for the word.

"Eat it."

He bit into the torte and chewed it slowly before swallowing.

"Who are you?"

He could felt her breath on his cheek. "Jake doesn't exist except for you, Mistress." He felt her move away.

After a few moments she spoke. "Take your clothes off, slowly."

He opened his eyes and was thrown to the floor by her fist.

"Take your clothes off slowly," she repeated.

Keeping his eyes closed, he stood and slipped out of the shoes. He bent each leg up to remove the socks. He paused between each button on his shirt, then slowly let it slide off his shoulders. *I can't look too good now.* He unbuttoned the pants and stepped out of them. The bikini briefs fell to the floor.

"You can ask me one question every night and I'll answer honestly. What's your question for tonight?"

Jake kept his eyes closed and asked, "How did you know that starving me would break me?"

"I read your history in your legal file. All of it. Never doubt that I know how to handle you and what makes you tick," she warned him.

He waited naked in the cold of the room.

Jake followed the guards through the slave corridors. They stopped in front of the infirmary. He went in and found a man and woman sitting reading magazines. "Where is the medic?"

"We're them," the woman replied, setting aside the magazine. "How can we help you?"

"I was sent by Princess Yvonne. I'm Jake Monroe. Princess Yvonne's slave," he added slowly when the woman just stared at him.

"The one she starved, huh?" the man said as he stood. "I'll go get the file."

"Yeah. She wants to see if I'm in good health," Jake threw the words out and sat down on the chair the man had abandoned.

The woman stood up and was about to speak when the man returned. "Let's look and see what she wants done," the woman said, flipping open the folder. "A full exam. Guess he's yours, John."

"Okay." The man pointed to a door. "In there, and take all your clothes off."

Jake rose slowly and went through the doors. *Typical exam room.* He took his clothes off and sat on the exam table. "Come in," he said when the knock came at the door.

The male doctor entered with a shy smile. "This is only my second month here. Says on your chart that you're new, too." The doctor frowned. "Says you were denied food for thirty-one days. Whatever you did, I'd suggest that you'll not do it again. That's not good for your body. Let's weigh you first."

Jake got on the scale. He looked at himself in the mirror next to the scale. *I look pretty good.*

"You've regained most of the weight you lost. About three pounds less than your weigh-in. Let's check the body fat."

Jake hurried to Yvonne's office after his exam. He knocked on the door before entering. She was speaking to two gentlemen, who ignored him as he entered and stood three paces behind her chair. He kept his eyes forward and listened silently. When Yvonne moved her cup toward him, he went and got the tea set. He poured her another cup and silently offered the gentlemen more.

After about an hour, the gentlemen rose and left. Yvonne remained in her seat, looking over her fingertips. After a moment she moved to rise. Jake slid her chair back and replaced it when she walked to the window. He waited silently by her desk.

"Give me the doctor's report," she commanded, holding out her hand.

Jake took the envelope from his back pocket and handed it to her. He waited by the window while she read.

"Good," she stated softly. She left through the slaves' entrance.

Jake followed her through the corridors to her main suite's slave entrance.

"Hold out your hands," she ordered, turning to face him. She fastened the handcuffs hanging from a nail on the door over one of his wrists.

Jake followed her into the room and removed his clothes when ordered. She dialed the kitchen on her phone and told them to bring lunch, dinner, and breakfast up to her room. He stood silently as she lifted his hands over his head and fastened them over a rod hanging from the ceiling. She moved his legs two feet apart and strapped them to the floor. Then she disappeared down the hallway to return a few minutes later with a small suitcase.

Yvonne opened the suitcase and laid it on the bed. "Your question gets to come early today. What is it?" She removed her jacket and took off her tie.

Jake looked straight at her; he had learned that this was allowed during his question time. "Why are you going to do this to me?"

"What do you think I'm going to do to you?" She looked through the suitcase.

"You can do whatever you want to me at any time. But I think you're going to torture me and I want to know why," he asked, then jerked back in anticipation of a slap.

"I am angry about the meeting, about the war. You're going to help me get rid of that anger." She approached and placed a blindfold over his eyes. "Don't fight it and you might enjoy it."

She pressed a few buttons in a hidden panel and raised the rod so he was stretched taut. First she simply walked around him, touching him with a feather every now and then. The feather's touch became more frequent until he was gasping from laughter and pain.

"Please, Mistress..." He flinched from the touch but couldn't move far. "I can't...breathe."

"Who can't breathe?" she asked, increasing the touches so he couldn't answer for several seconds. "Who can't breathe?" she repeated, slowing her tickling.

"Jake...can't...breathe...Mistress...please." He cursed inwardly at forgetting to refer to himself only in the third person in her presence.

"You have to breathe," she said and stood back.

Jake tried to control his gasps as his body stopped sending double signals to his brain. Just as his breathing returned to normal, he jumped from the feather's return to his rib cage. "Oh, please," he gasped. *What's going on? No, it can't be.* He felt his penis start to rise. "Please...no...please."

"I don't think you want me to stop," she whispered. "I can see that you like it," she added, running the feather over his now long shaft.

"Oohhh…" He shook his head, wishing he could thrust. Suddenly she stopped. He listened closely and heard her open the slave door. She set something on the small table.

"Time to eat," she announced.

He felt his arms lowered a bit. Next he felt his ankles unstrapped. His arms were further lowered so he had to kneel in order not to be hit on the head with the rod. He blinked as the blindfold was removed. The light indicated she had opened the curtains; the light breeze indicated open balcony doors.

She unlocked one of the handcuffs, which allowed him to lower his arms. He took the sandwich she handed him and ate it in silence. He ate another sandwich and an apple and washed it down with a mug of spiced wine. He went to the bathroom to empty himself and brush his teeth as commanded. When he returned the food platter was gone, and she waited by the now-higher rod.

He raised his hands and felt the other cuff locked around the wrist. Without a word, he spread his legs and felt the strap placed around his ankles. *If it gets her off to tickle me, it's no tough job. Here it comes,* he thought as the blindfold was tied over his eyes. "Aahhh!" he screamed as something cut through the back of his knees. He regained his posture after a few seconds passed and he realized that his knees were still there.

The blow landed on his buttocks. Whack! Whack! Whack! Then a pause. The next blow fell across his shoulders. Whack! *Staff…wooden.* His mind registered what the weapon might be. Five years of fighting his sentence had given him experience with many instruments of torture. He started to count the blows to focus his mind. After he reached ninety-four, the blows stopped. His skin felt hot and he could feel welts rising. Sweat dripped down his face.

"You like this. I knew you would," Yvonne touched his hot cock with one of her fingers and was rewarded by his moan. "I can feel the anger slowly start to leave me."

Swish, crack! He tried to bend over to protect his chest but only found his arms lifted higher by the rod. Swish, crack! *Whip.* Swish, crack! "Yip!" he squealed as the next blow struck his nipple. The blows stopped when he reached twenty-seven, all on his front.

"Please," he gasped. A moment later his mouth and throat were filled with something hard. *Leather; must be a gag of some type.* He braced himself for the next blows. These came on his back. *Swish, crack!* He tried to scream and almost gagged on the object in his throat. *Swish, crack!* He counted forty-eight more before they stopped. His sweat flowed freely now, and he felt the unmistakable trickle of blood on his back.

His ankles were freed as his arms were raised so he hung limp above the floor. He felt himself swinging backwards for a few feet. He thrashed in the handcuffs as the icy water hit him. Twice more the sharp waves of water fell on him. He was left dripping until he started shivering violently. Then he was swung forward a few feet and lowered to this knees. He pulled his hands from the unlocked handcuffs and shaded his eyes as the blindfold was removed. The sun was setting. *It can't be that late.* He glanced at his penis, which stood up stiff. He glanced at her boots directly in front of him.

"Clean them."

He bent and licked each boot ferociously. The rubbing of his penis against his thighs and stomach almost made him come.

She gripped his hair and forced his head back. "You need your hair cut again. You'll go to the barber tomorrow while I'm at a lunch meeting." She brought her other hand around and held it in front of his eyes. "This is a little something to make sure you last the entire evening." She quickly placed the cock cage over his penis.

Yvonne sat down on the floor across from her bruised and beaten slave. "You thought you were so tough. I know you've had the cane and even the whip before. Most of your other owners stopped the beatings when you didn't break after ten minutes." She leaned toward him and lowered her voice. "You're already broken to me, right?"

"Yes, Mistress," he answered quickly. His breath increased its pace. *Oh God, what's happening to me?*

"This isn't only for me either," she told him, indicating the cock cage. She leaned back on her pillows. "You're going to beg me by tomorrow morning." She glanced at the slave entrance. "Bring them in!"

Two kitchen slaves entered, carrying two large platters. They laid these between the two of them on the floor, then withdrew silently.

"Eat up." Yvonne picked up a roast chicken breast and tore into it with her teeth. "Come on. Eat. You're going to need energy."

Jake picked up a chicken leg. Once he took one bite, he started eating everything he could get his hands on. His stomach felt like an empty pit. The only thing that slowed him down was the pain caused by reaching for the food. He whimpered when the kitchen slaves returned and collected the platters.

He was allowed to relax a few minutes when she left the room. He rose as quickly as his legs allowed when she called him into the bathroom.

"Run me a bath and brush your teeth. I'll be back in a few minutes."

He turned the water on and tested it with his elbow as he had been taught the past week. He took his toothbrush from his cup and carefully brushed his teeth. He rinsed his mouth several times. He finished just as the tub was filled to the height she liked with bubbles. He started to leave, but his way was blocked by the most beautiful female body he had ever seen. He stepped back as it entered. "Mistress," he whispered, sinking to his knees.

Yvonne walked past him and stepped into the tub. "You will help me wash."

Jake rose and took the washcloth from her hand. He washed each part of her body, except her genitals, which she did herself. Then she lay back in the tub and let the water flow around her when he turned on the whirlpool.

"Hop in the shower and make sure you get completely clean."

He soaped himself up and rinsed off twice, but still she was frowning. He reached for the shampoo for the third time when her voice stopped him.

"Put that nozzle on the showerhead and give yourself an enema." She sat up in her tub when he shook his head. "You really don't want me to do it to you. Believe me."

Jake swallowed. "May I pull the opaque curtain closed, Mistress?" he asked quietly.

"Please do. And make sure you soap down and rinse off afterwards," she added.

He placed the nozzle on the showerhead and removed it from its post. He clenched his teeth as he did to himself what they had done to him in jail before and after sentencing to check him for drugs.

Yvonne smiled as she heard his soft weeping. She got out of the tub and wrapped herself in a towel. "Come to the bedroom when you are done," she ordered, leaving the bathroom as she heard him starting to expel his waste.

Jake returned to the main room ten minutes later. He saw her sitting on her bed in a red negligee. He swallowed in fear when she motioned for him to approach. *Damn it!*

Don't do that! he cursed his cock as it pushed against its bonds. He held out his hands as she held up the handcuffs.

"Kneel down and lay your upper body across the bed, arms straight."

The handcuffs were strapped to a ring on the other side of the bed. She stepped from the bed. Her feet kicked his legs wide. She strapped his thighs to the bed frame. He screamed as she shoved something up inside his asshole. This device was attached with straps to the cock cage in front.

Yvonne threw a blanket over him and climbed back into bed. "You can come in now," she called. From the dark of the room another female figure emerged.

General Corriger! Jake watched this woman slip out of her robe and climb into bed naked. He couldn't see what they were doing, but their moans caused him to strain against the bed.

Jake woke up when he felt his arms relax. He looked up to see the handcuffs removed. She climbed over the bed toward him and lifted his head up. "Drink this," she said, putting a glass of water to his lips. He pushed himself up by his arms to drink but found his thighs still strapped to the bed frame.

She took the glass and set it somewhere out of his sight. She stood on the bed and shed her negligee. "Now it's your turn to make me happy." She lowered herself so her crotch was directly in front of his face. "You couldn't help but hear how happy I was last night." Yvonne spread her legs. "See if you can do better and you'll get two questions tonight."

Jake thought for a moment. *It's been five years since I've made love to a woman but not like this. What does she want me to do?* Just then she gripped his hair and forced his face into her clitoris. *Okay.* He flicked out his tongue and was rewarded with a small thrust from her hips.

His tongue slowly licked along each side. He quickened his pace gradually until she started to rock. Jake placed his hands on her hips and pulled her closer. He worked his tongue down to the edge of her vagina. He stuck it in quickly.

"No," she said sharply.

He moved his tongue back up her inner lips. Slowly. Quickly. Slowly. Quickly.

"Yes!" she ordered, pulling him so close he couldn't breathe.

He licked faster and faster. His hands slipped from her hips and clenched the bed sheets. He bucked against the bed. Just as he thought he would pass out, she shuddered and thrust him from her.

He tried to slow his breathing. He glanced at her. She, too, was trying to slow her breath.

"Not too bad," she said, getting off the bed. She unstrapped his thighs. "Do you want to get off?"

"Yes," he said. He fell off the bed from the force of her blow. "Yes, Mistress. Please."

"Follow me." She led him to the bathroom and had him kneel in the tub. She handcuffed his hands to a bar over his head and hoisted them tight. "Do you want to get off?"

Jake remembered what she had said before the evening started. "Yes, Mistress," he begged. "Please let your slave come, Mistress."

She smiled and loosened the cock cage. "You only come when I say to." She reached behind him.

Jake's eyes widened as he felt his ass vibrate. After a few seconds, he started thrusting. "Oh, oh, please." He closed his eyes and concentrated on her voice. *Wait, wait for her!* The vibrating lessened and he took a breath only to feel it increase again. "Aaahhh…"

"Come," Yvonne whispered. She laughed as he shot his

load over the entire wall. She removed the buttplug and the cock cage. "Take a shower and come out to eat." She washed her hands, put on her robe, and left.

Jake showered quickly. He looked in the mirror and noticed another bruise forming on his face. *My ass is sore.* He walked out to her bedroom and found her eating breakfast.

"Sit down and eat. You are probably very hungry. I know I am." She smiled, the first truly warm smile he had seen on her. He knelt slowly, wincing from the pain. "You'll get used to it," she said and tossed him a roll.

Jake stopped his laps when he saw her limo drive up the road to the palace. He thought about running to meet her, then decided to finish his last two laps.

After the three miles, he headed back to the stables. There he took a quick shower to wash the sweat from him before he met her. He glanced in the mirror and nodded at how much he thought his body had improved in the three weeks she had been gone. *I can handle more tonight.*

Jake hurried through the slave tunnels to her bedroom. Finding it dark and empty, he opened the curtains slightly. He went to the bathroom and ran a hot bubble bath. He opened the closet with the torture instruments and picked out a two-inch leather collar. This he fastened around the metal collar already on his neck, along with the two matching wristcuffs. He glanced in the bathroom mirror when he turned off the water. *I hope this isn't too forward.* He heard the lower-level door open.

Yvonne trudged upstairs. Though she was mildly surprised when she found her slave prostrated a few feet from the stairs, Yvonne stepped over him to throw her pack on the bed. She ignored him and went to the bathroom. After a few minutes, she walked out to the bedroom and stood at his head. "Did you run that bath for me?"

"Yes, Mistress," he answered, but remained prostrate. He braced his body on his arms as his hair was grabbed and his head forced up. He tried to look past her naked body.

Yvonne bent and run her finger along the leather collar. She nodded slightly as she noticed the cuffs. "You want it, don't you, slave?"

"Yes, Mistress. Please," he heard himself whisper. His arms caught him as she let go of his hair.

"Help me with my bath," she ordered as she turned on her heel.

Jake jumped to his feet and followed her. He kept his face blank as he assisted her into the water. "Is the bath to your liking, Mistress?"

"It will do," she replied. She looked at him for a moment. "Remove all your clothes." She lay back in the water and bubbles, watching him disrobe. *Looking better.* "How many miles do you do now?"

"Three, Mistress," he replied, laying the last of his clothing on the floor in a neat pile. He could feel the leather more clearly now that it was his only covering. He caught the sponge that she tossed him.

"Wash me," she ordered, holding out a leg. She watched him dispassionately as he washed each limb, her neck, face, hair, and back. She took the sponge from him before he even thought of touching more of her body. "Call the kitchen and order some food. Tell them I'm in the bath and they'll know what to send up. When it gets here, bring it in."

Jake waited impatiently for the tray of food. "Thanks so much for hurrying," he snapped when the slave door opened and one of the kitchen hands entered. "I'll take care of this. Don't come back until we call you," he added as the boy left.

He found his mistress in the same position he had left her, relaxing in the now-fading bubbles. He laid the tray on a small stand and moved it to the tub.

"Are you hungry, slave?"

"No, Mistress. Not yet," he replied, uncovering the tray to reveal meats, cheeses, breads, and various fruits.

"Good. There are some hooks in the bathtub. Slip the rings on the cuffs over them. Facing away from me." She took a bunch of grapes as she watched him slip the cuff rings over the hooks placed at the opposite ends of the shower so his arms were spread away from his body. Taking a remote control unit from underneath her head, she pressed the button that made the hooks close.

Jake tried the hooks and found them to be strong. He glanced over his shoulder in fear and hope only to see her eating grapes in the tub.

"Tell me how you spent these three weeks," she ordered, reaching for some cheese.

"I did as you commanded, Mistress. Each morning at sunup I rose, dressed, and broke fast in the kitchen. Then I asked the steward for work. Sometimes he had chores, sometimes he didn't. If there were chores, I did them, but if not then I wandered around the palace." He paused when her chewing stopped. He felt her gaze on him. "I thought that learning about the palace would enable me to obey you more quickly." He sighed in relief as she murmured her agreement and resumed eating. "After a noon meal, I went to the stable to run laps. After that I went to the library to read the books you set aside for me." He felt his penis rise as his mind touched on the books.

"You enjoyed those books."

He wondered whether it was a question or a statement but decided to answer anyway. "Yes, Mistress. I hope they help me please you."

"I'm only here for this evening, then I'm off again. The next time I return, I hope you will be ready to accompany me on my station tour."

Yvonne stood up and exited the tub. She wrapped a towel around her and pulled the plug to let the water out. Closing the shower curtain with one hand, she turned the water on lukewarm and pointed it so it hit his body.

She left the bathroom and went to her torture closet. She dropped the towel and picked out the leather vest, chaps, gloves, and a small bag. She put the clothing on, then, smiling, she returned to the bathroom. She turned off the water and released the hooks with the remote, which she placed on the chaps' belt. "Come out to the bedroom."

Jake slipped his cuff rings from the hooks and stumbled from the shower wet and shivering. He went to the bedroom and stopped dead went he saw her. Quickly he lowered his eyes, which now saw his penis rising again.

"On your hands and knees, slave!"

He assumed the position and felt her standing behind him. He opened his mouth as she placed the bit in front of his lips. The reins rested over his shoulders. *She's going to ride me.* He tried not to fight, knowing it would be pointless. *You want this. Don't fight her. You really liked those pictures and the last night she was here. You're hers, go with it and you'll get to come.*

"Good, you're not fighting," she whispered. She knelt behind him and forced his legs slightly apart with her own. She took a tube from the bag and squeezed the jelly into his anus. "You are my slave," she whispered, slapping his buttocks. She took the strap-on dildo from the bag and fastened it around her waist. "The guards told me you liked them a lot."

Jake whimpered and tried to move but found the bit pulled back tightly. He closed his eyes and tried to relax as he felt his ass slowly being penetrated. Once it was in so deep he felt as if he would explode, she stopped pushing. He let out a breath through his teeth as she slowly pulled it out, stopping before it left him completely. Slowly back in him and slowly out. This continued just as slowly until he had counted thirty. He now felt a very pleasant pressure in him and found the bit loosened enough for him to glance down between his legs. His penis stood horizontal to the floor.

"Very good," Yvonne complimented him and patted his back gently. Suddenly she slapped his right buttcheek and pulled the plug out all the way.

Jake bucked as she slapped him again and pushed it in quickly. As he struggled, his head was forced back tightly. Slowly, he tried to relax as she pumped in and out rapidly. The pressure in him rose and a sweat broke on his skin. After a while his hands slipped so he landed on his forearms. She accommodated this new angle by loosening the bit and raising up onto her knees.

"Ahhh, oohh," he moaned through the bit as he felt his penis strain. Then she exited. He found the reins resting on his back and looked up at her. "Please, Mistress," he begged. He found himself filled but this time with something longer that just touched his prostate gland. He pushed back but found nothing there.

Yvonne lifted his head by his hair, taking the bit from him. She lay on her back and spread her legs. "Bring me to orgasm and maybe you'll come before I leave again."

"May I use my tongue and fingers, Mistress?" he asked, sliding lower to the floor so her clitoris was at eye level.

"Just the tongue, slave."

Jake touched her outer lips, licking all around them. *I hope that book is good.* Slowly he licked inward in circles to the inner lips and down her shaft. When he reached the

...agina he could taste her juice. He returned to the outer lips and licked a little faster. He wanted to repeat the cycle more and more quickly but could feel his own need pressing on him for release. He returned to her shaft and licked at an increasing pace. Soon her thighs clamped over his head and she started to moan her pleasure. Encouraged, he increased his pace until she was bucking into his tongue, then shuddering. He licked her clean without command while her breath returned to normal. He kissed her inner right thigh. "Please, Mistress," he begged.

Suddenly his ass started to vibrate softly, then more strongly. He moaned and tried to rub himself on the floor but found her hands holding the leather collar he wore. After several minutes he felt the device stab his gland and his penis explode in pleasure.

"Clean it up, then take another shower," she commanded as she removed the plug.

Jake started to rise but found her foot on his head.

"Use your tongue, slave. Hurry before it dries."

Jake felt a comment rising in his throat but shoved it down as he licked up his ejaculate slowly.

Jake went to do his laps near the stables. He had awakened that morning at sunrise to find the cuffs, collar, and mistress gone. He took a few breaths before beginning the run. As he turned the first curve of the track, he thought about what he had been through since arriving there. Weeks without seeing her, then hours of torture or simply following her around. *Is she doing this on purpose? Yeah, that's it. She's trying to break my will.* With that realization, he sped off to finish five miles without a thought.

"You were running from the devil out there," Mike the stable lad stated as Jake stumbled into the stable and fell onto the floor. "Bad move, 'cause I've got a job for you."

"Fuck you," Jake managed to say as he gasped for air.

"The princess's orders. I'm supposed to teach you how to care for her gear and horse." Mike stood above the gasping man. "As soon as you get your breath, come to the hay bin."

Jake focused on slowing his breath. Propping himself up on his elbows, he looked up at the ceiling. He remembered putting on the collar and cuffs before he had even seen her, and dug his fingernails into the dirt. *That's not going to happen again.* He stood up and headed for the hay bin with a frown. "So what am I supposed to do with her stuff?" he demanded when he found the stable hand shoveling hay from one pile to another.

"First you learn to pitch the hay." Mike stopped and handed the pitchfork to him.

"What does this have to do with her stuff?"

"Horses eat hay whenever it's available so you have to learn how to care for it. It's really easy."

"No, no, no." Jake threw the pitchfork on the ground. "You said that she wanted me to learn to care for her gear and the horse, so I ain't doing your work for you," he said and turned to leave.

"You will do whatever Mike tells you to do." Jake found himself face to face with the chief groom. "Pick up the pitchfork and do your work."

"Who's gonna make me?" Jake stood as straight as he could and clenched his hands into fists.

The chief groom stepped aside with a wave of his hand. "I'm not going to make you do anything. We're all slaves here. We should obey orders, but if you don't want to, I'll just have to tell her about it."

Jake felt his stomach tighten. "Just because you don't like to do your own chores, right?"

"No. Because she'll ask me what you did when she gets back just like she did yesterday."

Jake's face turned white.

"Oh, I see," the chief groom chuckled. "You think you're earning her trust. Why would she trust a drug dealer?"

Jake's face now turned red at the truth the groom spoke. He picked up the pitchfork. "So show me what to do," he said to the stable hand.

How long is she going to be gone? Jake pulled on some clean clothes. He now ate the sandwich he had picked up in the kitchen before returning to her suite to shower. No one objected to him showering there instead of the stable, so since he slept on the cot next to her bed he thought it would save time. *Save time for what?* he asked himself as he walked down the spiral stairs. There on the one chair were the books he was supposed to be reading. Confident he could ignore them for the third day in a row, he sat in the chair next to them and ate his sandwich. His eyes glanced at the title of the top book, *Sam's Submission. Why would I be interested in that?*

He finished the sandwich and sat silently for a moment. "I'm not going to read it!" he announced to the room as he stood and went to the windows. He watched the sun set and, when the last rays disappeared, felt a tug at his heart. He turned back to the chair. Flipping on the light, he sat and opened the top book. He read until the sun rose.

Jake looked out of the lower-level windows. *Ten days. God, I wish I had a watch.* He went to her desk and looked at it. He ran his hand over the top and closed his eyes. He pictured his mistress standing over him. Her hair pulled into a braid that rested over one shoulder. A black leather teddy on her body and thigh-high leather boots, one of which she placed on his knee. He imagined himself touching that boot, then opened his eyes.

Jake hurried to the books left for him, only one of the

three left still to read. He picked it up and ran his hand over the cover: *Taken or Given: Twelve Short Erotic Tales.* He opened it eagerly and sat on the floor to read under the floor lamp. The first two books had aroused him against his will but now he did not fight himself as he read.

Jake had unbuttoned his shirt and was leaning against the desk as he neared the end of the third story. He didn't hear the door open.

"You are to come with me!" The steward's voice caused Jake to throw the book in the air from fright.

"Shit! Don't do that, you fuckhead!" Jake exclaimed, scrabbling to his feet. At the steward's frown, he remembered his buttons. "It's hot in here."

"Of course," the steward replied with a sneer. "There is a bag packed for you in that closet," the steward stated, pointing to the coat closet. "Get it and follow me."

"Why?" Jake asked as he tucked in his shirt.

"She just sent orders for you to be brought to her." The steward walked to the open door. "Are you coming?"

Jake nodded and hurried to the closet. He grabbed the large khaki canvas bag and lugged it to his shoulder. "What's in this?"

"I don't know." The steward led him from the room, then locked the door to the princess's suite. "I'm to take you to the doctors first before you leave."

"Why?"

"She didn't tell me," the steward answered.

Jake grabbed the book and stuffed it in the bag.

They took the main stairway down to the clinic. After knocking, they entered. "You know what to do?" the steward asked the two doctors.

"Yes, we just received the letter," the man answered, taking the bag from Jake. "You can wait out here for him," he told the steward.

"Come with us," the female doctor told Jake.

Jake followed them into the room where he had been examined months ago. "Another physical?"

"We'll start with that," the female doctor said, taking the letter from her partner.

Jake stripped and did as he was told. When told he was in better health he smiled. "I'd better be after running those laps every day."

The female doctor took something large and black from the bag he had brought. The male doctor held it up and straightened all the straps of black leather.

"What's that?" Jake asked, though he knew from the books what it was.

"You're to wear what we put on you until you reach the princess's camp and are told to remove them." The man motioned for Jake to step down from the exam table.

Jake didn't struggle as the straps fit over his shoulders. He saw the woman hand the man several small locks. Straps were fastened around his upper arms and thighs. The three straps in back were tightened and locked. Next, a collar, wider than the last he had worn was locked around his neck. He couldn't move his head now so he just watched the items as they were handed to the man and felt them lock on him. First, cuffs were locked on his wrists.

"Wait," the woman said. "We should drain him before doing the rest."

The man nodded and helped Jake lie back on the exam table. Jake felt his arms and legs restrained.

"No!" he screamed as he felt his ass and urethra invaded. He continued screaming as he felt water pumping into his ass and being sucked from his bladder. Then the water was sucked from his ass. He kept screaming until he didn't feel any more pain. He opened his eyes to find the woman looking down at him with a frown.

"That was for your own good, idiot," she said angrily. She nodded to her partner, who silently spread Jake's asscheeks.

Jake clenched his teeth as something large was pushed into him. Then he felt a strap pulled around his semi-erect cock. He heard the click of two more locks. Then he was lifted to his feet by both doctors.

He put his clothes on as commanded; glancing at himself in the mirror only made him strain against the cock straps. The man helped him put on his socks and shoes. "You'll get used to it on the journey," he assured him.

"Do you know why I have to wear this?" Jake asked. He felt shame creep over him as the man stood up to face him.

"So you don't misbehave or get used before you reach her."

"She's the only one with the keys," the woman added. She opened the door to the waiting room. "You can leave now. The steward will show the way."

Jake followed the steward to the stables. He noticed the steward seemed amused but bit his tongue before saying anything. *He knows. Everyone knows.* Jake looked at the wagon that he was led to. "I go in there?"

"Yes, the guards will take you to the princess." The steward threw the bag into the wagon and watched with a smile as Jake struggled inside. As the wagon pulled away from the palace, the steward chuckled to himself.

Jake drank the shake that the female guard had given him. *No solid foods until we reach the camp,* he thought bitterly. He watched the male guard closely. *I know him.* After the guards finished eating, this guard came to him, unbuttoning his pants. Jake tried to stand but was stopped when on his knees. "Don't try it!" he spat at the guard.

The female guard stood behind the male guard. "He's

got a chastity device on. You might as well leave him alone."

"I had him that way before." Jake froze at the memory of one of his rapists. "I'll have him another way now."

Jake fought back as the man tried to force his head down. He relaxed when the guard released his grip, only to find himself tackled onto his back and the guard straddling his head.

"Hey, hold his feet and I'll help you get some action, too," the man said. Jake felt his kicking feet grabbed and held to the floor. "Open it!"

Jake clenched his teeth and shook his head. He tried not to give in when his nose was closed but finally had to gasp for breath. He felt the huge cock forced into his mouth. In rage, he closed his teeth.

"Bastard!" the guard screamed, then pulled out and hit him on the jaw. He grabbed the slave's head and held the nose again. "Do it nice or I'll kill you here and now!"

Jake gasped for breath and felt the cock shoved deeper into his throat. He didn't bite but struggled for breath.

"Just open your throat and let me do it so you can breath through your nose!" the guard ordered.

In Jake's mind some of the pictures from the books flashed before his eyes. He tried to relax. *Just let them do it and get it over with. You'll be there tomorrow.* Telling himself this seemed to relax his throat and he felt his breath flowing from his nostrils. He started counting the thrusts. *Five, six, seven.* He struggled again when the warm slimy come started filling his throat. The guard got up after a final thrust and rolled him over. Jake threw up.

He felt something kick his feet. "I don't want him after that!" he heard the woman complain.

"I'll rinse his mouth out for you," the man said.

Jake felt himself pulled away from that area to a more

grassy one. The woman pushed him into a sitting position. "You bite me and I'll rip it off!" she promised. The man gave him something medicine-tasting to rinse his mouth with several times. Jake even managed to gargle and get some of the filth from his throat.

Jake lay back down on the woman's lap. "Your turn," he snipped at her. She let his head fall as she stood up. She removed her pants and underwear, then straddled his face. Before she said anything, he licked her already wet and swollen clit.

"Hey! He must like you," the man said, squatting down to watch.

Jake continued to lick and suck at his own pace even after the woman grabbed his hair and tried to force him to go faster. *No. I do it my way.* He brought her to the edge of orgasm and started to back off when she stood up.

"Get it out!" he heard her order. Jake managed to sit up and watch as the man took down his pants and grabbed her. He watched in anger as they fucked in front of him. Jake wiped the drying juices from his face on his sleeve. They didn't notice that he had returned to the wagon until the next morning.

Jake blinked in the afternoon sun as he was jerked from the wagon by the two guards. His eyes focused clearly and saw the too-familiar figure in black fatigues. He pulled his arms free and prostrated himself as she approached. Her black boots stopped in front of his face.

"Stand up!" Her voice sounded strange. Yvonne grabbed his hair and forced his head up for her to view. "Open your mouth!" She looked inside and saw a red rash and bruises. Yvonne released him and pointed to the large tent from which she had come. "Go in and wait for me." She pushed past him and went to the guards. "Corriger!"

Jake paused once he was near the tent. He watched the general join his mistress. "Yes," he whispered when the male guard was thrown to the ground by the princess's blow. He went into the tent with a smile.

"No one touches my property without my permission! General Corriger!" Yvonne yelled loud enough for everyone in camp to hear.

"Yes, Your Majesty." Valerie glared down at the guard in anger.

"She used him too!" the male guard stated, pointing to his partner.

Yvonne turned to the woman. "Is that true?"

"I told him not to..."

"Is that true?"

The woman turned deathly white under her liege's cruel gaze. "Yes."

"Execute both of them," she ordered just loud enough for those nearby to hear.

"Are you sure?" Valerie asked with a glance at the two guards. "You don't want a trial?"

Yvonne looked at the soldiers gathered around her. "Did you hear them confess?"

"Yes!" the soldiers answered almost in unison.

"I believe the law says that I am within my rights, General."

Valerie smiled. "Your sentence will be carried out." The general watched her liege return to her tent, then turned to the two condemned guards. "How could you be so stupid?"

"You said you wanted him scared...," the man began.

"But not touched!" The general glanced around and signaled for two soldiers. "I'll try to make it quick," she whispered.

Yvonne stormed into her tent. She walked past the prostrate slave and poured two goblets of wine. "Stand up and drink this," she said.

Jake rose slowly and took the goblet. "Thank you, Mistress."

She watched him silently while they finished drinking. "They forced you?" she asked, taking the goblet from him.

"Yes, Mistress," he answered, eyes respectfully focused over her shoulder.

"Are you lying to me?"

Jake focused his eyes on hers. "No, Mistress." After the answer, he returned his eyes to the empty space above her shoulder.

"Take your clothes off and close your eyes."

Jake quickly did as he was bid. As he stood motionless, he heard the locks unclick.

"Open your eyes. Behind that curtain is the bathroom. Go in there, clean everything up and off, and put on the clothes you find there before returning here for supper."

Jake bowed and went behind the curtain. He slipped out of the straps. The buttplug hurt as he removed it. He washed the leather and plastic off with a cleaner sitting on a small table. He then took a quick but thorough shower, using the nozzle for an enema and the razor to shave his body. Stepping out of the shower, he heard voices in the tent. He glanced out of the curtain and saw the general standing and speaking seriously to the princess.

He returned to a chair that had his clothes folded over them. *Nice stuff. I wonder what she wants.* He put on the silk underpants, cotton pants, and silk shirt. The pair of sandals with matching brown vest finished the outfit. He looked at the mirror set up in the room. The blue pants and white shirt were clearly rich material. *I guess I better go find out.*

When Jake entered the main area of the tent, he found

his mistress alone. She was facing away from him, so he softly cleared his throat.

Yvonne spun around. "Very nice. I hope you feel comfortable in them."

What? "Yes, thank you, Mistress." Jake waited for a few seconds before approaching her. "May your slave do anything for you, Mistress?"

"Yes. Guard!" One of the two guards at the opening of her tent entered. "Take my slave to the cook and then bring him back with my meal. He'll learn the way after this."

Jake bowed and followed the guard out. These were soldiers, not the palace guards who had raped him. *They wouldn't do anything against her,* he decided. They led him several yards away to another large tent; this one had all the flaps open and delicious scents drifted out.

Jake nodded at the cook when he was introduced.

"Are you allergic to any foods or preservatives?" the large man asked, wiping his hands on his apron.

"Not that I know of," Jake replied with a smile. *I might like this guy.*

The cook nodded. "Good, because the baskets are ready to go." Two youths handed Jake two large baskets. "You can carry those, can't you?" the cook asked as the slave struggled to grip them.

"I got them." Jake looked around at the kitchen help and noticed they all wore uniforms very similar to the guards who had brought him here. "You're not slaves?" he blurted out.

The kitchen staff laughed. "No. Everyone here is free," the cook replied with a grin. "Except for you and any captives we might pick up along the way."

Jake felt his face turn red. He turned on his heel and hurried from the tent as fast as the baskets allowed. The guards soon caught up with him. *I hate them all.* "I can carry it!" he snapped when one of them tried to take one of the baskets. "I'm the slave, aren't I?"

"Hey, I don't care," the guard replied.

They hurried back to the tent. Jake went inside as soon as they started to part the tent flaps.

"Did you learn the way?" Yvonne asked, not looking up from the papers she was reading.

Jake glanced angrily at the guards. "Yes, Mistress." His voice did not betray his anger. "Get out!" he mouthed at the guards, who left with a shrug.

As he went to the large table in the room to set the baskets on it, his head was snapped by her slap. He dropped the baskets on the table and sank to his knees, head on the floor in front of her boots.

"You have a problem with my soldiers?"

"No, Mistress," he said, then found his head forced up by his hair.

"I know everything that happens in this camp and in my palace. I'll ask the question once more. You have a problem with my soldiers?"

Jake felt his face drain of all its color. "Yes, Mistress." As soon as he said it, she released his hair.

"What's the problem?"

Jake looked up at her to find her sitting on the edge of the table. He sat back on his heels and focused his eyes over her shoulder. "I thought the kitchen staff would be slaves too. I just didn't know I was your only one here, Mistress."

"This is an army. We work through mutual respect and need. I wouldn't have brought you except you can take care of my little needs so that more troops are free to fight and live their own lives." She got off the table and sat in the chair. "Serve the food."

Jake slowly stood up. He glanced at her as he unpacked the baskets. One had the plates, silverware, napkins, goblets, and a bottle of wine. The other held the food in various containers. As he dished the food onto her plate and poured the wine, he almost spoke a couple of times.

"You have a daily question so ask it now if you want," she reminded him as she started eating. "Don't waste it. The other plate is for you, so eat up."

Jake muttered, "Thank you, Mistress," then filled his own plate. There were three other chairs, but he remained standing to eat so he could serve her. After he refilled her goblet, he spoke, "They said that you pick up slaves on your missions."

Yvonne frowned slightly. "Is that a question?"

"No, Mistress," he explained quickly. "I don't understand. I thought only criminals could be enslaved. Would you explain this to me?"

"That's your question?"

"Yes, Mistress."

Yvonne set her goblet down. "Well, our citizens can only be enslaved for crimes. But our enemies aren't protected by our laws. I don't enslave enemies often. Usually I just ransom them back to their relatives to ensure good relations with people I may soon rule. Or I have them executed." She sipped her wine again and looked him over. "Of course, if you stop pleasing me, then I might just choose someone new."

Jake set his chicken leg down and looked at her. "What would happen to me then?"

"You only have one question per day," Yvonne reminded him with a cold smile. "Use your imagination and finish your food."

Jake entered the tent and bowed after returning from the mess tent. He waited for her invitation before kneeling next to her chair where she sat reading. He stayed there when she stood up and went to the bathroom. She returned, tossing him the book he had packed with him.

"You're not finished." Yvonne sat down in her chair and picked up the field reports. "Read one story, then stop."

"Mistress?"

"Yes."

"I was at the end of one story when I was called away. May I finish it and read another?" He braced himself for a kick or blow for asking another question.

"No, just finish that one."

Jake waited but no punishment came. He opened the book and tried to read the last three pages slowly. His pulse was racing and his skin was covered with perspiration by the time he read the last word. He glanced at her chair, then jumped to his feet. *Where is she?*

He went to the entrance and stuck his head through the tent flaps. "Has her majesty left the tent?" he asked the two new guards.

When they silently shook their head, he hurried back to the center of the tent. *Oh, shit! Damn it!* He almost fainted when she emerged from the bathroom in khaki pajamas. "Forgive me," he begged, crawling to her feet as quickly as he could.

"Did you enjoy the story?" she replied with a slight grin.

"Yes, Mistress." He looked eagerly up over her shoulder, bracing himself for a beating or the feel of leather on his skin. His heart sank when she simply walked past him empty-handed.

"Take your clothes off and lay them on one of the chairs," she ordered flatly.

Jake scrambled to his feet and faced her, his hope returning when he saw her sitting on the top of her bed. He removed and laid aside his clothes as soon as possible.

"There's a black case in the bathroom on the table. After

you've used the toilet, brushed your teeth, and washed up, bring it to me."

Jake hurried and prepared for the evening. He combed his hair neatly and smiled at himself in the mirror when he noticed how large his cock already was. He touched the black case but decided not to open it.

Yvonne took the case from her slave and told him to spread his legs and close his eyes. She fastened the chastity device on him again but not the butt plug. "Open your eyes." *Very good*, she thought, noting his expectant look and how his cock pushed against the leather cage. "You sleep at the foot of my bed. There's a blanket for you."

Jake opened his mouth in surprise when she crawled under the covers and pulled the light out. In the darkness he was tempted to touch her. *Damn! This is the punishment!* He felt his way to the end of her bed, found the blanket, and curled up on the rug.

He pulled the blanket around him, trying to block out his thoughts. Scenes from the story kept invading his mind. Soon these merged with the experiences he had suffered under her hand. He tried to awaken but found himself further and further into the dreams.

Yvonne sat in bed, smiling into the dark as his moans increased in volume and desire. She placed one finger to her lips to keep from laughing as she praised the doctors for supplying her with the tranquilizer lotion she had spread on the chastity cage.

Two weeks! Jake sat the breakfast basket on the table in the mess kitchen. *How long is this punishment going to last? What can I do to make her touch me? Even her fist against my jaw would get me off.* He touched his caged cock absently, then hurried from the tent.

"Watch where you're going, slave!"

Jake looked into the hate-filled eyes of General Corriger. He smiled. "I'm sorry, General. I'm just so tired from last night I must have dozed off while walking," he lied with ease. "I'll try to be more careful where I walk."

Corriger grabbed his silk collar and pulled him to his toes. "Keep your eyes open, slave!" She released him with a push that almost made him fall.

"Bitch," he whispered as she stormed away. *At least she ain't getting any either.* He straightened his shirt and returned to the tent.

Yvonne threw a bit and reins at him. "Saddle my horse!"

Jake caught the bit and reins. "My question from last night. Are we leaving, Mistress?"

"I'm leaving on a raid with my best soldiers. Now go saddle my horse."

"Yes, Mistress." Jake hurried to the stable, where he found her black mare eagerly pacing her stall. He brushed the horse down and saddled her as he had been shown back at the palace. Just as he led the horse outside, the reins were taken from his hands.

Yvonne quickly strapped her saddlebags on the mare, then mounted. "Pick up your meals as always. There's a new book for you on the table in my tent. Read as much as you like," she added with a smile.

Jake watched her gallop away. After he could no longer see her, he returned to the tent. There he found a leather book without a title sitting on the table. He picked it up and opened to the table of contents. *Introduction. Ted. Brian. Roger. Bill. Scott. Neal. Dean. Alex. Zach. Trent. Lyle.* He set the book back on the table. *Later.* He went to collect the laundry to take to the camp cleaners.

Jake gripped the book with both hands as he finished "Roger." It had been four nights since she had left, and he had read one section of the book each night. *I want to go there,* he thought about the school described in the book.

After four nights of reading, he found himself now opening the bag he had brought with him. He looked at the mirror in the bathroom as he placed the collar around his neck. *I wish the metal one was off so I could feel it better.* Then he put the wrist cuffs on. Unable to fasten the straps behind his back, he put the body harness back in the bag.

Next he took out a set of nipple clamps and snapped them on slowly. "Ooohhh...," he moaned as they burned him. After a few minutes the pain dulled. He looked in the mirror and noticed his cock turning a dark red as it pushed helplessly against the cage.

He took out a thin but long buttplug. His hands trembled as he smeared it with lube. Then he bent down at the knees and spread his legs. He closed his eyes as he pushed it into himself. As he slammed it in and out faster and faster, he heard himself crying out, "Mistress. Please. Please." Finally the plug touched his prostate and he felt sudden release.

After regaining his footing and his breath, he removed the plug and stumbled to the sink to clean it off. He noticed his penis was still enlarged but didn't hurt as much. He didn't know what happened but he felt a little better as he went to sleep at the foot of her bed.

"Oops!"

Jake glared up at the general as he picked up the remains of his breakfast, which she had knocked to the ground for the sixth day in a row.

"I'm just so clumsy," Corriger said, kicking him in the rib cage and knocking him on his butt. "Oops! I did it again."

"That's it!" Jake jumped to his feet. "You watch where you're going, you bitch!"

"What did you call me?" Corriger smiled at the soldiers who accompanied her.

"A bitch." Jake rolled up his silk sleeves and took a fighting stance. "You're just jealous because she's chosen me over you." Jake didn't see the kick that knocked him to the ground.

"Get him!" Corriger ordered her soldiers.

Jake fought against the two men, but only found himself with a bloody nose. He let himself go limp so they had to drag him to the middle of the camp, where the general waited with a mounted soldier. Jake's hands were tied together and the rope given to the mounted woman.

"Take him for a good run!" Corriger glared after the horse and the slave running after it. "Faster!" She turned as the soldiers around her took up the chant. "Faster!"

After three gallops around the entire camp, the rider returned, the slave stumbling behind her. "Look at this," Corriger clicked her tongue. "Look at these lovely clothes that she gave you and now they're ruined." She grabbed his hair and forced his head back so he had to kneel in order to breathe. "She's going to be very angry with you."

"Bitch," he spat into her eyes. He stood up shakily as she backed away from him.

"Strip him and bind him to the pole!" she ordered two of the soldiers. "Do it!" she yelled when they hesitated. "You! Go get me the biggest whip you can find! One of the horse whips!"

Corriger walked around the pole so she could glare at his face as he was tied to it facedown. "You will beg me to stop. You will call me Mistress, too."

"Never. I exist for her." When the words left his lips he felt a weight fall from his body. "Do your worst, bitch!" he screamed. His head struck the pole as she slapped him.

Jake braced for the blows. *I can take anything you got,*

bitch. His body arced in pain when the first strike fell. He clenched his teeth to keep from screaming. *One. Two. Three. Four. Five. Six. Seven. Eight. Nine. Bitch! Ten.* "No!" he screamed finally.

"Beg me to stop," she ordered, signaling the soldier to stop the whipping.

Jake braced for the next blows. "Never!" After a few more, he was screaming wordlessly with every strike. He felt something hot and wet running down his back. *Blood.* His mind ran through his options as his screams became weaker.

"Beg me to stop, damn you!" Corriger yelled at him as the blows fell. She grabbed him by the hair and looked at him. "Call me Mistress."

Jake just blinked his hate-filled eyes and bit his lip as the blows continued. Soon all he saw was darkness.

"What's going on?" Yvonne asked the scout returning from the camp. The young woman sitting behind her tightened her handcuffed hands on her captor's jacket.

"The general appears to be beating someone to death, Your Majesty."

Yvonne narrowed her eyes. "Come on!" she ordered her troops as she galloped into camp. Seeing the camp gathered around the whipping pole, she quickly slipped the woman off her horse, then dismounted, throwing her the reins. The crowd grew silent as she pushed through it. Upon seeing the bloody body of her slave tied to the post, she struck the soldier handling the whip in the neck, sending him to the ground unconscious.

"What the fuck is going on here?" she demanded from the general, who walked angrily around the pole.

"Yvonne," Corriger's face turned white. "Your Majesty. I was just…ummm…punishing him…"

"For what?" Yvonne walked to her frightened lover. Her

elite troops ordered the other soldiers back and made a circle around their liege, the general, and the pole. "Take him down and to the medical center."

"He wouldn't obey me while you were gone and was balking at my authority in camp."

"He's not your property, nor is he a soldier." Yvonne turned to the soldiers, glancing over the shoulders of her elite troops. "Did my property disobey any camp rules while I was gone?"

Yvonne nodded as all gathered around murmured in the negative. "He obeys me and no one else," she said.

"He was disrespectful!"

Yvonne laughed. "I know. That's why I like him. And that's why I'm going to be lenient with you, Valerie. Ann!" The woman who had ridden behind her emerged through the crowd. "This is a present I brought back for you. Take her and go to your tent." Yvonne turned to a few of her elite troops. "Escort General Corriger to her tent and make sure she stays there until further notice."

Corriger took the woman's cuffed hands and led her away. They stopped at the sound of her name.

"Valerie. You better pray he lives."

Jake glared at the nurse as she took his temperature for the third time that day. "I feel fine!" he insisted.

"Well, we'll see when you get your tests results back." She handed him a glass of ice water. "Drink this."

"Yeah, yeah," he said taking a sip for her benefit, then setting it on the table next to him. He remembered being brought back to the palace clinic a few days after the beating. How many weeks it had been he wasn't too sure. She hadn't stopped by once. *Shit. She's going sell me.*

"What are you thinking about?"

Jake jumped up from his bed at the sound of his

mistress's voice. "About you. You came. Mistress. Please, sit down," he said, motioning to the bed.

"You, too. You're still weak," she said, sitting on the cot next to his.

"I'm ready for your use, I mean I'm ready for service, I mean…"

"Sit down," she insisted.

"Yes, Mistress." Jake sat and couldn't tear his eyes away from her. She wore a light green dress, the first he had ever seen her in, brown boots, and a wide hat. He felt his cock rise, then remembered his eyes and focused them over her shoulder.

"I brought you something," she said, taking a leather book from her shoulder bag. "You didn't get to finish it."

Jake took the book and moaned when he recognized it.

"You don't like it?"

"You're not going to sell me, Mistress? I hope I've saved up enough nights for several questions," he added quickly.

"I thought I told you that if I ever get sick of you, I'll just kill you."

Jake nodded and looked at the bookmark sticking up from the book. "My collar's gone so I thought you might be selling me or killing me, I guess."

"That had to be removed for medical care. As was your chastity belt—as I'm sure you've noticed and taken advantage of."

Jake shook his head.

"Oh, please. How many times have you gotten off since you've been here?"

Jake looked her in the eyes. "None, Mistress. I didn't have your permission."

Yvonne smiled slightly and moved to sit next to him. "Looks like you can still do it," she said, nodding at the bulge in his pajama bottoms. She reached and opened the pants to let the cock jump free. "We'll have to get you a new collar."

"Mistress," he continued as she nodded approval. "I would be honored, though unworthy, to wear a leather collar or anything you wish at any time."

Yvonne moved closer to him and grabbed his hair to bring his face closer to hers. "Why?" she demanded with a pleased glance at his now purple-red cock.

"Jake doesn't exist except for you," he answered with all his being, freed from all concerns outside her voice and body.

Yvonne released him and moved slightly away on the bed. She nodded as he sat up to try to remain near her. "Come!"

Jake felt his body arc with the power of the orgasm that had been waiting for over a month. After a minute or more, he lay gasping on the bed. "Thank you, Mistress," he whispered.

"Sit up!"

Jake sat up on his knees, ignoring the still-warm ejaculate that covered his sheets. He smiled as she showed him the two-inch leather collar with his registration as her slave on it in gold. He stuck his neck out eagerly as she fastened it around his neck.

"Report to my suite when they release you, slave!" she ordered, rising to her feet.

"Yes, Mistress." He cried tears of joy as he jumped off the bed to prostrate himself at her feet. He remained there until he could no longer hear her footsteps.

Yvonne stopped outside the door to meet with the doctor. "He'll be able to join me by the end of the week?"

"Yes, Your Majesty," the woman bowed. "You were right. He did break without using drugs."

"Using drugs? Why doctor, that would hardly be the proper punishment, now would it?" Yvonne placed her arm around the doctor's shoulders and led her through the clinic. "He accepts who he always was."

"That hardly seems like a punishment. To live as he always should have."

"Who said he was going to live, doctor?" Yvonne stopped at the front door. "I'll send you instructions as soon as I hear he has a clean bill of health. You will follow them, doctor, won't you?" She ran her finger along the doctor's gold collar as she stared coldly into the frightened eyes.

"Yes, Mistress," the doctor replied and bowed as the Butcher of the United Lands left.

Responsibilities and Privileges

The marketplace was not very crowded even though it was the monthly slave auction. Today the market had been roped off to allow only the royal family and the highest class of citizens access. Most of the aristocracy seemed more intent on following the two birthday girls and hoping to make themselves noticed without interrupting their shopping than on looking at the slaves themselves. Here and there the merchandise was laid out in semicircles, grouped according to the slaves' classification, ranging from cooks to heavy laborers to caretakers of children. Only the most highly rated dealers in each area of specialization were allowed at this special auction. Common citizens stayed outside the market itself, content on this special day to view the items on monitors; a few would lean over the ropes to pinch an asscheek and laugh at the man's reaction.

Semiramis, heir to the Unamisian throne, walked with

her cousin Zerlinda, heir to the duchy of Verelande, around
the market. The two girls giggled as they marked their sale
lists for each slave. As they walked, the wealthiest citizens
whispered at how alike the two girls looked— the one with
a tinge of brown in her red hair was just slightly taller—and
took bets on who was the princess.

Those who bet on the shorter girl would have won.
"There are so many!" Semiramis exclaimed as she paged
through the booklet of listings. "I didn't think the slave
market was this active."

"I bet that everyone is trying to sell because they know
you're looking," Zerlinda said. "It would be an honor to
have their former property in the hands of the heir to the
throne."

"Or in the hands of the future Duchess of Verelande,"
Semiramis pointed out. She released the booklet and let it
swing on the golden chain at her waist so she could grab
her cousin's hands. "Oh, just think; in one day we will be
women, Zerlinda!"

"Yes! With all a woman's responsibilities and privileges," the royal cousin added as she looked up at the slave
hanging before them, her eyes sweeping over his almost-
naked body.

Semiramis looked at the man also but shook her head
and marked a zero next to his number. She stood for a
moment, then her face fell as concern filled her thoughts.
"Hey," she grabbed her cousin's shoulder, "what if our first
choices are the same?"

"The way things are going," Zerlinda said, marking the
lot number, "that doesn't seem too likely."

"Yes, but what if it happened?" the princess insisted.

"Then you would get him, because you are the
princess," Zerlinda replied quickly. She kissed her cousin
on the cheek. "But I doubt it's going to happen."

"You're right," Semiramis agreed. She looked at the sign above the group of slaves they were looking at. "I'm getting tired of looking at all of them. Let's go find the sex slaves and make our choices there."

"Sounds good to me," Zerlinda replied with a giggle. She took her cousin's hand and the two girls ran across the market to the area designated for sex-specialized slaves. "It's not like we're looking for a cook," she added as they ran.

The market manager for the sex block hurried forward as she saw the most richly dressed figures in the square rush toward her display. She turned to the slaves, whose wrists were attached to poles over their heads and whose ankles were staked slightly apart; waist-high benches were placed half a foot before each. "Behave!" she growled at them. With that command she signaled for her assistant to stand ready and hurried to greet the two aristocrats.

"Your Highnesses," the market manager addressed the two girls as she bowed low.

The girls giggled, then the one with redder hair spoke. "Arise, worthy merchant; we have come to view your merchandise."

The market manager bowed again and rose up. "You honor me with your presence."

"We are looking for coming-of-age gifts," Semiramis informed the woman, hoping it would stop the fawning.

"These are the best items the market has seen in decades," the manager stated as she led them to the first slave. "May I or my assistant offer you refreshments while you browse?"

"No, thank you," Semiramis answered politely.

"We prefer to browse alone," Zerlinda insisted when the women did not leave immediately.

"Oh, yes, of course." The manager and her assistant

bowed and hurried to stand a short distance away so they could watch but not disturb the girls.

"You didn't have to be rude," Semiramis commented quietly as they walked to the next lot.

Her cousin did not reply but pointed to the one they stood before. "He's a local," she stated, pointing to his plain bare feet.

"And our age," Semiramis added with a nod at the placard that hung around his neck.

"Aahhh..." Zerlinda moved closer to the boy, who looked directly back at her. She fingered his black hair, which hung in curls to his chin, a sure sign that his sale had been planned for months. She ordered him to open his mouth and inspected his teeth.

"May I be of assistance?" the manager asked with a bow.

"Yes." Zerlinda turned with a smile. "It says he has only had one owner," she said, pointing to the placard.

"Yes, Your Highness," the manager replied as she went to stand on the opposite side of the boy.

"Isn't that impossible? I mean, it would be immoral for a mother to train her son as a sex slave," Zerlinda added with a frown of suspicion.

The manager paled slightly as she pointed to the small print. "His mother died in childbirth and I bought him, Your Highness. He has had the best training money can buy," she added with a hint of pride in her voice.

"I bet," Zerlinda said softly as she walked behind him. "Let me look at his hole," she ordered.

The manager pulled the chain off its hook on the pole, allowing the boy to lower his chest to the bench as directed.

Semiramis sighed, uninterested in further examination, and started down the line of merchandise on her own.

Zerlinda pulled the plug out of the slave's asshole and nodded in approval of its width. After replacing it, she felt how firm his muscles were and tweaked his balls from behind. "He's very nice," she commented as she smiled at the manager. "Don't you agree, cousin?" Zerlinda frowned at the empty space where her cousin had stood. "What number is he?" she asked, turning again to the manager.

"Number 1579, Your Highness. Thank you for honoring me so," the manager added hurriedly to the girl who ran after her cousin.

Semiramis looked at the blond boy who stared at the ground, unlike the other slaves who stood straight, their eyes directly ahead. She read his placard silently: *number 1588; age 20 years; height 5'7" with a few inches to grow; previous owners— one, two, three; oh my goodness, that's ten.* She looked at his body briefly then continued reading. *Special talents: good voice.*

"Hey, you just ran off," Zerlinda declared to her cousin, tapping her on the shoulder.

Semiramis looked up with a sigh. "We don't have the same taste," she admitted, then returned to look at the boy.

"Obviously," Zerlinda stated after one glance at the boy. "Ten owners!" she exclaimed after a quick study of the placard around his neck. "You can't be interested in this?" she insisted, following her cousin as she circled the boy twice and ended up behind him. "Tell her what a waste he is," she ordered the manager, who had now joined them.

"Oh, Your Highness, he is worthy only for the poorest buyer," the manager stated with a glare at the boy.

"He looks abused to me," Semiramis said as she held up a finger covered in powder.

"You've used make-up on this slave!" Zerlinda stomped her foot in anger. "I should report you to the commerce council!"

"Oh, please, Your Highness, his owners have done this injustice. I will have him washed off immediately," she stated with a wave to her assistant.

"I want to examine him completely," Semiramis stated. Both the manager and her cousin stared dumbly at her. The princess stood up as straight as she could and placed her hands on her hips. "Show me his hole," she commanded.

The manager looked at the other girl, who simply nodded and stepped back to stand with her cousin. "Bow for the lady," she ordered the boy as she lowered his arms.

The cousins heard the boy moan slightly as Semiramis slowly pulled the plug out. "It's smaller than the one back there, and he's two years older," Zerlinda pointed out.

Semiramis didn't reply as she pushed the plug back in and firmly felt his butt, thighs, calves, and balls. "Have him stand again," she said as she walked back to his front. "Open your mouth," she told him. "He's missing one tooth, but the rest are in good shape," she told her cousin, who also looked.

Semiramis turned to the manager in exasperation. "Why doesn't he look ahead as is proper?"

"He has been this way since he was delivered," the manager replied with a shrug of her shoulders. "If you command him, he will obey you," she hesitated to add.

"Look up, boy," Semiramis commanded in a gentle voice. She almost gasped at the bright green eyes that immediately peered straight ahead. "Beautiful," she whispered. Touching the skin under his right eye elicited a moan from him.

"Wash him off now!" Zerlinda ordered the manager's assistant, who stood with hose ready.

The manager hurried the cousins to a safe distance while her assistant sprayed the boy with water, causing the powder that covered him to wash off into puddles at his feet. The boy gasped loudly as the cold water pounded his thin body.

"He's covered with bruises!" Zerlinda stated, her arms folded angrily.

"That cheat!" the manager exclaimed, one fist pumping in the air in anger. "How can I sell this?"

Semiramis walked forward until she reached the puddle of water and looked over the boy once more. "Look at me," she ordered firmly.

The boy's green eyes met hers briefly. They were surrounded by tears and water running down from his very short blond hair, indicating that he had not been sold that long ago.

Semiramis marked something on her sales booklet and turned to her cousin. "We haven't much time," she stated, indicating the watch on her wrist. "Let's continue browsing."

"Yes, I have much better merchandise," the manager said as she hurried beside the girls.

"Then show us your best," Semiramis instructed, with a sigh.

The boy shivered as the assistant manager sponged him off and placed a board under his feet so they could be cleaned and remain so.

"You have finished looking?" the woman with graying hair asked the two cousins as they joined her at their horses.

"Yes, Radella," Semiramis said, handing her the sale booklets. "I saw many good items."

"I too," Zerlinda exclaimed, a blush just starting on her cheeks.

The tutor looked over the lists quickly. "Indeed! But at least you numbered them one through twenty." She clicked her tongue at the lists. "Now you must return to the palace; your honorable mothers await your arrival."

"Can't we stay for the auction?" Zerlinda whined.

"Of course not," Semiramis answered her. "Then we would know which gifts we are getting and how much our mothers were willing to spend."

"That is correct," Radella agreed. She signaled the two guards who held the heirs' mounts. "They will escort you home," she stated, her eyebrow cocked so that the girls would not question her wisdom on that matter.

"Good-bye," Semiramis said, kissing her tutor's cheek.

"Tell Demida good-bye for me," Zerlinda instructed as she, too, mounted her horse.

"I will," Radella said as she waved to the girls. Soon they disappeared, kicking up clouds of dust in an attempt to outrun their escorts.

"Oh, I just missed them," the tutor of the heir to the dukedom of Verelande said as she rejoined Radella. "How are their lists?"

"Many choices, but yours is more complicated," Radella answered, handing the proper list to her fellow tutor.

"Oh, dear, wish we could have advised them on a few of these choices," Demida stated after looking over the final page containing the top twenty.

"Yes," Radella said as she stared at choices one through three, all marked with the same number: 1588. She looked at the sun, rising to its zenith, and led the way to the auction block.

The tutors nodded to each other as another lot was sold. "I don't know if it is a privilege to be sitting this close or not," Demida whispered and waved her fan again to rid her nostrils of the body odor the merchandise and buyers created. "Hasn't she wanted any of them?"

Radella glanced at the other tutor. "You have yours; you are free to go," she pointed out, with a slight smile.

"And allow you to have all this fun? Oh, no," Demida insisted, adjusting her velvet cushion beneath her.

Both women fell quiet as the next lot was announced. "Ladies, here is today's bargain," the auctioneer said. A bruised and cowering boy was led onto the stage, and the chains on his wrists were fastened to the post at the center of the stage. A large placard with his number printed on it was placed above his head.

"Who would buy that?" Demida shuddered.

"Who will make an opening bid?" the auctioneer asked.

After a few silent seconds a voice called from the cheaper section of the crowd, "ten silver!"

The auctioneer frowned, because everything else that day had started at least one gold piece. "Only ten silver? Who will give me more. Come now, ladies, this boy is only twenty, and any of your strong hands could surely train him for great things. Ten silver going once."

"Twelve silver!" Radella called out, after but one rechecking of the sales booklet.

"Are you insane?" Demida asked as softly as shock allowed her. "How can you possibly bid on that?"

"Fourteen silver!" Radella countered another bid and handed the princess's list to the other tutor.

"Oh, Goddess save us," the other woman whispered, placing her hand over her heart. "You best get it to at least a gold piece," she advised when the bidding from the crowd stalled at seventeen silver.

Radella nodded and waved her handkerchief. "One gold piece!"

The auctioneer sighed in relief as the bid was raised to decent levels. "One gold piece from a wise woman. Who will make it two? One and a half? One and a quarter?"

"Let her have him and bring out something better!" a voice from the poorer section called out. Voices from all sections of the crowd agreed.

"Very well, then," the auctioneer smiled weakly as she pounded her gavel. "Going once, twice, sold to the lady on the royal podium!"

The two tutors rose and walked to the cashier, where Radella paid the one gold piece and received the ownership papers. Silently the women went to get their goods.

"Boy!" Demida called to the black-haired slave who stood waiting by her horse. The boy rushed and knelt in the dirt before her. "Beautiful," the tutor commented with a smile to her colleague.

"Yes," Radella admitted with a sigh. She motioned to the guard, who led her purchase toward her. "Thank you," she said to the guard, tipping her one gold piece and receiving a low bow of thanks in return. Radella looked down to find the boy cowering on the ground before her. "Stand up, boy!"

The boy stood up, but his head remained bowed. He shook when the tutor's hand gripped his chin and lifted his head.

"You're not much to look at," Radella stated as she looked up his body. "Except," she gazed into his emerald eyes, "for those eyes." She released his chin, and his head returned to its bowed position. "What did your last owner call you?"

"Sorry," the boy whispered.

"What? Speak up, boy!"

"Sorry," the boy spoke up but did not raise his head.

"Are you apologizing, or was that your name?" Radella asked with a bemused look.

"My name, Mistress," the boy replied, his voice shaky but rich.

"I'm not your mistress and that's a terrible name." Radella looked at the ownership papers she had been handed, then back down at him. She touched his shoulder, and he practically collapsed to the ground, kneeling on his knees. "Hold up your hands, boy." She tied a rope around his wrists and commanded him to stand. "Follow my horse," she instructed as she mounted.

"Why?" was the single question Demida asked as she joined the other tutor.

"For his eyes," Radella responded. "It had to be for those eyes." She spurred her horse, and the two tutors, two guards, and two slaves headed out of the market stables at a very slow pace. As they rode, the older tutor began thinking how best to represent the situation to the queen.

Radella led the boy to the check-in center for slaves at the palace. Demida and the gift she had bought had separated a few miles back to head to the duchess's local house. Radella pushed the boy toward the slave steward who was waiting for them. The woman's face whitened at the sight of the skinny, bruise-plastered body. "This is a joke, lady?"

"No, this is the princess's coming-of-age gift. Whoa, boy." Radella placed her hands on the boy's shoulders to calm him down. "He didn't know who he was for until now," she informed the steward.

The steward clucked her disapproval as she turned the boy around and looked at him more closely. "What choice was this?"

"Her first, second, and third choice," Radella replied as she sat in the chair her own slave brought to her. "Thank you, Dwern." She held up one leg, and her slave quickly removed her boot. "He doesn't have an appropriate name, which should please her. And his eyes are quite stunning."

The steward nodded and frowned. "There's not much I can do for these bruises by tomorrow night."

Radella stood up when her palace slippers were once more on her feet. "Have a complete physical done and written up and a complete history run on the best paper. We'll get the best clothes, but that is all we can do. The rest will be her responsibility."

"It's not an appropriate choice," the steward muttered but found her arm in the harsh grip of the tutor.

"He was her first, second, and third choice," she restated.

"I obey the laws, as you will obey me." So saying, the royal tutor left the check-in center, her slave following with her boots.

The boy started to follow the woman who had bought him but was stopped by the chief steward. "Boy, you stay here. We have a lot of work to do before tomorrow night."

Semiramis looked out the window until her tutor's measuring stick struck her book. "Just because it's your birthday today doesn't mean you are allowed to forget your studies," Radella reminded her. "This is the last scholarly test of your entire life. So let's finish, shall we?"

"Of course, Professor. Forgive me." Semiramis picked up the black pen and finished filling in the corresponding ovals on her test form.

In half an hour she was finished and out of the classroom. She ran down the hallways and out into the sunlit garden to meet her cousin, who had just arrived. "Zerlinda! I'm finished with school!"

"Me, too!" the other screamed with delight.

The two girls hugged each other and spun around in joyous circles, their pinafores blowing out. Collapsing in a dizzy pile, the girls giggled at the sky. Zerlinda propped herself up on her elbows. "Tonight we become women."

"Yes," Semiramis said from her place in the grass. She lay there and closed her eyes. "It will be so wonderful to be women," she sighed.

"Especially with our gifts," Zerlinda added, her voice husky. "I feel like I have been waiting for this night my entire life."

"Since you were a babe?" Semiramis questioned with a guffaw of disbelief. "But yes, I have been looking forward to this for many months," she admitted, placing her hands over her abdomen and feeling her breath rising and falling.

The princess closed her eyes and remembered the tutor sessions on choosing a man. Her mind pushed aside the small collection of books she had read, focusing instead on the hands-on lessons during the last few weeks. Her hands clenched now as she remembered the feeling of skin beneath her fingers as she examined some of the palace slaves under the gaze of her instructor and the chief steward. She had been allowed to feel their hands and tongues on her neck, arms, legs, and digits. It had stirred her, as it stirred her now, but Radella insisted that her complete pleasure must wait until her birthday.

Semiramis's mental images twirled to form a row of the eighteen men she had listed on her auction sales list. Each was different, most beautiful and young, each claiming to have a skill that a princess must have. All but one. That one had only two sad emerald green eyes. A feeling of uncertainty now filled her stomach.

"What time is it?" she asked suddenly, sitting up.

"Oh, no!" cried her cousin, checking her watch, "We've only four hours until the guests start arriving!"

Semiramis scrambled to her feet, helping her cousin up. "We have to start getting ready!"

The steward threw up her hands in frustration. "Listen to me, boy! You will look up and stand at attention properly or I'll beat you black and blue!"

"A useless threat, I believe." The tutor had hurried downstairs after grading the princess's final exam to make sure things were progressing properly. She tilted the boy's head up with her hand and straightened his shoulders. "Boy," she said in a gentle yet firm tone of voice, "you are the gift for a very important young woman. You must behave in the best manner possible. Do you understand?"

"Yes, Mistress," the boy replied and kept his stance as steady as he could.

"Did you give him anything to eat?" Radella asked the steward.

"Some dried toast last night and this morning. The palace doctor said not to feed him more," the woman explained.

"Let me see the report," Radella said as she watched the tailor put the finishing touches on the boy's jacket, which was a color to match his eyes. The boy's hair had been trimmed evenly, making it even closer to his scalp, so it stuck up without assistance. His bruises had faded quite a bit with the aid of healing ointment. But he was obviously thin and scared. Radella looked over the physical report. "At least there wasn't much internal damage," she stated tiredly.

The tutor turned to the tailor, who had removed the jacket, leaving the boy in cotton shorts and shirt. "Are you finished with him?"

"Yes, lady," the tailor replied with a bow as her assistant took the jacket from her.

"I'm taking him to the hall to show him his duties for the evening. No need for him to be any more frightened," she added to the steward in a whisper.

"He might pass out from it," the steward replied.

"Boy!" Radella touched his shoulder. "Follow me!" The boy immediately fell in step behind her. The tutor looked down at his bare feet. "Where are his sandals?" The steward handed them to her, and she handed them to the boy. "Put them on, then follow me."

The boy slipped into the sandals and followed the tutor at a two-pace distance. He gasped when the tutor stopped and turned to him.

"Three paces, boy!" Radella commanded softly.

"Yes, Mistress," he said and made sure he now followed at three paces.

"You will be brought into the Great Hall through this back door," Radella indicated as they passed through the door into an enormous ballroom being decorated by dozens of slaves and ladies of the court. "You will be brought out onto this platform and presented to your owner, Princess Semiramis."

The boy placed one hand on his chest as he felt panic rise again.

"Calm down," Radella ordered firmly and met his eyes until he lowered his hand to his side. "You'll be waiting right outside the door, which will be open, so you'll see a similar presentation take place earlier in the evening," Radella continued. "Now, you know the rules of etiquette for meeting your new owner?"

"Yes, Mistress," the boy whispered.

"Pretend I am your new owner and demonstrate this etiquette," Radella instructed him as she took several steps away from him.

The boy knelt and bowed his head to her shoes. At a motion from her right shoe, he sat up straight and kissed the offered hand. She motioned him up with her hand, and he rose, stepping back three paces and standing straight with his arms folded behind his back.

Radella walked around him, looking him over closely. "Very well done, boy. Very well done indeed." She frowned as she looked more closely into his face. The boy closed his eyes, bowing his head with a twitch. "After the presenta- tion, you will follow the princess, at three paces unless otherwise instructed, and serve her every whim for the rest of the evening," she added with a sniff.

The tutor walked away from the boy and stared into the center of the room. "This is, of course, her coming-of-age party, so afterwards you will go to her bedsuite and satisfy her every desire. This will be your life for as long as you please her. Do you understand?" Radella waited for a few seconds before asking again. "Do you understand?"

Finally she turned around to find him unconscious on the platform. She pressed the intercom button on her wrist band. "Doctors report to the Great Hall immediately."

"What do you think?" Zerlinda asked as she held up her dark blue gown. Their gowns were not the full-skirted ones of childhood; they had straight skirts which only flared out enough to hug their body contours before touching the floor.

"Beautiful," Semiramis exclaimed. "I'll show you mine."

"Oh, no, you don't," Radella interrupted the girls. "Zerlinda, you are to go to your own suite and get ready there."

"Radella! We want to get ready together," the girls insisted in unison.

"That would be against tradition," Demida said as she entered the princess's suite. "Come, Zerlinda. Your mother is waiting for you."

The cousins sighed, kissed briefly, and said good-bye.

Semiramis turned with a frown to her tutor. "Did I pass all my tests?"

"Of course; you always do very well on tests," Radella replied, helping her out of her pinafore.

"Will Mother be coming?" Semiramis asked as she sat down in front of the vanity that had been delivered that morning.

"Yes, in a few minutes." Radella brushed out the girl's hair, which fell beyond her waist even though it was full of bouncing curls. "Now for your bath, Princess."

Semiramis stood up and headed for her bath. At the doorway she turned toward her tutor. "Will I like him?"

"You're the one who chose him," Radella replied.

"You don't approve of my choice," Semiramis said in surprise.

"I didn't say that, Your Highness," the tutor replied evenly.

"I thought he was," the princess paused as though searching for the best word, "intriguing."

"That's an interesting choice of words," the tutor commented softly. "I'm just concerned that he will need more from you than he can give back."

Semiramis sat down at her new vanity and brooded silently for a few moments before turning back toward her future chief advisor. "And who would you have chosen, Radella?"

"Someone older, someone wiser, someone whom you wouldn't have to train at all," she replied. Radella took a seat on the couch and looked seriously at the young heir. "You'll have time for fun later in life. You need to learn now and grow so that you can handle the realm when your time comes."

"That's quite a way away," Semiramis insisted.

"I pray so," the tutor replied. She stood up, a soft smile on her face. "Now go take that bath, Princess. Your people await."

"How do you feel, boy?" the doctor asked as he finished the drink they had given him.

"Fine," he whispered, looking around the palace clinic with worry.

"Is this going to cause problems?" the steward demanded.

"No," the doctor said as she rose to her feet. "The drink contains only nutrients his body will use; there will be no waste by-products," she explained.

The steward nodded and motioned for the boy to rise. "Come on. You have to get ready now, boy."

The boy followed the steward back to the room he had slept in the night before.

The queen entered her daughter's bathing chamber and motioned for the girl to remain in her bath. The queen sat in a chair one of the court ladies brought her and signaled for everyone to leave the room.

"Good evening, Your Majesty," Semiramis greeted her mother formally.

"Tonight I am a proud mother first," the queen insisted with a wide smile. "I must go out soon and meet the guests as they arrive. I gave Radella a gift for you to wear this evening. I am very proud of you," the queen restated as she stood up. She knelt and kissed her daughter's wet cheek. "See you in an hour and a half."

Semiramis sat in the bubbles of her bath after her mother left until her tutor's voice woke her out of her daydreams. "Yes, you're right, Radella. It is time to get ready," she called back. She rose and took the towel offered by one of the junior court women. Quickly she dried her body off, then allowed the woman to wrap the towel around her and lead her to the changing room, where many servants waited to assist her.

Semiramis looked in awe at her reflection as her hair was finished. The red curls had been piled up on top with a few strays hanging down around her neck and forehead. A tiger eye jewel sat in the middle of the bangs, suspended from delicate gold ribbons. "Is that me?" she asked in a whisper.

"Of course," Radella replied. "You are a beautiful young woman now."

Semiramis smiled at her reflection. "All of you but Radella leave," she commanded in a firm voice. She held up her hand to the women's protests. "It is only my gown and shoes. Radella and I can manage quite nicely." She stood up and turned around. "Go enjoy the party."

The women bowed and hurried from the room.

Radella held up her gown and helped her into it. The

gown was a russet color with gold flower outlines in the skirt to match the gold ribbons in her hair. The brown of the gown heightened the red of her hair.

Semiramis stepped into her matching russet slippers and held up her skirt as her tutor laced them up. She stood still as Radella smoothed out her skirt. "Didn't Zerlinda look beautiful?" she asked, referring to the scene of her cousin's presentation almost an hour earlier on the video monitor she had set up in her suite.

"Yes, but not as lovely as you," the tutor insisted diplomatically. "Your mother gave me a gift for you." She held up a beautiful tiger eye gem the size of a hen's egg on the end of a gold chain.

Semiramis opened her mouth in awe and turned so the necklace could be placed on. She turned to look at her full reflection in her mirror. "It's gorgeous!"

The tutor stood for a silent moment. Then, wiping away a tear, she opened the suite door. "It's time to go, Your Highness."

Semiramis walked down the hallway beside her tutor, then stopped by the entrance. "My speech," she gasped, taking hold of the older woman's sleeve. "It's back in my room."

"No, it's on the podium, just as we planned," Radella reminded her gently.

Semiramis closed her eyes and placed her hand over her heart as she prayed for guidance. At the sound of her name, the tension seemed to melt from her body, and confidence radiated from her as she walked out onto the platform.

The princess curtsied to the queen, then to the guests, either nobles or the wealthiest ladies of the realm.

"My daughter and heir: Semiramis!" the queen announced again. She stepped aside as the princess walked to the podium.

The princess's speech lasted the proper ten minutes exactly and was followed by the traditional standing ovation.

The steward double-checked the boy's clothes and hair as they waited offstage.

The queen was now at the podium speaking. "Since you are now eighteen, a woman, you have earned the right to the pleasures and responsibilities of womanhood. One of these is the ownership of a man, the inferior half of our species, so that you may learn how to deal with your future consort. Therefore I would like to present you with your gift."

"That's you," the steward hissed at the boy, who paused, then slowly walked out onto the platform.

The room grew completely silent as the boy walked up to the princess and perfectly performed the rituals of presentation. When the boy finally stood at the proper three paces behind and to her left, the queen's face paled at the sight of his thin body.

Semiramis's face glowed as the crowd of women fell completely silent. "Thank you, Your Majesty," she stated clearly into the microphone.

The queen smiled slightly, then asked the guests to be at ease and to enjoy the party.

"To my office," the queen snapped, just loudly enough for the princess, her sister, her niece, and the chief members of her court to hear. The queen waited until everyone was present and the door to her office shut before pulling the trembling boy forward by his arm. "What is this?" she demanded of the tutor.

Radella remained calm as she spoke. "It is the princess's first choice, Your Highness."

"That's impossible!" the queen said but took the offered sales list from the tutor.

"You wanted him?" Zerlinda asked angrily. "How could you want him?"

"Be quiet!" the Duchess of Verelande ordered her daughter, then turned in horror to the princess. "What does this creature possess that made you want him, niece?"

Semiramis felt her face flush in embarrassment and anger. "He has beautiful eyes," she insisted, tilting his now bowed head up so that the room could see the two emeralds.

"That is hardly enough," the queen replied shortly.

The princess looked at her tutor briefly, then at her cousin, but both women only shook their heads. Then Semiramis's face relaxed as she remembered the placard. "His voice is lovely. His singing is like that of angels," she stated as convincingly as she could.

The queen stood up. She looked the boy over. "Then he will sing for our guests." Without another word, the queen led the women back out onto the platform.

Semiramis turned to her new property. "That placard better have told me the truth, boy. You better get out there and sing for your life, because if you don't, I will have you executed within the hour. My honor will demand it," she added.

The boy stared back at his new mistress and felt his heart sink. The princess walked out onto the stage and he followed at the three-pace interval.

Semiramis stepped up to the podium. "Ladies, while my slave may not be a beauty to behold with your eyes, his voice shall delight your ears as they have never been delighted before."

The boy stepped up to the microphone as instructed. He turned to his new owner, his stomach turning and his head spinning. He stepped back quickly as she returned to the podium.

"He needs a song to sing," she explained quickly, her face flushed as she felt her mother's eyes boring into her. "Any requests?" Semiramis asked, then nodded to the Duchess of Farlington.

"The Mother Moves Through the Wind," the elderly woman said with a smile. "Everyone knows that one."

"The Mother Moves Through the Wind," Semiramis replied. She stepped back and let the boy step up to the podium.

The entire hall fell silent as they waited for the boy to start.

The boy looked around the room, then swallowed and closed his eyes. The women gasped as the first crystal-clear notes fell from his lips. The boy sang all five verses, only opening his eyes on the last note. He stepped away from the podium and knelt on his knees before his new owner. His body was shaking visibly as he took great gulps of air and tried to calm himself.

Radella clapped slowly, and soon the entire room vibrated with approval. She smiled at her student and nodded toward the queen.

Semiramis raised her right toe and the slave hurried to stand behind her. "Beautiful," she whispered as he passed her.

"Incredible," Zerlinda commented when the two cousins finally were able to get a moment apart from the crowd. "Who would have thought that such a voice could exist in such a body," she added. She took her fan and fluttered it out in front of her lips as she whispered, "Will you be able to sample him tonight?" She looked over her cousin's shoulder at that same slave, who kept glancing at the women and their slaves around them. "He doesn't look too good."

"The medical report should be in my room. I'll have to look at it," Semiramis replied. She ran one hand down her cousin's blue silk sleeve and changed the subject. "I had them bring me a video monitor. You looked wonderful, lady."

"Not as good as you, Your Highness," Zerlinda added with a curtsy. Then she giggled and motioned for her gift to step up next to her. "What do you think of this?"

Semiramis smiled at the boy, the first her cousin had looked at in the sex slave corner of the market. His blue eyes sparkled with the lights of the room and seemed darker because of his blue jacket. All the slaves in the room wore white pants and shirts and white sandals, but most differed in jacket color. His ear had been pierced already, and an earring decorated with the Verelande coat of arms hung from it. His black hair was the traditional short length. "Very nice," she commented and added with a wink, "I bet you want to cut out of here fast."

"Yes, of course," Zerlinda whispered back. "Let me get a closer look at yours."

The boy stepped forward, head bowed until his new owner touched his chin, then he stood at attention. He tried to breathe as little as possible as the other woman examined him closely.

Semiramis nodded in satisfaction when she realized that under the bruises and skinny frame, he might be rather attractive. The green jacket brightened his eyes, and his hair was a medium shade of blond.

"He hasn't been pierced yet," Zerlinda commented once she had made a complete circle around him.

"I'm to take care of all of that on my own," Semiramis explained. "He isn't bad, now, is he?"

"No, he's fine," Zerlinda admitted out of politeness, "just fine."

Semiramis led the way into the dining hall. As the boy pulled out her chair, she whispered instructions to him. "You'll stand by the wall with the others. Just do what they do and you'll do fine."

"Yes, Mistress," the boy replied as he pushed her up to the table.

Semiramis looked down the long table at her mother at the other end. As a woman and therefore now the official heir, she took the opposite end of the table. Semiramis grinned at her cousin sitting on her right, just as the Duchess of Verelande sat to the right of the queen.

The boy stepped backwards until he was against the wall right next to the slave who had been given earlier to the heir of Verelande. The boy bowed his head in embarrassment as he noted how poor he looked when compared to this slave and the others. He glanced up when a troop of elegantly dressed slaves entered, carrying huge platters of food. "Go," the slave behind him hissed. The boy turned and followed the slave in front of him.

The slave escorts entered a large kitchen and sat in the nearest chairs they could reach. The boy made sure he stayed close to the slave who had been presented earlier. They sat at a table near the door to the Great Hall. The boy blushed when the slave who had removed the boots of the woman who had bought him sat directly across from him. This slave appeared to be in his thirties at least—his black hair had a few gray hairs—and he was dressed in a simple black jacket. "Congratulations," this slave said quietly. "Congratulations to you both," he added to the heir of Verelande's slave.

"I'm still in shock," the black-haired youth replied with a smile. "I'm still not clear who my mistress is."

"She," the older slave spoke with an air of authority, "is the heir to the dukedom of Verelande. That's a very fertile farming area about three days' journey from here. You'll probably be leaving tomorrow after spending the night at their cottage a few miles away." The slave turned to the skinny slave with a gentle smile, "You are the luckiest of all."

One of the cook's assistants rang a bell, and all talk stopped. The young woman looked around at the slaves distastefully. "Is there anyone here who has been told to eat a special diet?"

The boy raised his hand slowly.

"Speak up!" the assistant cook ordered.

"Thirteen," the boy replied just loud enough for the woman to hear.

The woman looked at his skinny form and still-visible bruises and nodded. "Anyone else?"

The boy slumped in his chair. He placed his head in his hands and wept silently.

"Hey, now," the older slave said, "don't do that. It will make your eyes puffy."

The slave of the heir to Verelande took the boy's hands from his face and shook his head with a frown. "You must stay as attractive as possible. That voice won't get you by for long."

"A few pounds on him and I think he will be fine looking," the older slave stated. The other slaves at their table rose and walked to other empty chairs, leaving only the three of them. "Guess they were jealous," the older slave stated. "I'm Dwern, slave of Radella, tutor and now advisor to your mistress, the Princess Semiramis," he introduced himself.

"Well, I don't know if my name will be the same after tonight," the younger black-haired slave said."

"What was your last name?" Dwern asked.

"Aaron," the slave replied. "Do you think she'll like it enough to keep it?"

"It's a very unusual name," Dwern said thoughtfully. "I'd say there was a good chance it will remain your name."

Aaron turned to the blond slave. "What was your name?"

"Sorry," the boy whispered and bowed his head to the table.

"It was obviously a joke," Dwern said quickly. He patted the blond head, which elicited a violent jerk back. "I'm sure Her Highness will come up with a better name," he added as he pulled his hand back onto his lap.

The food was brought out. Everyone except the blond boy received plates of steaming meat and vegetables with a large chunk of brown bread. Bowls of gravy and butter were placed on each table along with a pitcher of cheap wine.

"This is the best meal I've ever eaten," Aaron said in astonishment.

"The royal house takes good care of its men, especially when they are having a party," Dwern informed them.

The boy glanced up at the assistant cook as she set a plate with one hard-boiled egg, one slice of toast with a light spread of jam, and a glass of warm milk before him. "Eat this slowly, boy," she told him and patted him on the head.

Aaron paused in his eating to frown at the simple fare. "When was the last time you ate that good?" he chuckled in an attempt to lighten the mood that had suddenly fallen on their table.

"Weeks," the boy said as he gingerly bit into his toast.

With a shake of his head Dwern cautioned the other slave not to speak, as he himself asked the next obvious question. "When did you eat last? And don't include any food you've been given here at the palace," he added.

The boy looked up in surprise, then counted on his fingers. "About four days, I think."

Dwern nodded. "You'd best eat that slow then."

The boy followed the line of slaves back into the Great Hall and stood along the wall. His eyes focused on his new mistress and on the food that she took. His stomach felt full, but his mouth watered as she took a slice of layered chocolate cake from one of the serving slaves. He looked at her rich clothing and the bright red hair pilled up in perfection. He looked down at his feet, then back up suddenly to find her blue eyes focused on him and a slight frown on her lips. In response, he pulled himself up straight, eyes ahead, as was proper etiquette.

When the last course had been taken away by the serving slaves and a final toast made to the two young women, the slave escorts moved forward. The boy carefully pulled out the princess's chair. He stood back with bowed head as she turned and left the dining hall to return to the ballroom.

"Oh, I'm stuffed," Semiramis declared to her cousin when they had once more managed to find some solitude from the guests, who were eager to prove their loyalty and love.

"That cake was divine," Zerlinda replied. "But I think I need a small drink to calm my nerves." She motioned to her slave and the boy knelt next to her feet, his face turned upward in full attention. "Fetch me a drink from the bar; something soothing."

"Yes, Mistress," he replied and rose to his feet.

"Wait," Semiramis ordered, and her cousin's slave paused. "Boy," she said, turning to her own gift, "get me the same drink."

"Yes, Mistress," the boy whispered and bowed low before following the other slave to the bar. "Be careful," he whispered over and over to himself. When they had their drinks, the black-haired slave hurried back to his mistress. Semiramis's boy walked slowly, his eyes focused on the drink, until he bumped into another slave, dropping the glass.

Everyone stopped chatting and turned to look at the boy standing dumbly over the puddle of alcohol and broken glass. Semiramis approached quickly, her cousin with her own slave at her heels. She looked at the boy, anger flashing in her eyes briefly, until she registered the bruises he already had and forced her fists to remain clenched at her sides. "Go get a towel to clean up this mess and bring me another drink," she ordered evenly.

The boy looked up in fear but nodded and hurried from the ballroom to the dining room, where a slave handed him a towel. The boy hurried to the ballroom and quickly wiped up the drink, placing the glass shards in the towel. He noticed that the women had returned to their conversations and were now ignoring him. He returned the towel to the slave who had handed it to him and went back to the bar. This time he balanced the drink in one hand and watched the people around him. Several slaves and even a few ladies seemed to step directly in front of him on purpose, but he simply waited until they had passed. When he reached his mistress, he knelt slowly and silently held the drink up to her.

After a moment, Semiramis took the glass and sipped it. "Well done, boy," she briefly commented.

The boy bowed his head to the floor, then rose at the tap of her right foot and stood back from her. He touched his forehead and found it covered with sweat. The other slave shook his head sadly. The boy just straightened to attention.

Semiramis waved her fan as she led the way back to her suite. She paused in front of her door and turned to the boy. "This is my bedroom suite," she told him. "My new office and library is across the hall."

She opened the door and entered her suite. "Help me out of this gown," she instructed after she had locked the door behind them.

The boy's hands trembled as he unbuttoned the gown and held it as she stepped out of it.

"Hang it up over there," Semiramis instructed as she went behind the dressing screen that had been placed in her suite after she left that evening. She kept one eye on the boy as he hung up the dress and rebuttoned it, then zipped up the plastic protector around it. She came around the screen dressed in a new nightgown and matching robe and slippers. She smiled at the boy, who tried to smile back. "Brush out my hair," she said, sitting down at her vanity.

The boy stepped up behind her, took the ribbon with the jewel from her hair and handed it to her. Then he stared at her hair and touched it briefly. Crying out loud, he threw himself to his knees, head pressed against the floor. "Forgive me, Mistress, please. I don't know how to do this," he pleaded.

Semiramis touched the boy's head, causing him to cease crying for fear any further sound might elicit a worse punishment. "Go pull that rope," she said, pulling his head up by his hair and pointing to a silk rope hanging from the ceiling by her door.

The boy rose to his feet and did as he was bid as soon as she released his hair. In a few minutes there was a knock at the door. At his mistress's nod, the boy opened the door and a young woman dressed in a nightgown hurried in. "May I be of assistance, Your Highness?" the woman asked.

Semiramis smiled at her hairdresser. "Yes, Marzine. Please demonstrate how to brush out my hair."

The woman nodded and motioned for the boy to stand next to her. "This is very simple. In a few years, you'll be able to style her hair as well as I," the young court lady added with a smile.

The boy watched and did as he was instructed until he was brushing out the long curly hair by himself.

"Very good," the hairdresser said, stifling a yawn.

"You're excused, Marzine. Sleep well," Semiramis said quietly.

"The best of dreams to you, Your Highness," the woman said and left the room.

Semiramis let the boy brush out her hair as she looked over his medical file. "That's enough," she said when she had finished scanning the entire collection of papers. The boy set the brush on the vanity and stepped back as she stood up. She looked down at him; he was only two inches shorter, but his cringing made him very short indeed. "You know that tonight you are to please me sexually?"

"Yes, Mistress," he replied softly.

"However, that is not a hard-and-fast rule." She looked over the last paragraph of his medical report. "It is obvious that you were ill-used by your last owner, so I will grant you a week to recover before using you thus."

The boy looked up briefly, then fell to his knees. "I will heal quickly, Mistress. I promise," he added, placing a small kiss on the top of her bedroom slipper.

Semiramis smiled, then sobered her face. "You broke a very expensive glass this evening."

The boy lowered his head to the floor in silence.

"But I know it was an accident, so I'm not angry."

The boy looked up in surprise.

"I'm very tired, so I'm going to take you to your room." Semiramis led him out the suite door to one right next to it. She unlocked the door and motioned him inside.

The boy looked at the shelves that lined one part of the right wall. On it were several sets of clothing and a small alarm clock. A narrow, low bed sat by the other wall. Across from it were several pegs on the wall, one holding a plastic protector bag. He turned back to his mistress. "For me?"

Semiramis laughed. "Yes, this is where you will sleep

and change your clothes. This is wired so I can ring you at any time and the clock has been set to wake you in the mornings, starting the day after tomorrow. Tomorrow I'll wake you myself because I don't know when I'll be rising." She motioned him out into the hallway again. "There is a bathroom for you across the hall. I've asked Radella to lend me her slave, Dwern, and he'll teach you all the rituals you need to learn for your service to me."

She turned to go, then paused. "You don't have a name yet. Tell me, what did your last owner call you?"

"Sorry, Mistress," the boy answered with downcast eyes.

The princess paused for a few minutes, then frowned. "Sorry was your name?" Semiramis shook her head when the boy nodded. "Okay. Then your owner prior to her, I know you had ten before me," she added.

The boy frowned as he spoke, wanting to sink into the floor. "Idiot, Mistress."

Semiramis shook her head again. "Just tell me all the names you've been called."

The boy rattled off a list of joke names, ranging from insults to his intelligence to insults to his body. The very first name had been simply Boy.

Semiramis shook her head and crossed her arms. "I'll have to give you a new name. Those will never do. Not at all."

The boy smiled to himself and stood patiently as she paced the hallway, thinking.

She stopped in front of the boy. "Look up, Linden."

The boy looked up slowly, urged by her fingers in his hair.

"Repeat the name," she ordered.

"Linden," he said.

Semiramis smiled and patted his head. "Go to sleep, Linden."

The boy waited until she was in her suite and the door shut behind her before entering his room. He took a survey of the shelves, finding they contained two pairs of brown pants, one pair of black pants, three plain off-white shirts, underclothing, and a pair of tan sandals. "Linden," he repeated the name, and found it sweet to his ears. Carefully he removed the fancy clothing and placed it in the plastic bag, putting the white sandals on the bottom. He touched a bruise on his inner thigh and sucked in his breath in pain. "Linden," he said again. He touched his ass and made sure the plug which the steward had placed there prior to the party was tight, then climbed into the bed, pulling the coarse blanket over him.

The tutor stood at attention as the queen sat silently brooding for a moment. Finally the queen cleared her throat and asked the obvious question. "Why did you buy that for her?"

Radella looked directly at her ruler. "He was her first choice, Your Majesty."

The queen arched her eyebrows. "Surely she had at least ten choices, you could have bought her number two," the queen stated.

"That boy was listed as her top three choices," the tutor replied.

"I thought you instructed her in these matters," the queen said, her voice on the edge of yelling.

"I tried, Your Majesty," Radella replied evenly.

"Obviously not enough!" the queen screamed as she stood up. "He is not an appropriate gift for…" the queen waved her hands in frustration, "…anyone, let alone my heir!"

"Perhaps he will train well and fill out once he puts on some weight," the tutor offered with a forced smile.

"For your sake, tutor," the queen replied, "I hope you are correct."

"How is he doing?" Radella asked her young liege as they finished going over the expenses that the palace had incurred for the party a week before.

Semiramis laid down the folder and put her feet on her desk. She now wore the adult pants that her party had declared her ready for. "Linden?"

"Yes, how is he doing for you?" her advisor pressed with a slight grin.

"I should ask you—Dwern is teaching him the ropes around here," Semiramis countered. She raised her eyebrows in jest, then smiled. "Actually, he is very prompt with my breakfast each morning, and he hasn't spilled anything since that incident at the party."

"I think that was mostly nerves," Radella suggested.

Semiramis nodded. "I think he is looking better as well, don't you?"

"Yes, the bruises on his face have all but vanished, and he seems to have put on a little weight." Radella leaned forward in her chair. "You read his background." The princess nodded. "He's been mistreated since day one."

"I couldn't believe it when I read that his last owners had been an entire gang of ruffians!" Semiramis declared, setting her feet on the floor. "He's still terrified."

"Have you done anything about that?" Radella asked, looking the young woman directly in the eyes.

Semiramis stood up. "I've mostly left him alone. I don't think I should do anything until after he's been used as was intended. I think I deserve that much, if not more." She smiled at her advisor. "Tomorrow night, hopefully."

"Well," Dwern said as he walked the young blond man back to his quarters, "I think I have taught you everything you need to know, except for things I can't, like tomorrow night's activities."

Linden tried to return the smile, but instead found his hands shaking. "I'm going to fail tomorrow," he said and slid to the floor, his back against the wall.

"I told you to stop talking like that," Dwern ordered, crouching next to him. "Radella told me that you were purchased from the sexual section of the market, so what are you worried about?"

"I think that was a joke," Linden said. "This last set of bruises was a good-bye gift from the Running Demons for all the mistakes I made in the sack, or I should say sacks." Linden buried his face in his hands for a moment, then slowly looked back up. "How many owners have you had again?"

Dwern rolled his eyes. "Three, remember?"

"I've had ten. Must mean that I'm a real screw-up," Linden added. Then he turned with a childish grin and begged, "Tell me about how Professor Gaxas bought you." He pulled one leg up and rested his chin on top it.

"Again?" Dwern sat down on the floor. He nodded at the other's insistence. "All right. I was placed in the same market as you by my second owner, who had trained me as a copyist. I was only fourteen, but she felt that it would be the right time to sell, because then a new owner would have the opportunity to train me further. Well, you know how it feels to stand there in the market."

"Like dirt," Linden replied, glancing away.

"Yes," Dwern agreed slowly as he remembered the event. With a shake of his head, he smiled and continued speaking. "It was getting late in the day when this woman who looked far more distinguished than her clothes stopped in front of me. She started to speak to me, asking me questions about the placard around my neck and about my former owners. Then she just disappeared into the crowd.

"When I was taken up to be auctioned, I didn't see her or hear her voice. The bidding was winding down when suddenly she stepped through the crowd and upped the bid." Dwern's brown eyes twinkled as he spoke. "She and another bidder competed for a while, but she won. I was scared to death when I was presented to her at the cashier's desk. She didn't speak, only tied my hands and led me away behind her horse."

Linden nodded at the familiar sequence of events.

"She took me to a little house she had just rented. She asked me my name and said it would remain so after I answered. She trained me to read the things I was copying," he said, lowering his voice. "I've learned how to read her every desire and anticipate her every need. But it took me years—sixteen years."

"You're so lucky," Linden said, his voice dreamy.

"You, my friend, are the really lucky one," Dwern insisted. "You are serving the future queen of this nation, the largest nation on the planet. This could turn into the greatest honor and the greatest position any of us can hope for."

Linden nodded slowly. "And I could blow it tomorrow night."

Dwern was about to place his hand on the younger man's shoulder when he sensed the door to the nearby office opening. He stood, and Linden followed suit just as the door opened.

Radella nodded at the two slaves standing at attention across the hallway. "Dwern, attend me," she ordered and left the princess alone with her gift.

Linden knelt before his mistress, pressing his head to her boots, rising when her right foot moved. He stood silently, his eyes straight ahead.

"Dinner time," Semiramis stated and headed down the hall.

Radella looked down at her bedmate as they relaxed from their evening's passions. She ran her finger along his inner arm, causing him to pull on the chains that held his hands above his head as he laughed out loud. Her finger retraced its path and ventured to his chest, where it ended up hooked in his right nipple ring.

Dwern opened his eyes wide and tried to slow his breathing. He opened his mouth but didn't speak words, only sounds of pain and pleasure.

"How is he going to do?" Radella asked as she gently pulled up on the ring.

Dwern blinked twice before replying. "Mistress?" he asked, then nodded when she cocked one eye at him. "He learned everything I taught. He is doing very well." Dwern gasped as the ring shot another arrow of pain through him.

"But how will he do in bed?" Radella asked, twisting the ring halfway, causing him to arch up in an attempt to relieve the pain.

"Mistress, I don't know. I cannot foretell," Dwern pleaded, his voice now edged with pain and a fear that he hadn't felt in the last few years of his service to her.

"He'd better do well," Radella replied. "She risked her reputation on him that night." She released the ring and placed that hand on her slave's chin. "If he doesn't work out, I'm giving you to her," she stated, releasing his chin and standing up.

Dwern sat up onto his elbows, as far as the chains would allow. "What?" he asked loudly.

Radella lit a cigarette and turned away from him. "You heard what I said, boy," she spat out the last word.

Dwern felt his skin grow cold as he stared at her back. He said nothing as she turned around and walked up to the bed.

"Repeat it!" she ordered, knocking some of the hot ash from her cigarette onto his upper arm.

Dwern screamed at the pain he hadn't felt in several years. "You'll give me to her!" he cried out, falling onto his back.

Radella smiled and noted that at the same time he turned to face the wall. She sat down next to him and waited for a reply. After a few minutes, she held her cigarette close to his face as she spoke, "Look at me or I'll burn a hole in your pretty little face, boy!"

Dwern quickly turned his head to face her. He held his breath as she moved and put the cigarette out in the ashtray on the night table. His eyes followed her as she got the key and undid the chains. As soon as she moved away from the bed, he scurried to his knees. "Why, Mistress?" he asked, his voice breaking.

Radella couldn't face him as she spoke. "She'll not let him go even if he doesn't work out in bed. She would lose too much face. She'll just lock him up and take him out to parade him around on special occasions. But I won't let her be lonely during the next five years. It's not normal for a woman to wait until her mating years for a good roll in the bed."

Dwern got down from the bed, throwing his arms around her knees and pleading, looking up at her face, "Why me?"

"Because I know you'll do a proper job," she replied, looking straight ahead.

"It's been twenty years," he stated, anger now on the edge of his voice. "Please don't do this, Radella."

The royal advisor looked down slowly, her eyes flashing. She bent and ripped his arms from around her knees, throwing him to the floor. "Go sleep in the living room!"

Dwern glanced up, then crawled out of her bedroom and into the main living area of the suite. He took the afghan from the couch and crawled to the furnace, which was leaking heat now that the first frost of the fall had happened the night before.

Dwern brought in her boots, bowing himself to the floor before placing them on her feet. All morning he had performed his duties in utter silence, answering only briefly to specific questions, allowing himself to cry only when not in the same room as the princess's chief advisor. As he finished buckling her second boot, his hair was grabbed and his face was forced close to hers.

Radella glared at his puffy eyes. "Crying makes you unattractive!" She released him and stood up. "You will stop crying and attend me all day! When we see the princess, you will greet her as you do me each morning!" She paused, but he didn't reply. "Is that understood?"

Dwern looked up and nodded, "Yes, Mistress." He hurried to the door, slipping into his sandals as he held it open for her.

"How is he?" Semiramis asked the doctor who led the slave back out to her. The princess noted that he walked a little differently but smiled at the doctor.

"Very good. The ribs have completely healed and most of the bruises have disappeared," the doctor said with a satisfied smile. "I would advise against anal use for at least a week more. I removed and destroyed the plug; he is in terrible shape. Also, I suggest replacing the nipple rings. I think an infection is just dying to break out there."

Semiramis nodded, now understanding his slightly bowlegged walk. "But everything is okay now?"

"Yes," the doctor signed her report and handed it to the princess. "I would like to continue seeing him on a bi-weekly basis to keep track of his weight. Malnutrition can have long-term side effects."

"Of course; I'll make sure he keeps regular appointments." Semiramis signed the report and returned the doctor's copy to her. She headed out of the clinic and walked down the hallway to the elevator. Entering, she watched her gift as he pushed the third-floor button, noting that the few pounds he had gained had indeed proved her suspicion that he was good-looking.

As they left the elevator and headed down the hallway, they were met by her advisor and her slave. The slave came forward and performed obsequious moves before her normally reserved for one's owner. Semiramis looked at her advisor, but noted that the woman only nodded. She raised her right toe, and the slave rose and stood off to the side of the two women.

"What's going on?" Semiramis asked, when she joined her former tutor.

"You are the official heir now, and he has been told to show you proper respect," Radella stated simply. She smiled and placed her hands behind her back. "What will you be doing today?"

"What I've been waiting a week for," the princess replied with a grin. "No business today, Radella. I'm out to lunch all day." With a clap on her advisor's shoulder, the princess continued down the hall. The slave at her heels threw one pitiful glance at Dwern, who stared after them.

"Come, boy," Radella instructed her slave and headed back toward her own suite.

Semiramis sat down on her bed after her boots had been removed. She looked at her slave as he stood before the bed. "Take off your clothes slowly," she instructed him.

Linden stepped out of his sandals first. Then he unbuttoned his off-white shirt and slid it off his shoulders.

Semiramis smiled as the silver nipple rings caught the

light from the open window curtains. *Much nicer than in the market*, she thought.

Next, Linden unbuttoned his pants and let them fall to the floor, where he easily stepped out of them. The bikini briefs were still a little loose, so they slid off easily. He waited, his breathing increasing in proportion to his nervousness. Tentatively, he stepped forward.

"Hold still," Semiramis ordered. She got up from the bed and walked around him in a tight circle, then sat in front of him on the edge of the bed. "We have all day, so there's no rush. I just want to look at you." She laughed at his puzzled look, then at the blush her reaction caused. "Owning a man is a great responsibility, but it's also supposed to be great fun," she said.

She touched the silver rings in his nipples gently. "When did you get these pierced?"

Linden took a deep breath as he remembered that day. "About six months ago, Mistress."

"Ah, from the Running Demons," she said.

"You know about them?" he asked, then clasped his hand over his mouth.

She waved her hand in dismissal. "Forget it. I want to talk with you for a while." She stood and retrieved his history folder from her vanity. "I got a complete record of your life—well, complete in the facts of who owned you and when." She peered at his nipples, then straightened up and frowned. "They look swollen all right."

Linden gritted his teeth together as the rings were removed. Then he gasped out loud as she applied rubbing alcohol to the nipples.

"It burns, huh?" Semiramis agreed. She tossed the rings in her wastebasket. She knelt before him, took his slightly erect penis in her hand and looked at the ring pierced through the urethra and glans. "This looks okay. When was it done?"

"Two owners before the Demons," Linden replied, embarrassed that his cock was hardening even as she held it.

Semiramis stood up and smiled at him. "Undress me," she ordered simply.

Linden obeyed with trembling hands. When she was naked, she led him to her bed and climbed up facing him. He looked at the bed, then up at her face. "Mistress?" He tried not to look at her pale skin and rounded hips and bosom but found his own mouth watering.

"Yes," she said, her voice husky with desire.

"What do you want me to do?"

Semiramis grinned. "What I got you for. Touch me everywhere and bring me to orgasm." She lay back on the pillows she had piled up at the head of the bed. She lifted one leg and lay that foot on his shoulder.

Linden quickly scanned his memory for all the times and all the mistresses he had pleased. He chose to follow the pattern of his fourth owner, the one who had first used him sexually, the only one who had not hit him often, the one who had died in an accident, the one he sometimes cried for at night.

He turned his lips to the foot on his shoulder and ran his tongue and lips along the arch. He took it gently into his hands and sucked each toe briefly, then took the other foot she offered him. Slowly he licked his way up each leg, making sure to spend equal time on both and pausing when she commanded him to stay. He briefly licked her clitoris, then traced the outline of her curly red pubic hair. His tongue skipped over her belly after she chuckled at his first touch. Her nipples were already erect, so he concentrated on licking and sucking these equally, bringing out her first moans of pleasure.

After several minutes on her breasts, he traced up her collarbone swiftly and licked her neck. She grabbed his face ᴛʜᴇɴ, and he noticed she was covered with a light sheen of perspiration.

Semiramis stared into his emerald eyes. She could feel his arms, which were mainly supporting his weight, shake. "Get down there and do it," she whispered the order.

"Yes, Mistress," he replied. He worked his tongue back down her body, then settled his head and shoulders down between her legs. He glanced up as he started licking her clit very gently. She tossed her head back with a moan. He watched and listened carefully, knowing from experience that different women needed different stimuli. He continued to gently lick the tip of her clit and soon her pelvis pushed him off the edge of the bed as she convulsed with orgasm.

Semiramis sat up immediately and giggled at the slave kneeling at the end of her bed. "Wonderful," she said and pulled him up onto the bed. She climbed on top of his chest. "Can you do that when I'm on top?"

"Yes, Mistress," he said and licked the edge of her clit when she had positioned it within his reach. His hands were moved to her hips by her hands as she moved further up so he could continue more easily.

This time, Linden worked quickly, knowing that in this position he could lose his breath. Within a few minutes she arched her back and pulled away from him. He looked up at her and watched her roll off him and back onto her pillows. He waited, still and silent.

"Wine," she ordered with a little cough.

Linden jumped out of bed and poured her a goblet from the decanter on the table by the window. He looked outside and smiled at the snowflakes falling in a gentle shower. Returning with the goblet, he knelt by the bed, offering it to her.

Semiramis took the goblet and took several sips. "Sip," she said, holding it out to him but not releasing the goblet.

One small sip made him choke. "You've never had wine before," she said, sitting up. She patted the bed, and he climbed up next to her. She finished the wine and set the glass on the night table. Swinging her legs under her, she looked at him. "Pull the blankets up around us," she ordered as she placed one arm around him.

Linden complied and found himself cradled in the crook of her arm, his head on her breast. He moved away and mumbled an apology.

Semiramis turned on her side. "On your hands and knees, facing away," she ordered.

Linden complied, trying not to tense up as she parted his asscheeks. But instead of pain, he felt a coolness spread through him as she spread some type of cream on his hole. At her word, he turned around and lay down on his back. His mind whirled as he tried to figure out why she had done that and what she was planning.

Semiramis touched his nose and giggled. "I want to know all about you. All about your past."

"Why, Mistress?" he asked innocently.

She touched the bruise under his eye, still visible at this close range. "Because you're afraid of me."

Linden cocked his head and closed his eyes as he quoted the familiar scripture, "A man shall serve his mistress in fear and trembling."

"Well, yes, but only to a certain level," Semiramis insisted. She traced another barely visible bruise on his upper arm. "You've had a rough life, little slave boy."

Linden nodded. "I'm a fool, a clumsy idiot, a moron, a begging asshole," he said, but found his lips closed by her fingers.

"Tell me about your mother," she commanded. "I want to know about all the women who've owned you before me."

Dwern had fallen asleep as he sat out in the hallway in front of his mistress's suite. "What?" he said as the alarm on his watch rang. He glanced at the door, then hurried down to the kitchen. "Professor Gaxas's meal, please," he told the assistant cook. He took the familiar tray and headed back to the suite. The door was still locked, so he knocked. After a few minutes it opened, and he was let in.

Dwern set the tray on the table in the living room and looked around him at the disorganized room. "Mistress, would I be able to help?" he asked hopefully.

"Sit down!" Radella ordered as she sat at the table and lifted the cover of the tray.

Dwern sat down where he was and waited for his mistress to finish her meal. At her signal, he took the tray and left the suite. A tear fell down his cheek as he heard it lock behind him.

"Okay." Semiramis had changed into her nightgown as her gift spoke and now she held up her finger for him to pause. "Let me see if I got this straight. Your mother sold you at the age of five to pay for a gambling debt; she had called you Lucky that last year, but before that it was simply Boy. Your second owner had you sweep up her bar and casino, but she only beat you when she was drunk, just like your mother. She called you Dirtboy." Semiramis shook her head as she tossed him his shirt and underpants. "The third owner bought you when the second went bankrupt. She had you take care of her dogs, called you Puppy Face, and only beat you whenever her dogs didn't win a race."

She crawled back into bed with his file in one hand. "You liked number four?"

"Yes, Mistress," he said, but bit his lip and finished putting his clothes back on.

"Why?" she pressed. "Tell me about…" and she looked at his history record, "Anita Drawon."

Linden took a deep breath. "She came to the racetrack and saw me crawling out of the dog kennel. She approached my owner and bought me. She told me later that she needed someone to help out in her video store."

"Porn shop," Semiramis corrected him with a slight grin.

"Yeah." He looked down. "She rarely hit me, and only if I broke something. She taught me how to please women and let me practice with some of her customers. She didn't wake up one morning, and the next thing I know I'm in the market for the first time," he said with a faraway look.

"She didn't have any relatives?" Semiramis asked.

"No, so the state put me up for sale." He took the goblet of wine she offered him and took a slow sip, his eyes blinking at the unfamiliar alcohol rush.

"How old were you?" the princess asked as she sipped her second glass.

"Twelve." he said, taking another sip.

"Twelve? You were sexual at the age of twelve?" Semiramis shook her head. "I mean, I know that's what men are for," she said as she tried to cover up her shock at this information, "but it seems rather young to me."

Linden didn't know how to respond, so he took another sip and continued his story. "A construction worker bought me at the auction. She had these two little girls that I was supposed to watch during the day that summer. They broke my arm one afternoon, and my mistress broke the other one to punish me. As soon as it healed I was back in the market."

"Terrible, just terrible," the princess said, pouring more wine in each of their goblets.

"That gets me to the advertising agent who was looking for a nude model for her latest ad campaign," he said.

"That ad for Passion Prisoner Parfum?" she interrupted.

"Yes, Mistress. It was a very successful campaign," he

added, smiling a little too wide as he sipped his second glass of wine.

"Did they really do that stuff to you?" she asked, recalling the scenes of torture the ads employed.

"Yes, Mistress. It was a very successful campaign," he restated blankly, taking a deep swig from the goblet.

Semiramis nodded. "Okay, that brings us to number seven," she said as he continued drinking his wine.

"Yeah." he looked into the goblet and frowned, then downed the last few drops. "Number seven. The rock singer, in a tiny little band. I was the whole band's roadie—moving all the equipment on and off stage. That lasted a full year," he added, his eyes arched in surprise.

"Did they beat you?" she asked.

"Oh, no," he said with an exaggerated frown. "Only Mercury could hit me, because she was the one who paid for me."

"Yeah, but how often?" the princess asked, with a frown into her own goblet. She grabbed the decanter and poured the rest of the wine into their two glasses.

"Thank you, Mistress," Linden replied. "Let's see, how often? Oh, after every performance, because something always went wrong and it was always my fault."

"You made a lot of mistakes," Semiramis said gravely.

Linden nodded soberly. "I guess so. I was fifteen when the band broke up. Mercury had to sell me to pay some bills. Lynnel was the next one. She was an old woman who had me lead her around the shops and run errands for her. But I always dropped some change or missed an item. She could swing that cane really well," he added, downing his wine.

"Who was nine?"

"Okay, that would have been the jewel thief. That only lasted a week, because she was caught." He stopped talking and pulled his knees up to his chin.

"So that brings us to the Running Demons. Tell me about them," Semiramis ordered as she leaned back onto the pillows.

"What do you want to know?" the slave asked, his voice suddenly faint.

"How many of them were there? Did they all own you? How did they treat you? Why did they sell you?" She paused for breath. "Everything."

"There were ten members and they all chipped in cash for me," he begin. "They bought me on the western side of your realm. Over six months we rode to the market where I was bought for you. Every night they'd gamble to see who got to use me first. They each had their favorite activities." He glanced up with sad eyes. "Whatever you want me to do or endure, Mistress, they taught me the basics. Anyway, by the time we got here, they were getting tired of me. Seems like I was doing something wrong every second of the day. And I tried, I really tried." His voice almost broke as he said those words, as though begging. "So when they saw the market ad, they covered me in make-up and gave me to the sexual section of the market that very morning."

Semiramis placed a hand on his shoulder and felt him shudder in response. "That's when I saw you," she said. She felt him shaking. "Linden, are you okay?"

He turned a pale face up to her, his hands clutched at his stomach. "I don't feel too good, Mistress."

"Come with me," she instructed, pulling him from the bed and into the bathroom just in time.

"How did things go?" Dwern demanded, turning the princess's slave around when he stopped him in the kitchen picking up supper.

"Oh." The boy was still pale from his previous ordeal from the wine. "Well, she gave me some wine, and I drank it and made a fool of myself by getting sick."

The older man's eyes widened in terror. "You got drunk? You drank wine!" Dwern pulled the young slave out of the kitchen into the hallway. "You never really drink that stuff when they offer it to you!"

"But she insisted," Linden explained.

Dwern paced a few feet, then grabbed the boy again. "But how did the sex go?"

"She seemed pretty happy with me. Then I got sick," he added, his shoulders slumping in sadness.

"Just go get the food and try to make the rest of the evening good," Dwern suggested firmly. He followed the boy into the kitchen and took a rather large tray. "It's going to go well, it has to," he commented as they walked down the hallway for one wing before going separate ways.

Dwern knocked anxiously on the suite door. It was opened immediately. "Mistress, the cook says she gave you extra rolls as you requested and some extra butter as well." Dwern stepped back silently as Radella sat down and began to eat. He waited for a few minutes, then cleared his throat.

"What, boy?" Radella's voice held the same displeasure as the evening before.

Dwern knelt by her chair as he spoke, "What did I do, Mistress? Please tell me so I can correct it or at least beg for the appropriate forgiveness?"

Radella's eyebrows shot up in ire. "You seem to be forgetting that you are my property to do with as I please!"

Dwern bowed his head. "I am sorry, Mistress. I did not mean to sound that way. I am yours," he added, glancing up hopefully.

"Go to the kitchen and eat," she ordered.

The slave bowed his head to the floor, then backed out of the room on his hands and knees.

Semiramis looked at Linden closely before offering him one of her rolls. "Do you think you can keep this down?"

"Yes, Mistress," he said, taking the roll. He sat on the floor by her chair and ate it as slowly as it took her to finish her entire meal. As he cleared away the plates, he glanced up and saw her walking behind the dressing screen. "Shall I take this to the kitchen, Mistress?"

"Yes, and hurry back," she called out.

Linden took the tray back to the kitchen, thankful that he didn't meet the older slave until he was heading back to the suite. "Hey, what happened to you?" he asked at the other's frightened look.

Dwern shook his head. "She set this outside her door. All day she's only let me inside her suite to deliver food."

"Maybe she's just in a bad mood," Linden offered. "The princess commented about the tax year ending soon and having to get all the records together."

The older slave started to explain the real problem, then decided not to and simply nodded. "You're probably right. She's done this before," he lied. "Got to go."

Linden watched the other slave disappear into the kitchen, then hurried back to his owner's suite. He knocked as he opened the door. His eyes were covered with something as soon as he entered. He heard the door shut behind him. He followed his captor's lead, and soon he felt the mattress beneath him and a weight on his chest.

"Let's see if you can do it blindfolded," Semiramis said.

Linden could smell that her clit was near his mouth so he reached out tentatively and was rewarded by her moving up closer. She didn't place his hands on her hips this time, so he grabbed the sheets instead. His face was soon covered in her lubrication as he worked steadily at her clit with his tongue.

Semiramis felt the pressure building in her pelvic area. She rocked her hips to his rhythm until she cried out with the pleasure of another orgasm. She rolled off him and wiped off his face with a tissue. Then she leaned over him and ran her fingers along his jawline.

Linden sighed silently, sensing that she was pleased with him once more. He felt her unbutton his shirt and lay it open. He moaned in pain but kept his hands clenched in the sheets as she touched his still-sore nipples. He felt her hand continue down his stomach and dip under the waist of his pants.

"How does this feel?" she asked, grasping the firm cock in her hand.

Linden's eyes moved back and forth in the darkness, looking for the proper response. She pulled slightly on him, and he heard a moan escape his throat.

Semiramis laughed softly. "I am pleased with you, Linden." She released him and removed her hand from his pants. "Take off the blindfold and come with me," she ordered.

Linden removed the blindfold and followed her out the door, buttoning his shirt as they walked. She took him to a part of the palace he remembered Dwern telling him it was best to stay away from. He paused in the doorway of the basement room marked ONLY AUTHORIZED PERSONNEL ALLOWED.

"Linden!" Semiramis called to him, a smile on her lips.

He walked to her slowly.

"Knock," she ordered.

He lifted the brass knocker on the door and knocked twice. Then he stepped back.

Soon a woman he didn't recognize opened the door and stepped back to let them in. Linden looked around the dimly lit room, remembering the scenes from the ads he had done and feeling his heart drop to his feet.

"Sit down," Semiramis said, pulling out a chair.

The boy sat down on the chair. He felt his mistress's

hands on his shoulders. The woman looked at his right ear and he felt a tap on it.

"This will be good," the woman commented. "Gold or silver?"

"Gold," Semiramis said, "I like it better, and it will go better with his eyes."

Linden glanced up but found his head was pushed back down. He felt something cold on his ear, then a brief sting. Suddenly his ear seemed to grow and grow.

"It's okay, boy," the woman said with a smile. She held up two larger rings within his line of sight. "Are these what you want?"

"Yeah, but he seems to be infected," the princess answered.

The woman parted the slave's shirt and touched his nipples with something that burned intensely for a brief second. "Yeah, just apply this every day, and in a few days, when there is no pain from it, you can just slip these in."

In a few moments, the woman held a mirror up to the slave's face. There, through his right ear, was an earring; the hanging part carried the crest of the royal house. He looked at it, then up at his mistress, who now stood in front of him with a smile of satisfaction.

"Looks good," Semiramis said to the woman. "Thanks a lot."

Linden rose and followed his mistress upstairs and back to her suite. In the doorway she turned to face him.

"Good night, Linden. Go to bed, and don't play with that earring," she added before shutting the door.

Linden looked at the door, placed one hand on the cool surface, then shrugged and went to his room.

Linden knocked on the suite door with her breakfast that morning to find the princess already dressed and on the telephone. He set the tray down and moved to the wall to stay out of her way.

"Yeah, well, thanks a lot!" she screamed into the receiver and slammed the phone down. She turned to the slave, who now was cringing against the wall next to the door. She took the lid off her breakfast and tossed the slave the orange. "Here, eat up."

Linden caught the fruit as he moved to her. He sat down next to her feet and glanced up at her in silence.

"Bad start to the day. The main supplier of our firewood says that two of her men have fallen ill, so she won't be able to deliver her shipment on time," she told him. "That means that Radella and I will be in the office all day looking for a new supplier."

Linden crawled to the wastebasket and threw the peels in before pulling off a slice of orange and eating it.

"So, you just need to be outside the office ready to get us drinks and meals," she added.

"Yes, Mistress," he replied. They quickly finished eating in silence.

"After you take this back," Semiramis said as she stood, "get Professor Gaxas and bring her to my office. I'll meet you there."

Linden bowed and put the cover on the tray. He hurried to the kitchen, where he was almost run over by the professor's slave.

"Linden!" Dwern grabbed his tray and set it on one of the kitchen's many tables. "She won't let me in this morning! I brought her breakfast, and she wouldn't open the door, so I set it on the floor in the hallway. But when I came back, nothing had been eaten!"

The blond slave nodded, his face pale with the memory of finding his fourth owner dead. "Did you tell the steward?"

"Yes," he replied, but shook his head. "She says she can't open the door for me. What if something happened to her?" Dwern suddenly got a wildly fearful look in his eyes.

Linden smiled weakly and grabbed the older man's hand. "I'm supposed to get your mistress and bring her to the princess's office. Maybe she'll open the door for me."

"And if she doesn't?" Dwern's face was very pale; even his lips were a deathly pink shade.

"We'll tell Her Highness, and she'll find out what's going on," Linden said with confidence.

The older slave paused for a moment, surprised by the boy's composure, then nodded and mumbled agreement.

The two slaves hurried to the professor's suite. Linden knocked on the door and said, loudly enough for anyone inside to hear, "Professor Gaxas? Her Highness, Princess Semiramis, requests that you come with me immediately to her office." There was silence, and the door didn't move. Linden raised his voice and knocked louder.

"She's not coming," Dwern said, slumping against the wall.

Linden grabbed his arm and hurried the older slave down the hallway to the princess's office. He knocked and at the order went inside, the black-haired slave in tow. "Mistress," he said with a quick bow.

Semiramis looked up from her desk with a frown. "I said I wanted Professor Gaxas!"

"Yes, Mistress. She isn't answering her door, hasn't answered at all this morning," Linden quickly explained.

Semiramis turned to the terrified older slave, making her voice gentle but firm. "Is this true, Dwern?"

"Yes, Your Highness." The older slave said, then sank to his knees. "She locked me out of the suite yesterday except for meals, but this morning she won't let me in at all."

Semiramis stood up and grabbed a key from the top

desk drawer. "Let's go see what's going on," she said, pushing past the men and hurrying down the hallway. The men reached the suite as she finished pounding on the door. "Radella! Open the door! It's Semiramis!" The young woman frowned, as there was no reply. "Open this door in the name of the queen!"

"I'm going to open it up," she stated, fumbling with the key. "Radella!" she called loudly as she opened the door. The room was empty of anyone. The older slave brushed past her and ran into another room.

Soon Dwern returned. He leaned against the wall as he spoke. "She's not here."

Semiramis looked around the room. "Maybe she went out."

The slave shook his head as he walked toward her. "The closet doors and the bureau drawers are all open and empty." He knelt before her, bowing his head to the floor.

Semiramis ignored the slave at her feet and hurried to the other rooms. Linden stood in silence at the open suite door, unable to move.

Semiramis returned to the room with a folder. "She's gone! The only thing left is this folder with my name on it!" She threw the folder on the floor and ran her hands through her hair in frustration. "Okay, Dwern. Tell me what happened in here!" When he didn't respond, she hurried to him, forcing him to look at her as she crouched in front of him. "What happened? And you'd best tell me true!"

"She's gone," Dwern replied in tears.

Semiramis sighed and released him. "Get the steward," she said to her own slave. "Now!"

Semiramis stood up and tapped her right toe so that the slave would straighten up. "Dwern? Why wouldn't she let you in yesterday?" she asked more gently.

The slave looked up and wiped at the tears falling from

his eyes. "She said she was going to give me to you," he began.

Semiramis wrinkled her nose. "What?"

"Give me to you because he couldn't give you pleasure," Dwern continued. He paused and choked on a tear before looking at her. "Do I belong to you now?"

Semiramis realized that the slave was in shock, acting as her brother had as he was sent away to one of the southern border realms to become consort to the new queen. She stood up and turned to the door just as the steward rushed in.

"Your boy tells me that Professor Gaxas has disappeared," the steward stated with a quick bow of respect.

"So it appears," Semiramis replied. "Ask everyone in the palace if they saw her leave or heard anything at all about this." Semiramis waited until the steward had left, then slammed her fist on the table. "Damn that woman!" She hurried through the suite door and yelled back, "You two hurry it up! We have work to do this morning!"

Linden helped the older slave to his feet. "Wait," said Dwern, and paused and picked up the folder his owner had left behind.

Both men hurried into the open office. Dwern found another folder thrown at him; he caught it by reflex.

"You can read, so you get to take her place today!" Semiramis stated, picking up the phone. She glared back at the men, whose mouths were hanging open in shock. "She told me a long time ago," she explained quickly, "so stop gaping and read me that first number!"

Dwern opened the folder, read off the number, and read the name next to it, "Wilson Lumber Company."

Linden was busy all day, hurrying from the kitchen to the office with drinks and light snacks, his mistress and the other slave too busy for a real meal. Upon returning at sundown, he was greeted by a warm smile from the princess.

"Found a replacement for the next three weeks!" Semiramis told him as she took the proffered coffee from his tray. She clapped the other slave on the back and sat down in her chair. "I need to relax," she said bluntly.

Dwern immediately stepped behind her chair and began rubbing her neck and shoulders. He stopped when her hand went over his.

"That's Linden's job," she stated with a nod at her own slave.

The blond slave stepped into place as the older slave walked to the window. Soon both young people could hear the older man's weeping.

"Dwern?" Semiramis placed her feet on her desk as the slave turned around. "My feet hurt too," she told him in a gentle voice.

Dwern wiped away the tears and bowed. "Yes, Lady," he whispered as he pulled her shoes off and started rubbing her feet.

Semiramis entered the queen's chamber as she heard the command to enter. She bowed and hurried to sit next to the queen on the couch. "Mother, I need your advice."

The queen frowned slightly as she kissed her daughter in greeting. "I thought that was Radella's job."

"Exactly," Semiramis said, "but she disappeared this morning. Packed up all her clothes and more personal items and left the palace."

"What? When?" the queen demanded, looking to her own advisor, who simply frowned and strode from the room.

"The steward talked to everyone, and only the stable boy saw her leave. But of course he didn't question her," the princess pointed out.

The queen stood up and walked to the blazing fireplace.

"Why would she leave suddenly? If she needed time away with her boy..."

"She left him here," Semiramis answered. "In fact," and she took out the folder the slave had given her when she had dismissed both men to go for a run in the gymnasium before sleep time, "she signed over her papers for him to me."

The queen took the document and glanced at it. "Why would she do this? You told me that things went very well last night."

"They did," Semiramis agreed, standing up also. "She also enclosed his last medical report, his history, and a letter to me asking me to take care of him while she is away. Which doesn't make sense, with her signing over ownership."

"No, it doesn't." The queen took the letter and examined it. "I'll have the lawyers look over everything in the morning." She sat down on the couch again. "Does the boy know?"

"He says that she informed him about this last night, but he didn't believe her." Semiramis sat back down next to her mother. "He's in shock. He's been with her for twenty years."

The queen nodded. "They always take this hard," she commented. "What are you going to do with him?"

Semiramis stood up. "I feel that I should keep him until she returns."

"Yes, but she might not return," the queen pointed out. "You're still young, and taking on another man is an incredible responsibility."

"I know." She sat down very close to her mother and whispered, "He can read and write."

The queen's face was flushed in shock. "She taught him?"

"Yes, and I've known for a few years now," Semiramis added. "He helped me through a supply crisis this morning."

"Crisis?" the queen was suddenly distracted by the more appropriate subject. "What's happened?"

"Oh, the firewood supplier got two of her men injured in an accident. I finally found someone to pick up the slack for the next few weeks." Semiramis stood up, then knelt on one knee. "I need your permission to keep the slave called Dwern, Your Majesty," she requested formally.

The queen placed her hand on the princess's head. "Permission granted." As her daughter rose to leave, the queen added, "Good luck. Try not to push yourself too hard, my dear."

Semiramis grinned, then bowed and exited the room.

She found both slaves standing next to her suite door; their wet hair told her that they had showered after their run. She stopped in front of the black-haired man, who knelt down, his head touching her shoes. She tapped her toe, and he rose to his feet. "Dwern, are there things you need to get from Professor Gaxas's room?"

"Yes, a few clothes and personal items," he said, and after a second of pause, he added the title, "Mistress."

"Linden will help you move the stuff into his room," she said with a glance at her first slave.

The men bowed and walked quickly down the hall. Linden only glanced at the older man, unsure what to say. The door was unlocked, so they entered.

Dwern went to the small closet to the left of the larger, now empty, one. He handed the plastic bag that held his formal clothes to the other slave. "Would you carry these?"

"Sure, I can carry more, too," Linden added.

The other slave smiled oddly. "Come on, you know we don't have much." He took his few shirts, pants, and undergarments and held them under one arm. He paused as he took out a small picture frame that held the photo of him and the professor from a few years earlier, taken at her fiftieth birthday party. He glanced at the younger slave.

"I'd keep it," Linden said. "I think it will be okay."

Dwern nodded and placed the frame between two pairs of underwear. Next he picked up the black bag that had been left in the bottom of his closet. "She must want the princess to have this," he stated. He traced the leather under the handle, then sniffed back the tears that threatened to fall.

The two men hurried back to Linden's, and now Dwern's, room. Linden noted that the single bed had been replaced with a bunk bed, similar to the ones in the band's bus. "Which do you want?" he asked the older man.

"I'll take the top," Dwern replied, setting his clothes on it, "if you don't mind."

"Sounds great to me," Linden said, attempting to smile in a manner that would make the older slave feel more at ease.

"I should give this to her," Dwern said, holding up the black bag.

"Sure." Linden led him to the suite. After being asked in, they entered and bowed, heads to the floor, until they heard her tap her foot. Dwern stepped forward and again knelt, holding the bag up.

"What's this?" Semiramis asked, taking the bag.

Dwern kept his back straight and eyes forward as he replied, "Professor Gaxas left these in her room, so I assume she wants you to have them."

"What is it?" the princess repeated her question.

"Her toys," Dwern replied flatly. He swallowed as the princess opened the bag and dumped the contents onto her couch.

Semiramis stepped back and looked at Linden. "I bet you know what this stuff is?"

The slave walked to the couch and nodded after a brief survey of the items. "Passion Prisoners," he muttered softly.

"Well," Semiramis suddenly felt uncomfortable, "thanks for bringing these to me. Why don't both of you go to bed? We've had a long day," she added. She stood up and looked at her gift with longing but waved him away.

Both men bowed and left the room. Dwern turned to the other slave when they were back in their room. "I'm not going to try to move into your territory," he assured them both.

Linden narrowed his eyes as he spoke, "You may be older than me, but I know that you'll move into whatever area she orders you, and so will I."

That night, when both men were asleep, Linden woke when he felt a hand placed over his mouth. He nodded and followed his mistress from his room into her own.

"I feel sorry for him, but I'm not tired of you yet," Semiramis told him as she ran her hands down his chest and to the hair of his pubic region. She smiled as he moaned when her hands traced the main vein down the front of his penis. "You got sick last night, and then I got tired. I don't think I'll drink that much for quite a while," she decided as she lifted up his balls in one hand.

Linden's eyes opened and closed as her hands continued to explore his body. He rose up on his feet when her hands caressed his butt firmly. "Did I please you?" he asked, using the privilege she had granted him at the end of the evening to speak freely when in her suite with her.

"That was last night," Semiramis replied. "But tonight is another night." She released his ass and stepped back. Standing just out of his reach, she loosened her nightgown until it fell to the floor.

"Command me," Linden begged as he felt his cock stretch toward her and his stomach tighten.

"I let you come once last night," the princess reminded him. "You told me that no one had allowed you to experience that in their presence before."

"That's true, Mistress," he replied. His skin felt uncomfortable to him as it burned with the new desire she had awakened in him.

Semiramis shook her head and pirouetted around once, her arms lifted above her head to display her figure better. "Maybe I made a mistake," she whispered. When he didn't reply, she continued to dance around the room slowly, circling him but never touching him. "You probably are only in this now for what you'll get out of it."

"No," Linden replied without hesitation. "It only happened because you commanded me. I only did it to please you."

Semiramis stopped directly in front of him and leaned close enough for their noses to touch. "I want to fuck you, boy," she whispered.

"Yes," he replied. "Yes, please." His voice was thin as his breathing increased rapidly. He sucked in his breath as her fingernails flicked his nipples.

"I want to get to know your body, because it's mine now," she whispered.

"Please," Linden begged. His vision was blurry as he tried to look at her mouth, wanting to drown in her voice.

"You want that, too?" she asked.

"Yes," he moaned as she twisted the least-damaged nipple firmly.

"But the doctor said I can't," Semiramis reminded him as she stepped back.

The slave forced his legs to remain steady as he felt the cold rush in to take the place her body had just occupied.

He fell to his knees, his mind spinning with unfamiliar and frightening desires.

The princess walked to her bed, noting with pleasure that he crawled after her. "That means that we're left with just focusing on me."

The slave stopped at the edge of the bed and looked at the foot dangling in front of him. He swallowed, realizing the game she was playing. "Please let me pleasure you, Mistress," he begged in earnest for the first time in his life.

"Someone told me once that after a while, there isn't a need for orders," Semiramis replied. She lifted her foot to his face and traced his lips with her big toe.

Linden opened his mouth and let the toe inside. His tongue now became active, licking and sucking on it. With a brief command from her, he gently took her foot in his hands. His fingers massaged her sole as his tongue flicked out and traced the outline of her toes, each one being sucked and caressed by his mouth before he moved to its neighbor.

Next he carefully nibbled his way up her legs, paying an equal amount of attention to each in turn. He paused as he looked at the flower of her sex and breathed in her scent. He nuzzled her inner thighs and worked his way up slowly to her center.

She pushed her hips forward, blocking any attempt to escape, and shuddered as his hot breath touched her lips. She arched her back as his tongue barely touched her, teasing slightly before she clamped her legs around his head, forcing him down.

The slave responded immediately, licking and moving his mouth quickly. He used his hands to caress her outer thighs. Her hands grasped his. Their fingers entwined. He held back his own moans as his cock pressed against the side of the bed so he could concentrate entirely on her body and her responses.

Semiramis's voice exploded out as her vaginal muscles pulsed violently. She released her grasp on the slave's hands and he scrambled back from the bed. They sat there for several moments, entirely silent. The princess's head spun and her entire body seemed to clench and unclench over and over.

Linden sat on the floor, his elbows supporting most of his weight. After a moment he shifted his position so he could run at a moment's notice. His breath did not slow as he watched her closely for any sign that would indicate his beating would begin. He jumped when she turned to face him, her chin resting on one shoulder as she looked back at him.

She pushed her perspiration-dampened hair from her face and smiled at him. "And she thought that you wouldn't be any good," she said as she held out one hand toward him.

The princess tossed a file on the desk before her former tutor's abandoned slave. Her gaze was met evenly and silently. "Since she's gone, you get to be my assistant, Dwern."

"If you wish, Mistress," the slave replied softly.

Semiramis sat back in her desk and sighed. "You are aware that she left your ownership papers behind and signed them over to me?"

"Yes, Mistress," Dwern replied. He sniffed back a tear and returned his gaze to the floor.

"I haven't signed it yet," she informed him.

The two slaves exchanged looks.

"I think we need to go through a type of mourning for Radella. I intend not to sign those documents until you are ready to let go of her memory, Dwern." She threw out these comments and watched the older man closely.

He opened his mouth and sighed audibly. "I thank you for your time, Your Highness."

"You know what the mourning period allows you?" she asked.

"Yes, Your Highness," he replied.

"Good." The princess picked up her own pile of files and nodded to her gift to leave. "Let's get to work then."

"You look anxious," Dwern said to his bunkmate as the younger slave faced the mirror in the bathroom.

"I am," Linden replied. "It's been a week, and the doctor gave me a clean bill of health this afternoon."

"You're not the frightened kid who came in two weeks ago," Dwern announced. "You bounce back quickly."

Linden turned and smiled warmly at the other man. "You gave me a lot of hope. You said to focus on her and it would work."

"I wouldn't place too much value on my words," Dwern commented as he ran a hand through the thin beard now growing on his face.

"How does that feel?" Linden asked as he reached out and touched the hair just enough for it to tickle his fingertips.

"Like a heavy burden," the older slave responded. "Not as heavy as my heart though." He helped the younger man into a fresh pair of pants and a shirt. "You ever had this done to you before, boy?"

Linden nodded gravely. "Many times, but everything is so new with her that it is," he paused and shut the door to the bathroom, "pleasant for me."

"Sometimes, with the right person, it can be very pleasant," Dwern agreed. He turned his back to the younger man and waved him away. "Don't keep her waiting, you fool."

Linden didn't reply. He just left the bathroom, closing the door shut behind him.

In the corner, Dwern knelt and pressed his face to the wall as the tears once more rushed forth.

Semiramis stood for several moments just admiring the firmness of his ass and the now-healthy pink of his hole as he bent over, hands placed on his knees. "Much nicer," she commented as she moved closer.

Linden focused on his breathing, as instructed by the doctor earlier. He tried to pay attention both to calming his breathing and steadying his nerves, and to following her finger from the opening up the small of his back. It finally stopped at the base of his neck.

"I don't know why this is so attractive," she said softly as her finger slid back down and rested just against his hole. She closed her eyes and moved her hand over each cheek slowly, squeezing his flesh so she could absorb his heat.

Linden felt a moment of panic when he heard the snap of rubber, then relaxed when some of the cream she had applied teasingly to him on the first night was wiped over his hole.

"I'm going to fuck you, boy," the princess whispered in his ear. "You still want me to, don't you?"

"Yes," he moaned his plea and thrust his ass up higher to show his need. He rolled his head down as he felt a finger push a large amount of cream into his anus.

Semiramis's eyes closed again as she felt his muscles loosen slowly around her finger. When his muscles relaxed more she pulled that finger back, but not all the way out, so that two could enter together, along with an added bit of lubricant.

Linden shuddered as he was stretched wider. His mind flashed several random colors as his hole started to tighten in fear.

"Sshhh," she breathed into his ear and moved slowly to one side of him. Her fingers turned slowly until the rest of her hand could rest on his ass. She ran her free hand through his hair and over his jawbone.

After several minutes, Linden began to moan and twist his head toward the fingers tracing patterns along his face.

"What do you want?" Semiramis demanded softly.

"More," Linden begged as his lips brushed against her palm and he flicked out his tongue.

The princess moved her fingers out slowly, then pushed them in very slowly. His body tensed as she increased her tempo of thrusting. Her fingers pushed apart, widening his hole as they plunged in and out now in a rapid motion. As his ass muscles tightened and signaled his nearing orgasm, she suddenly pulled her fingers completely free.

Linden stood completely still only because his mind fought desperately with his body. He felt so empty, a million times more than when he had been in a chastity plug for weeks. His body wanted to fall onto the floor and crawl after her, pleading to be filled again. He moaned when he heard the rubber glove snap and then plop into the trash can.

He nearly fell over when he felt her now naked body press up against his back. His hips responded to her own movements as she thrust against his ass, nothing entering him, tormenting his sudden need. He moved his hands from his knees but found them grabbed by her and returned to his previous position. Her hands and legs pushed against his own, pinning him in place.

Semiramis moved blindly, her body going where her mind led it, then abandoning herself to lust. She thought of how tight and warm he felt around her fingers and dug those two nails into his arm where she held him. Soon her body shuddered, and they fell over onto the floor in a heap.

They lay there, both breathing deeply for several seconds. Slowly the princess pulled her hands out from underneath him. "You okay?" she asked between breaths.

"Yes," he managed to croak. He rolled over and looked at her as she sat on the floor beside him. His hand reached out and caressed her knee nearest him. Unlike his previous owners, she didn't push him away when he sat up and started to use his mouth on the same area.

Semiramis let his hands roam up her torso and cup her breasts. After a few moments of fondling, she tapped her right foot. Immediately his hands and mouth withdrew and he sat back looking at her. "The privileges are pretty damn good," she commented, more to herself than to him.

"He doesn't look very presentable," the queen commented to her heir as they stood watching her slaves help with the winter festival decorations. "His face is so…hairy. And he still has her family crest," the queen said, pointing to the slave's ear.

"Mother," Semiramis sighed at the now familiar chant that her mother had taken up over the past month.

"People will talk at the party," the queen said, loudly enough for the two slaves to hear.

"Let them talk," Semiramis snapped back. "If anyone asks me, I'll tell them the truth," she stated as she marked her checklist and walked to the kitchens.

The queen hurried after her daughter. "You will not!"

Dwern looked up at the younger slave on the ladder and handed him more of the silver ribbon. "They're talking about me."

Linden stapled the end of that ribbon up and stepped down the ladder. "Probably," he said when he stood face-to-face with the man he now called his friend. The ten pounds the older man had lost over the past month seemed to have been transferred to him. The boy still seemed thin, though, because he had grown an inch as well.

"No one will recognize you," Dwern said with a smile

that pulled up on the tiny beard he had been allowed to grow in mourning.

"Me, what about you?" Linden asked as he moved the ladder to the next chandelier. "Two more and we are done," he announced as he climbed up the ladder.

True to her word, Semiramis did tell the assembled noble-women what had happened over the past few months, but with her own twist on things. "May I have your attention?" she asked from the podium. "Thank you, and welcome, gentlewomen!"

The crowd of women clapped, then whispered as a slave with a beard, dressed in a black jacket, walked up to the podium.

"If this slave looks familiar to you tonight, it is because he belonged to my former tutor, Professor Radella Gaxas!" the princess began. "Professor Gaxas has taken a leave of absence for an indefinite period of time. Until her return, her slave will be in my service. As you can see," she motioned to his face, "he is being allowed a mourning period, so please respect my wishes and do not ask questions of him this evening. Thank you for your understanding!"

Semiramis nodded at her mother, who simply stood with open mouth by the punch bowl, but went to join her cousin. "Zerlinda!" she exclaimed and kissed her cousin on both cheeks.

"My dear," her cousin replied. "It sounds like a lot has been happening since we became women. But you can tell me," she added in a whisper, "what really happened."

Semiramis found that she didn't care for the changes that had occurred in her cousin over the past months. The heir to Verelande now wore black lace on her beautiful blue gown and had outlined her eyes in dark black lines. She noted that Aaron, her slave, seemed far more nervous than he had been on the night he was given. "Why do you think something else happened?" she asked with as blank a face as she could manage.

"Fine," her cousin replied coolly. She walked to the older slave and turned his head so she could examine his earring. With a frown she stepped back. "Forgive me, cousin," she said with a slight smile, "I see I was wrong." Zerlinda snapped her fingers and her slave quickly knelt beside her. "Drink," she ordered.

"That sounds good." Semiramis motioned to Linden, who hurried to the bar. She next motioned to Dwern, who knelt next to her. "Get us a plate of food," she said.

Linden opened his mouth to speak to Aaron, but the other slave hurried back silently. "Brandy on the rocks," Linden told the barkeep. A crashing sound made him turn around.

Aaron had returned with the drink only to have it knocked from his hand. Linden couldn't hear what was said but noticed the familiar twitch of Aaron's body as the future duchess of Verelande wagged her finger at him.

Linden took the drink and hurried back. When he offered the drink to his mistress, her cousin said, "See, even he can fetch the proper drink! Go and get me another one!"

"Goddess, he has become clumsy!" Zerlinda exclaimed as she moved away from the spill so that the slaves Semiramis had had posted around the room could wipe up the mess.

The princess simply sipped her drink and took one of the sandwiches Dwern had returned with.

"Lady?" Dwern asked her cousin with bowed head.

Zerlinda took one of the sandwiches and frowned at the slave. "I hope you won't have that at my party in January," she stated to the slave.

"Party?" Semiramis asked.

"Unless you prefer to have the first one?" her cousin asked with arched eyebrows.

Semiramis shook her head. "I think you know a little more about these parties than I do. I'll throw the second one."

"Good, because I already started making the plans." Zerlinda took the proffered drink from her slave's trembling hands and tasted it. "Very good. Finally." She took her cousin's arm and led her outside. "You should have sneaked in with me when my sister threw hers. You would have learned a lot."

"Well, I had studies to finish," Semiramis replied. "May I ask you a question?"

"Of course," her cousin answered with a flick of her fan. Her slave barely bit back his cry as it stuck his cheek. "You're too close!" Zerlinda screamed directly into his face.

The princess raised one eye to her own men, then licked her lips before asking what she was sure everyone at the party was thinking. "What is all that stuff around your eyes?"

Zerlinda tossed back her head in a chuckle. "It's the latest fashion, my dear cousin. The latest fashion to make our elders' heads spin."

"Oh," Semiramis muttered as she sipped her drink.

"Aren't you keeping up with anything?" her cousin asked.

"I've been busy learning how the palace works," Semiramis replied.

"You must be kidding me," Zerlinda said. "You actually have to work here, with all your courtiers and servants?"

"I can't manage unless I know how it all works," the princess paraphrased her former tutor's words back at her cousin in reply.

"Well, you must learn something before you come to my winter party," Zerlinda stated. "I'll send some basic information with your invitation."

"That would be helpful," Semiramis replied, arching her eyebrows so only her slaves could see, thus forcing them to swallow the giggles this produced.

Semiramis kicked her shoes off upon entering her suite. She let the two slaves unbutton her gown and had the blond follow her behind the dressing screen while the older one hung up the formal dress. "It's early," she commented, rejecting the nightgown and instead slipping into loose pants and shirt. She and Linden returned to the living room to find the older slave waiting, as always, at attention.

Semiramis sat down on her couch and patted it. Linden knelt next to her, and Dwern knelt before her. "Goddess, what a party!" She leaned back, her arms across the back of the couch. "Zerlinda. What do you think is going on there?"

"The lady didn't seem too pleased," Linden remarked.

"Obviously," Semiramis stated. "But what happened to Aaron? A few months ago, he put you to shame, and tonight he couldn't do anything right."

Dwern opened his mouth, then closed it without comment.

Semiramis leaned forward. "You do that a lot," she pointed out. "Did Radella let you speak your mind often?"

"Yes, Mistress, when we were in her suite." He sighed sadly. "Usually."

"So speak up, then. I mean, aren't I worth as much consideration as she?" Semiramis hinted as she leaned back again.

The older slave just looked at her a second, then blinked once, slowly, as though trying to clear his head before answering. "I thought I was showing you more respect, Mistress. You never gave me permission to speak freely with you."

Semiramis nodded. "True." She slapped her knee. "You

have it then, same as Linden, when we are in here. And oh," she added quickly before he could reply, "you can have one more week, then I expect you to go get a shave and start using the cream again."

"Yes, Mistress," Dwern nodded and looked at her directly. "You have been most kind to me."

Semiramis's eyes twinkled mischievously as she asked a question that had nagged her for weeks. "Was Radella the only woman you ever pleased sexually?"

"No, Mistress. She had me please others on her command," Dwern replied with a slight blush. "She bought me when I was just fourteen," he added as an explanation.

The princess slid off the couch so she could sit on the floor closer to the two men. "Those things in that bag. Did she do that kind of stuff?"

"Of course, Mistress." Dwern looked at the ground as he spoke. "Don't you?"

Semiramis leaned back and glanced at Linden, who was trying to suppress a laugh. "Give him an inch and he takes a foot," she said with a grin. She reached across and patted the older slave's knee before he could protest. "Actually, no. I haven't used that stuff before. I need to learn, because I heard through the grapevine that this is the kind of stuff that happens during the party season."

"Party season?" Linden asked.

"Every year between the new year and the end of spring, the aristocracy between the ages of eighteen and twenty-one throw parties where anything wild and weird sexually goes on, or so Zerlinda has informed me." She sighed and decided to change the subject when the two men paled at the news. "Hey, I think we have time to go raid the kitchen before it closes."

Dwern rubbed his smooth face for the dozenth time that morning. He leaned against the wall, remembering his nipple piercing fourteen years earlier, an eighteenth birth-day present, Radella had told him. He clenched his fists in empathy for the blond slave who sat in the piercer's chair.

"Ouch," Linden let the moan slip out as the needle was pushed through the second nipple.

"Drink this," his mistress commanded, holding a mug of warm wine to his lips for a few sips.

"Almost done," the piercer stated as she now pushed the ring through. "He's got to take better care of these. A third time would be hell," she added, looking the slave directly in the eyes.

"It was mostly my fault. I've been so busy that I forgot to clean them and put the rings back in," Semiramis replied. "Will he be ready for heavy use in three weeks?"

The piercer glanced up over her spectacles. "Not on the nipples. Wait six weeks for those."

Everyone was silent as the piercer wiped the nipples with salve and put her equipment away. "Dwern!" the princess called, and the older slave helped her get her gift onto his feet.

Linden's feet started to give way beneath him, but the hands of his owner and friend supported him. He tried to focus on walking as he was led out of the piercer's office and made the slow journey back to his room. There he was laid on the bottom bunk on his back.

"You just stay there today," Semiramis ordered. "Dwern will bring your meals."

"Yes, Mistress," Linden replied, his voice sleepy from the warm wine.

Semiramis and Dwern left the room and went to her office. Dwern sat in the chair by her desk and took out the billing statements that were left from the previous day.

Semiramis sat down and looked at her budget records. "Okay. Where were we?"

"The bill from the flour mill," Dwern replied. He looked up and noticed the same smile he often observed her giving Linden play on her face. He cleared his throat to indicate that he had a question to ask.

"Yes?" The princess looked at him over top of the royal checkbook.

"May I ask if you have signed the ownership papers for me yet, Your Highness?" he asked softly.

"Are you ready for me to?" Semiramis asked bluntly.

"I've been calling you Mistress for several weeks now and it feels…safe." He added that last word after a bit of a pause. "You said that you wanted to learn about the toys in that black bag, but that you wouldn't ask me until you owned me," he reminded her.

"And my cousin's party is in three weeks," Semiramis finished his thought for him. "I've had people out looking for her, but no one has seen her," she added.

"I know, Mistress," the older slave replied. He opened the drawer on his side of the desk and took out the folder the former tutor had left behind. "Please, sign it. It would make me feel much better," he said with a tremble in his voice.

Semiramis opened the folder and looked at the ownership document. She looked at the slave, then took her pen up. Without a word she signed the document and dated it. "You'll report to my room after the evening meal," she informed him.

"Yes, Mistress," Dwern answered as he took the folder from her and placed it in the out box for papers going to the palace archives.

"She always did this?" Semiramis asked as she locked the shackles to the head of her bed.

"Not always," Dwern replied as he pulled on the chains and found them secure.

"It limits your movements," Semiramis observed as she ran her hand down the cold metal. "I can do almost anything I want to you now," she added, with a wicked twinkle in her eyes but a mischievous grin on her lips.

"Shackle my legs and I'm helpless," Dwern informed her, his voice still holding a touch of sadness.

Semiramis looked into his eyes and smiled weakly. "We'll just start with this." She ran her hands down his bare arms to his naked chest, pausing briefly to flick the silver nipple rings, which elicited a gasp from him. She sighed as she felt a twinge of pleasure at the sound.

Dwern kept his eyes open, knowing that if he closed them he would only see the face of his former owner. His skin tingled as he felt her hand move down to his stomach and thighs, pausing to touch his semi-erect cock.

Semiramis now straddled his stomach and looked at him. "Make me orgasm," she ordered, then moved up his chest until his mouth could touch her clitoris. His skin was slightly rougher than the blonde's, the ointment impeding the growth of hair but was not strong enough to end it completely. He worked quickly, faster than Linden, bringing her to a violent jolt of pleasure. She pulled back and sat down next to him, letting her body pulse with the now familiar aftershocks.

Dwern's eyes followed her, and he felt good that she seemed pleased. His mind went back to his last night with the professor and he realized that it hadn't been his fault at all. He focused his attention on his young mistress and said, "Thank you."

Semiramis smiled back and played with his side hairs, where the patches of gray were beginning.

"I'm getting old," he whispered.

The princess shrugged. "I hadn't really noticed." She moved her fingers along his sides and slowly circled his stomach in tightening rings until she dipped one finger into his belly button.

Dwern chuckled and stretched his legs a bit.

"Am I like her?" Semiramis suddenly asked.

Their eyes met as the slave shook his head. "No, Mistress. You aren't the same," he replied, guessing at the real meaning of her question.

"But she did this to you," Semiramis touched the chains attached to his wrists as she spoke.

"With you it's very different." He used the word—"different"—that Linden had used to describe his encounters so often.

Semiramis's grin widened. "I've only begun with you, slave. I suggest you keep such judgments until after you've pleasured me more."

Dwern arched his back, offering himself to her as her teeth grabbed one nipple ring and started to pull and twist it playfully.

The two slaves looked at each other with a surveying glance. Then they faced the mirror as the princess joined them. Each of them looked at their leather outfits and said in unison, "Passion Prisoner," then broke down in laughter.

"Okay, we've hidden in here long enough," Semiramis announced. "Let's go to this party. And boys," she placed one hand across each set of shoulders, "stay close to me. My cousin has gotten weirder, and her friends are sure to be the same."

The three of them just stood dumbly in the entrance to the ballroom of the castle of Verelande. They watched the scene before them in shock. To Semiramis, each woman looked like a creature from some old magazine, taken as booty during the Separation Wars a thousand years earlier.

To her slaves it seemed as though their darkest nightmares and most shaking fantasies had been fulfilled.

"Your Highness?" A male voice woke the princess out of her thoughts and made her turn around.

"Aaron?" she asked, not wanting to believe that the pale and thin creature, clad entirely in leather save for his head, could be the same gift presented to her cousin not many months before.

"Yes, Your Highness," the slave bowed very low. "If you please, the Lady Zerlinda awaits your presence."

Semiramis nodded and flashed her slaves two fingers.

Dwern shook his head as they fell just two steps behind their owner and followed her along the balcony to another stairway, which led to the stage.

"Cousin!" Zerlinda rushed forward when she saw her descend the stairs. "I was so concerned that you would not come."

"I would never miss your first party, cousin," Semiramis replied. "I hope we are attired appropriately."

Zerlinda laughed and pulled her own slave to her by his now fairly long hair. She gripped the back of his neck harshly, causing him to slump or risk choking in her grasp. "I like it. Simple, yet it fits in fine. Did he show you any disrespect?" she added, shaking the slave roughly.

"No, he was perfectly mannered," Semiramis assured her. She looked around and felt ill at ease. "Do I know any of these people?"

"Of course, at least their mothers," Zerlinda replied. She tossed the slave from her hand and he fell back, only catching himself before landing on his butt. He stood up and fell to attention immediately.

"These are very nice," Zerlinda exclaimed, taking the chains that ran between the nipple rings on each of her cousin's slaves to a leash the princess held in her hand.

"Would you like to try them?" Semiramis offered, getting two wide-eyed looks from her property before they lowered their eyes in submission.

"Really?" Zerlinda's speech seemed blurred slightly as she considered the offer. "But I only have that to offer you." She pointed to her own slave with a snort of contempt.

Semiramis looked at the black-haired slave carefully, then turned to her cousin. "For just a few hours," she amended her offer.

"Agreed, agreed," Zerlinda quickly accepted with a chuckle.

"Oh, cousin," Semiramis added as the other started to lead her slaves away. "Go very gently on the blonde's nipples or I shall be very angry."

Zerlinda paused and looked closely at her cousin. "As you say, Your Highness," she replied seriously.

Semiramis watched the group hurry toward the center of the room, where her cousin would surely show off her new toys. She looked at the shadow of the boy she'd seen for sale that day four months earlier.

"Aaron," she said and held out her hand. The boy just stood there looking at her. "You heard her give you to me for a few hours?"

"Yes, Your Highness," he replied.

The princess sighed, pouting out her lower lip so the air blew her bangs up. She pulled down on the leather crop top to adjust it slightly, but that did not cure the discomfort she felt. "So," she asked, trying to smile at the slave, "did you help decorate this place?"

"Yes, Your Highness," came the simple, formal answer.

Semiramis sighed again. "I bet you see everything from up on those balconies, huh?"

"Yes, Your Highness," he agreed.

"Good, then let's go up. You lead the way, boy," she

ordered, with a light tap on his arm. She watched his body closely as they climbed the nearest stairway. Even though she had not closely examined him that day in the market, she was sure his form had deteriorated since he had started living in Verelande. His body seemed tired but tense as he moved. The leather squeaked as he climbed.

At the top of the stairs he motioned to a couch set a short way off, where anyone using it could easily see over the railing. Semiramis nodded and led the way there. She sat there and intensely surveyed the crowd beneath her until she spied her two slaves and her cousin. At this point there did not seem to be abuse going on, simply her cousin showing off each man's body and pointing to the royal crest now hanging from each ear.

The slave standing at attention wobbled slightly, but steadied himself with the railing.

Semiramis noted one drop of sweat falling from his forehead as he bent his head for a brief moment. "Aren't you terribly hot in all that stuff?" she asked.

The boy paused before answering, but another drop of sweat seemed to force another brief reply, "Yes, Your Highness."

"So take some of it off," she commented as she noted that several guests were now swatting at her slaves with paddles. The men seemed to be enjoying the attention, so she leaned against the back of the couch and turned her attention back to her cousin's slave.

Aaron fingered the collar of the leather jacket but did not make a move to unfasten it.

"Go ahead, take some of it off," Semiramis ordered, now more firmly.

"I," the boy began to speak but had to swallow several times before continuing, "I wish I could obey, Your Highness."

The princess leaned forward and looked him directly in the eyes. "Why can't you obey, boy?"

"My mistress ordered me not to remove the clothing with my own hands, Your Highness," the slave replied quickly and turned his head way with a wince.

"Oh." Semiramis glanced back down to reassure herself of the activities below, then stood up. "So I can remove your clothes," she stated.

"Yes, Your Highness," he agreed.

"Shouldn't that be, if it so pleases you?" Semiramis pointed out as she placed a hand over his and touched the leather of the collar beneath their fingers.

The slave bowed his head and repeated the words, adding her title. He lifted up his face as one of her fingers directed.

Semiramis bit her lower lip as she suddenly realized that he seemed far more attractive to her now than he had in the market. She brushed his hand down and unbuckled the top strap on his jacket.

The slave shivered slightly as the air hit his damp skin beneath the leather. He grasped the leather of his pants with both hands as the remaining buckles were unfastened and his entire chest displayed.

Semiramis noted with distaste the silver metal collar locked around his neck. "Overkill," she muttered softly as she traced its length around his neck with her fingertips. She slid the jacket off his shoulders and to his wrist. "You have to let go if I'm going to get this off," she told him gently.

The slave immediately released his grip on his pants, and the jacket slid to the floor. He bit back his responses as best he could when her hands found his nipple rings and played with them. A gentle twist on each of them pulled a tiny moan from his lips. He bowed his head, his lips trembling as he pressed them firmly together.

Semiramis bent her head to his neck and very gently took a small fold of skin into her teeth. The body under her hands shuddered and grew warmer. She flicked the area she had just bitten with her tongue, then let it trail up the side of his neck to his earlobe. First she blew hot air into the channel, then licked all around his ear before placing her lips over it. "Do you like this?" she whispered.

Aaron closed his eyes and murmured an affirmative. His neck arched as she moved around him, licking, biting, and sucking on it. When she faced him again, he offered his neck up, as he had been trained to do for years, but then bit his lip, recalling the slaps he'd earned for doing so these past four months.

"I like to see your responses," Semiramis told him. "I want to hear your feelings spill forth."

Still tensed by fear, the slave opened his mouth and let out a wail, pulled from where he had buried his responses for months.

Semiramis pushed him to his knees and crouched over him. "The market manager told us that you were skilled. I wonder if you are?"

The slave arched his pelvis forward, giving her a place to rest her body. He looked at her skin and followed the leather straps of her top down and around each firm breast. "Command me, Your Highness," he barely whispered his request.

"Show me your skill, boy," Semiramis ordered huskily. She turned her head so that her hair fell back and bared one shoulder to his tender lips and tongue. Her hands reached down and unfastened his pants so that he moaned into her arm and had to pause in his attentions for the briefest second. As he bent his head and licked along the line of her top, her hands traveled back up his stomach to his chest. The fine curly hair there offered an easy target. He arched his body away from her slightly as she pulled several strands.

Semiramis blinked several times as her ears picked up a loud din from the ballroom. She placed her palm flat against his chest and pushed herself off him. She shook her head and stumbled up to her feet. Reflectively she patted his head as he knelt next to her legs and wrapped his arms around them for protection.

"I'm looking for Her Highness!" the royal herald announced loudly.

"I'm here!" Semiramis called back. She yanked the slave up by his hand and they hurried down the stairway. The crowd parted silently before her as she rushed to the herald.

The herald bowed low, then straightened and looked around at the crowd. "The queen is dead!" she announced.

The crowd responded with a volley of denials and groans of sadness.

Semiramis released Aaron and hurried to her own slaves. "What did you just say?" she asked the herald softly. She felt both of her slaves rest their hands on her shoulders for a brace.

"Your mother, the queen, was found dead a few hours ago. The doctors have just confirmed it was of natural causes," the herald added loudly.

This brought the crowd to a roar of denial and fear.

Semiramis placed her hands on top of her slaves and leaned back for support.

"Quiet!" the herald instructed the crowd. After several minutes of uneasy silence, the herald turned to the princess and handed her a document. Quickly the herald fell to one knee to make her final announcement. "Long live the queen!"

"Long live the queen!" other voices shouted out, and soon the entire crowd, except for the cousins, was kneeling and repeating the hail over and over.

Zerlinda looked at her cousin, then bowed her head and knelt also.

Linden exchanged concerned glances with the older slave.

Semiramis stood still for several minutes as her mind reeled with the news. It took both slaves to lead her out of the castle and back to the carriage. They rode home in full silence.

In a cave in the mountains that surround the land of Unamisia, a fire blazed. Demida paused in the entrance, waiting to be recognized. The figure by the fire turned toward her and motioned her in. The advisor to the heir of Verelande entered and sat by the fire.

"The queen died two days ago," she stated.

"Oh," the figure replied.

Demida looked directly at the woman, her mouth tight with anger. "Of natural causes," she added.

The figure just looked blankly at her guest.

"You know what that means?" Demida stood up in anger when the other simply nodded. "She needs you now, we all need you now!"

"No, she must do this herself," the woman replied.

Demida shook her head. "I have kept my word, Radella, and not told her where you are. She has asked, many times. I do not like lying to her."

"Does she think I'm dead?" the former tutor asked.

"No, but she wishes she could." Demida turned away and walked to the cave entrance. She paused briefly and threw back, "I wish you were."

Radella looked into the fire, reassured by what she saw there.

Linden double-checked his face in the mirror to make sure the entire beard had been removed. "It looks fine," Dwern replied as he combed his now almost completely gray hair. He looked at the bottle of hair coloring the doctor had given him earlier that day.

"It's been a year," Aaron stated as he joined them by the sink.

The two other slaves looked at their new comrade. A month earlier, the Duchess of Verelande had drunk herself to death under the stress created by the ritual suicide of all the Ladies of the Realm after the former queen's death. The elder daughter now held the throne and had sent the slave over to the queen as a gift. All of them had been presented as gifts at one time or another to Semiramis. None of them had been called to her suite since the night her mother had died. This morning they had received the summons and were all shaving in celebration.

"Do you ever wish Radella would return?" Linden asked as the older man scrubbed the hair coloring into his hair.

Dwern sighed and paused in his vigorous rubbing. "No," he answered slowly, then resumed the process.

Aaron looked into the mirror and smiled. "I look almost like I did when I was sold in the market. Do you think she'll approve?"

Linden sighed. "I don't know. I just don't know what to do about this situation. How are we supposed to act?" His voice had changed over the year and was now a rich baritone.

"We'll follow her lead," the older slave replied casually.

The three slaves entered the room softly after hearing permission given by the queen. At first they did not see her. Then, when she sighed, they looked at the windows and saw her standing there, her back to them. Just as they had, she had cut her hair very short as a sign of mourning, so that now it hung around her face in a tight halo of curls. When she turned to face them, the black velvet band holding back her hair made her face seem even more white and withdrawn.

Linden stepped forward first and approached slowly. When he was within three paces of her, he knelt down, bowing his head to the floor. Her right foot barely moved but his watchful eyes noticed it, and he rose to his feet immediately.

The process was repeated with the other two slaves, each in turn according to when they had been given to her.

For almost an hour the three men stood silent and watched their owner stare out the window. Finally, after a nod from his roommates, the blond cleared his throat and spoke softly. "Mistress, we were informed that we were to end our mourning rituals and report here this evening."

Semiramis glanced back over her shoulder and nodded. She walked passed the men and sat down on her couch.

Linden sighed softly and knelt in front of her. "May I ask why we were summoned, Mistress?"

"Oh," Semiramis began as she leaned back further into the couch. "I've been told that I need to relax."

The three men exchanged looks for several seconds before Aaron took the blonde's place at the queen's feet. "May I rub your feet, Your Majesty? I am sure it will relax you," he added with a smile. He fluttered his eyelashes briefly as he moved slightly closer to her.

A smile played at the corner of the queen's mouth as she nodded. Semiramis looked up at the other two slaves as she felt her slippers removed. "This has been a hard year," she commented. "A year of many changes. I assume Dwern has kept you abreast of the legal changes I and the Council have made?"

The slaves nodded but remained silent. All of the changes

in the legal status of slaves, giving them more protection and further controlling sales had made them happy. The other changes concerning transfer of land and inheritance, they did not really understand.

A tense moment of silence followed the queen's question. "May I be allowed to entertain you, Mistress?" Dwern asked with a sly grin on his face.

Semiramis arched one eyebrow as she agreed with a nod of her head.

Dwern glanced around him, then picked up several small glass figurines from the fireplace mantel. Slowly and carefully he tossed these into the air one at a time, then added more until at least two were in the air at all times. At her smile, Dwern bowed his head slightly and chuckled. "A skill I picked up in my spare time," he informed his audience.

Aaron smiled at the juggler, then raised one of the queen's feet to his thigh and began kneading her right sole. He sighed when her muscles began to loosen under his hands.

Linden now joined in with a jolly song he had heard at the casino where he had once lived and worked. He started softly, then increased in volume as the queen herself began to sing.

The three slaves all nodded at each other as their attempts brought a bit of color to their owner's face.

Semiramis felt her entire body relax and her mind suddenly brighten as she felt the warm hands on her feet, watched the tiny glass animals flying through the air, and heard the rich and lively words the baritone and her own soprano sang. When the song ended, she clapped her hands. "That was very..." she began, but her voice broke into a brief sob as she struggled to keep her sorrow at a distance.

"Mistress," Dwern spoke as he placed the figurines back onto the mantel, "have you cried at all this past year?"

The other two slaves moved away from the queen, shocked at their roommate's question.

Semiramis shook her head as she sniffed back the tears. "There hasn't been time."

"You've given us freedom to speak in your presence, here in your suite," Dwern continued as he came to the couch and sat next to her. He took one of her hands in his own and tenderly caressed it. "Don't you think you should allow yourself to be yourself here as well?"

Linden moved closer and stood behind the couch, resting his palms on her shoulder and massaging them gently. "You don't have to be the queen here with us."

"But I'm the mistress," Semiramis protested weakly.

"We know that," Aaron now replied as he placed one kiss on top of her feet. When she didn't answer, he let his lips linger and work their way across that foot to the other.

"You don't have to work when we're here," Dwern reminded her as he raised her hand and sucked on her fingertips.

"Let us do all the work," Linden whispered as he bent his head to her neck and brushed his lips against the skin right beneath her ear.

Semiramis felt she should protest, but when she opened her mouth only a soft moan came forth. She arched her neck, making sure he was able to reach her most sensitive spot. She pulled her fingers together and stuffed several into Dwern's open mouth. She lifted her foot and was rewarded with Aaron's wet tongue journeying underneath to caress her sole and heel.

Linden moved his lips quickly to the area she liked and followed the nerve ending along the base of her neck and up to her ear. Gently he sucked the lobe into his mouth, careful not to use his teeth. She moved her head and forced him to his knees so that he would not lose his grip. He moaned and followed when she pulled back a bit. When he placed one hand on her shoulder, she slapped it harshly, causing him to withdraw it quickly and place it behind his back.

Dwern sucked eagerly on the two fingers in his mouth and opened wider as she added a third. He slid off the couch and onto his knees so he would not choke on her thrusting. A slight sheen of sweat developed on his face as she stopped moving her fingers and he was forced to bob his head up and down to continue the motion. His neck arched up at a sharp angle as she tilted it with her one free finger and thumb. As he continue to impale his mouth, she hooked her finger up slightly so that her nails scratched his palate, forcing him to groan deep in his throat.

Aaron sighed as he was allowed to lick and suck each section of her feet. Her nails were well kept and her soles firm but not tough. He released one foot when she pulled it from his hand but gasped when it landed on his chest, pushing him down. He slid his body out flat so that he was lying on the ground directly beneath her feet. He placed his arms and hands at his sides as she shook free of them. Hungrily his mouth followed her feet, his tongue reaching out to lick any part within his range.

Semiramis smiled and opened her eyes. Her body tingled, alive with her sense of power. A year of starvation made her body burn in need, but her desire for control raged more rapidly. This she needed more than physical pleasure. Being queen had been a position of organizing this past year, responding to each.minor crisis and the frightened hysteria of provinces left without leaders. Responding was not control. She sat up straight and smiled deeply when Linden moaned as his lips were parted from her flesh. Dwern buried his head in the couch cushions as she pushed him back from her fingers. As she pulled her feet up underneath her, Aaron gasped and breathed heavily.

Semiramis stood up, careful to not let any of her slaves touch her. Her skin flushed as she felt their eyes follow her. She watched as they moved to lie prone on the floor, helpless against the feelings she had stirred. She sat on the vanity chair and swung one leg up to rest over the other knee. After watching them for a few minutes silently, she spoke. "So, when are you going to entertain me?"

All three slaves pushed themselves up to their elbows and exchanged confused looks. After firm nods from the two black-haired slaves, Linden rose to his knees and spoke. "Command us, Mistress."

Semiramis's eyes closed briefly as she considered the possibilities. In her mind, she recalled the last time she had visited Verelande before her cousin's death. While the scene she found disturbed her, she felt her blood rise now that she remembered the orgy she had walked in on. Opening her eyes, she noticed that each slave was now kneeling and looking anxiously at her.

"Aaron is the only one of you with real training in this area," Semiramis commented. The two other slaves looked down at the floor while the newest arrival beamed with pride. "I think he could demonstrate his talents for us all. Remove his clothes," she ordered.

First the blonde, then the oldest slave, looked up slowly. They glanced at the queen, then at the third slave. "Mistress?" they asked in unison.

"Stand up, Aaron," Semiramis commanded. "I think you know what I want." She directed her gaze and words at him.

"Yes, Mistress," Aaron replied as he rose. He lifted his arms away from his body and looked toward the blond.

A brief moment passed, then Linden nodded and touched the other slave's shirt. "I've done this before," he whispered as he slowly unbuttoned the shirt's front.

"Well, I haven't," Dwern hissed in fear as he took the offered wrist and unbuttoned that button.

"No talking," Semiramis cautioned them. She ran her fingers through her short curls, then let her arms fall back to rest on the vanity table. "Make it a good show," she commanded firmly.

Aaron rolled his head back as the two other slaves slid his shirt from him. He thrust his chest out slightly so the new gold nipple rings moved, catching the light from the full moon outside the open curtains. Soon a twinkle of light at his groin matched these as his lower body was bared.

Semiramis lifted her chin slightly as she noted how much better this slave looked after a short month in the palace. All his body hair had been depilated, so his own excitement was starkly evident to her eyes.

Dwern glanced nervously at the blonde, but followed his lead, matching the movements of his own hands to the others as they ran fingertips up from the bare feet to the nipples. The slave moaned as they pulled the rings out from his body, causing his nipples to jut forth.

"Do you like his body?" Semiramis asked.

Linden looked at his owner from under his bangs and nodded. "Yes, Mistress," he answered as he added a twist to the ring he held.

"And you?" the queen asked again when the other slave did not answer.

Dwern's face flushed scarlet as he looked at the naked body before him. His own cock was stirring, but his head felt heavy. He looked at the queen and noted the harsh glare now forming in her eyes. "I..." he began, then withdrew his hand and stepped back.

"He's shy," Semiramis commented as she leaned forward with a tight smile. "Dwern, you will now remove Linden's clothing."

At a motion from her hand, Aaron moved aside and stood watching the other two slaves. He held his body straight, not moving to hide any of it from view.

Dwern stood fidgeting with the fabric of his pants leg as the blond moved directly in front of him. His fingers moved under the other slave's as they directed him to the shirt buttons. After the second button, the older man's hands continued their task even though the blonde's hands now rested at his sides. As he slid the shirt down, Dwern noticed that his body was covered with a very light, pale, down of hair.

Linden turned his face to his mistress as he stepped out of his pants and felt the air encircle his legs. He opened his mouth and silently begged her for instructions.

"Now," Semiramis interrupted the men, "the two of you remove his clothes. Be gentle. Show him how this should be done."

Dwern looked at each man as he was surrounded. His skin felt clammy as they ran their hands over the fabric, touching every inch of his body before beginning their task. They let their fingers slide over his chest as the shirt was parted, and the stubble of his morning shave sent tiny shivers up his back. Just as he started to close his eyes, the two slaves moved back, leaving him naked and alone. He opened his eyes and found hers focused on him. Her gaze moved slowly down, then back up.

"Can you answer my question now?" Semiramis asked with a hint of sarcasm in her voice.

Dwern swallowed and felt his now-heavy cock bob slightly as his diaphragm expanded and contracted. "He is attractive, Mistress. Both of them," he added and felt his face flush.

"Good," Semiramis whispered. She rose and walked toward the oldest slave. She circled him closely, letting one finger trail over his body. Next, she moved to the other black-haired beauty and examined him gently. Motioning to her first gift, she fanned her palms firmly down his chest, her eyes holding the jealous gazes of the other men. "All of you are beautiful in your own way," she assured them. "I want you to be beautiful together. Do you know what I'm saying? I don't want to have to direct this theater."

The three slaves turned and watched her move to the bed and sit on the edge. She pulled all the pillows close and leaned back onto them. At her nod, the three slaves reached out tentatively for each other.

Aaron was the most comfortable and quickly positioned himself between the two other men. As his mouth caressed one's nipple, his hand reached back and teased the other's cock. He moaned freely as they returned his caresses roughly, encouraged by his earlier responses.

Linden caught the newest boy by his hair as he began to kneel between the other's legs. Without words, he pushed him toward the other slave. He caressed the exposed buttocks now facing him and remembered how wonderful such treatment felt to himself. Following his own desires, he ran his hands between the white thighs and pushed them wider apart.

Dwern knelt quickly as the mouth which now engulfed him was forced lower. His hands moved up his own legs and to his balls. There he felt the hot breath escaping from the slave's mouth. He thrust his hips forward slightly, causing the slave to buck.

Linden took this opportunity to slide his hands firmly around the hips, positioning them directly in front of his own cock. He watched as the slave sucked cock and rocked his hips back and forward with the thrusting of the older man. He raised his hand back, then let it swing, landing with a soft thud on the ass. One look at his mistress's face assured him he was doing as she wished, so he swung again, harder, eliciting a groan from both other men in response.

Dwern's eyes had closed the moment the wet, warm mouth had sucked him inside, so he used his hands to feel the puffed cheeks and taut lips. His fingers moved over the face and into the hair, which he grasped as well as its short length allowed. A gasp of warm air rushed over his balls as the slave responded to being pulled closer. The slave's nostrils flared as they worked hard to maintain his air supply.

Linden's cock ached as he held it in one hand and continued to slap the now-dancing ass. Soon precome leaked from the tip. This he gathered onto his fingers and spread on the rosy bud in front of him. As though starving, the hole opened and the ass thrust back. Not needing further arousal, the blond pushed his cock slowly into the awaiting opening.

Aaron's moans increased as both his holes were filled and he was fucked with increased roughness. His body, now healed from the abuse he had suffered in Verelande, responded of its own accord, thrusting and grasping with desperation. His balls ached and swung with each thrust, and his cock smacked against his stomach, hot with its need. He wiggled his ass, trying to position himself for maximum pleasure, but jumped as his thigh was rewarded with a sharp slap.

"Can you come together?" the queen's voice broke through the flood of sensations the slaves were feeling. Each mumbled a pledge. "Let's get more organized," Semiramis stated. "Stop, don't move." She grinned as three tortured moans met her ears. "You're going to thrust together, work together, and all come on my command."

Aaron gasped as the cock in his mouth moved out slightly while the one in his ass was driven in deeply. As soon as the anal sensation began to lessen, his throat was rammed by the other hard shaft. His fingers spasmed as he was rocked back and forth rapidly. When the warm liquid invaded his body, his own cock jumped violently and splashed his stomach and chest with sticky heat.

All three slaves drew apart slowly and lay on the ground, attempting to find spots dry of come and sweat.

"Here, clean yourselves up," Semiramis ordered as she tossed several towels on top of them. As she watched them dry themselves and each other, she slipped out of her court clothes and into her nightgown.

The slaves folded the towels and smoothed back their hair, breathing deeply and slowly as they knelt tiredly before the bed.

Semiramis climbed into her bed and moved into the center. "I'd like you to join me," she whispered.

First Linden crawled under the covers on her right hand side. He moved into the crook of her arm as she directed and curled his body close to hers. He watched as Dwern lay by her left side, on his back, slipping his arm under her so that she rested up against him. As Aaron slid in behind, Linden sighed, moving his legs so that the other slave's limp cock could press gently against one of his asscheeks.

Semiramis looked lovingly at each of her men and touched each face in turn. "I'm feeling much better," she announced as she closed her eyes.

Epilogue

The hooded figure handed the reins of her horse to the palace servant and walked purposefully toward the main entrance. She had little difficulty convincing the door guards to let her pass and less trouble ordering the chief steward to show her to the throne room.

The figure entered silently, opening the door but a crack, wide enough for her thin body to sneak inside. She hugged the wall and watched the activities of the room.

Today not being a normal hearing day, the three slaves had decided to bring the children into the large room to escape the boredom of their lessons and the dampness of the early spring air. The slave with gray hair stood and demonstrated juggling to the eldest of the children, a boy with sharp green eyes who appeared to be in his very early adolescence. The man chuckled and tousled the boy's hair when the other dropped the brightly colored balls. The other black-haired slave was running wildly with two children, a boy and a girl, trying to escape their hands as they shrieked and ran after him, their brown hair flying free. The third slave was attempting to comfort a wailing toddler who had fallen as she tried to keep up with her siblings.

The hooded figure stepped out into the middle of the room, and the oldest child screamed, dropped his juggling balls and whispered to the slave instructing him.

The men hushed the children together as the blond stepped forward, the child in his arms looking wide-eyed at the mysterious person. "Today is not a scheduled hearing day," Linden stated.

"I need to see the queen," the woman's voice insisted firmly.

The oldest slave slapped his protégé's butt, and the boy hurried out of the room.

The mysterious woman moved closer, walking directly toward the gray-haired slave, who held his ground.

"Who wants to see me?" The queen's voice made them all turn toward her as she entered, the boy close at her heels. Semiramis slowed down and motioned for her men to take the children out of the room.

"I always knew you'd have beautiful children," the woman said quickly.

Semiramis held up her hand, and everyone stopped. The queen moved closer to the figure, placing one hand on the hilt of the sword that hung at her hip in silent warning. "How did you get in here?"

"They all remembered me and allowed me certain privileges," the woman replied. "Don't you know who I am, Your Highness?"

The queen stepped back one step, but straightened her back up, thrusting out the hips and bosom four children had helped her develop. "Who are you? Take off that hood."

The figure reached up and slid back the hood. Behind the queen, the slave with gray hair gasped and placed his hands over his heart.

"Radella," the queen muttered in amazement. She looked at her former tutor and advisor, then sniffed and turned her back to her. "What are you doing back here?" she asked as she ascended the throne steps to sit in her place of power.

"I've returned to my job," Radella answered. Her back, now free from the cover of the cloak, was bent slightly with age, hinting that her life had not been as easy as they had all assumed.

"Your job?" Semiramis gripped the arms of the throne to keep herself seated. "You walked out on us. You abandoned your responsibilities to me, to this land, to the people! If you had come back in a few months, even the first few years, we would have welcomed you back! It's been fifteen years without your help. Now we don't need it, nor do I want it."

The old woman nodded slowly and turned her gaze toward the gray-haired slave. "I've returned. Is that any way to greet your mistress, boy?" she added with an edge of anger to her voice.

Dwern flinched slightly, his mind reeling from the shock. He glanced up at the queen, but found her looking directly forward. He looked back at his former owner and shook his head. "You're not my mistress anymore," he said as loudly as he could, his voice shaky.

Radella chuckled and moved closer. "I know you better than that," she told him, but found her path blocked by the other two slaves.

"Let him go," Semiramis directed them. "If he wants to go, he knows he is free to go," she added.

Linden and Aaron looked at their lover, their brother,

and in many ways, their father, before slowly moving away. They gathered the children around them and joined the queen on the throne platform.

Dwern's breath quickened as the old woman moved to stand as close to him as possible without touching him. He smelled the familiar scent of her skin invade his nostrils, making his head twirl with mixed feelings.

"I know how you work, boy," Radella hissed. "You've never been happy except with me," she told him.

Dwern's eyes flashed as he narrowed them. "No," he heard his voice speak his thoughts, "I've only been happy without you."

His head snapped to one side as her slap caught him off guard. Behind him he heard a couple of the children whimper. He turned, straightened up, and walked to the feet of the queen. There he knelt and laid his head on her lap, his arms wrapped around her legs. The children gathered around him and patted his back.

Radella frowned as their murmurs of "father" hit her ears.

"Get out of here before I call the guards," Semiramis ordered.

The old woman cocked her head thoughtfully to one side, then slowly nodded. As she turned, she heard the movements and sounds of a family comforting each other behind her. She allowed herself one small smile as she opened the throne room door and left.

A Simple Gift

The lights of the room exploded as his body shook from the pounding orgasm she tore forth. He felt her weight on top of him as she collapsed. Slowly his eyes focused on the canopy of white silk overhead. He drew in his breath as he felt her move. Her dark scarlet tresses brushed the side of his face and chest as she propped herself above him. Her green eyes filled his sight as she lowered her mouth to his. His mouth opened and submitted to her tongue. He lifted his head with a moan as she pulled away and sat up, straddling his chest. As she leaned toward the head of the bed, the scent of their sweat and their fluid filled his nostrils. His tongue flicked out and touched her quickly.

She clicked her tongue in disapproval and swung one leg over so that she was no longer straddling him. "Just for that, the legs stay," she said.

He felt his wrists released and slowly lowered them to

his chest. He watched silently as she got off the bed and disappeared into the bathroom. Soon the patter of water was heard. He lifted up his left hand and gazed at the ring on the third finger. He had made this ring himself, following her exact instructions. The delicate gold chain links had taken him weeks to perfect.

He lowered his hand after the water stopped. Soon she returned, his scent gone from her body. This saddened him slightly and he hated himself for feeling that way. She pulled the covers over both of them as she snuggled close to his body. His feet at the bottom corners stuck out, but he didn't care because her body was soft and warm wrapped around him.

"Good morning, Pierce."

He opened his eyes to her voice and her tongue probing his mouth. She guided his hands to her gentle breasts that pressed against his chest. His fingers were led along to the nipples as she sat up. She laughed and released his hands, which fell obediently to his chest. He felt his ankles released as he lay still.

"Time to get up," she ordered with a smack on the bottom of his right foot.

He sat up slowly, pulling his legs up, the muscles tight from being in one position all night. He watched her pull her clothes out of the closet.

"Don't just sit there," she said, looking over her shoulder at him.

He swung his legs off the bed and stood up. The room spun and he found himself on the floor, his head cradled in her arms.

"You know this happens when you lie in one position all night," she reminded him. "You need to be more careful."

He let her help him up and walk him around the room a

few times. As soon as he was able to walk by himself, she returned to the closet. He went into the bathroom and turned on the shower. The familiar sight of his clothing for that day laid out on the floor made his heart soar and his legs capable of stepping up into the shower. As he felt the water wash over him, he smiled contentedly.

When he had first encountered her at a nightclub, his friends all warned: "She's a gold digger. She knows you're kinky and she'll play you for everything you have." They were wrong. In two short years, their love was legalized at a tiny country church—the rings he made at her direction, blessed by the minister. That ceremony was for their families and straitlaced friends. Then that night they signed a contract in blood and he received a tattoo to signify her power over him. The year was ending now. He had to do something special for her. Give himself completely to her. But how?

His shower lasted precisely seventeen minutes, time enough to shave his body and make sure he was squeaky clean. As soon as he stepped out of the shower, she was there, standing in her bra and panties. His chest squeaked as she ran a finger over it. This won her smile. He watched with a deep sigh as she returned to the bedroom.

Quickly he dried off and pulled on his clothes—his worst jeans and a work shirt so he could continue on the landscaping today. As he walked past her, he noted that she was wearing one of her business suits. His heart sank at the thought of her going out and he pinched his thigh in punishment.

"Omelets," the note on the refrigerator read. The one underneath informed him that she was eating lunch in town, and the next one that she was in the mood for Italian. That probably meant they were going out for supper.

He had just placed the omelets on two warmed plates when she leaned over the kitchen island to blow him a kiss.

He smiled back and replied to the signal. "Good morning, Mistress."

"Yes, it is," she said, taking a seat at one of the stools of the breakfast nook. "You read the notes?" she asked, glancing at the refrigerator.

"Yes, Mistress," he replied. He placed one of the plates in front of her, the fork already on it. "Coffee?"

"Hhmmm," she thought aloud, tasting the omelet. "Irish cream. This is very good," she added, taking another bite.

He prepared her coffee and slid it in front of her. Standing opposite her, he ate his omelet, making sure to finish when she did. That wasn't a rule, but he felt he shouldn't make her wait. He took her empty plate and rinsed both off in the sink.

"Got to go," she exclaimed, glancing at her watch, the one he had bought her for her birthday two months ago. She picked up her coffee mug in one hand and her briefcase in another.

He followed her to the door, taking the mug after she had finished. He felt that evil sadness creep up inside of him as she opened the door. She paused and her lips touched his briefly.

"Be home around five. We're going out." She kissed him again, then hurried out of the door.

He watched her get into the Cadillac and drive off toward town. As he closed the door, he hit his head on it, cursing his feelings once again.

"So, your first year is about to end," his friend stated as he watched Pierce cart another wheelbarrow of wood chips to the back yard.

"Yup," Pierce answered as he stood up and wiped the sweat from his brow. "How long you and Marcy been married, Rick?"

"Oh, gee. Let's see," the man took his sunglasses out of his blazer pocket and placed them on. "Been with the old ball and chain for nearly three years now," Rick chuckled.

Pierce managed a smile. "What did you get her for your first anniversary?"

"Traditional is paper, but of course Marcy's tastes are higher than a mere card," Rick added. "I bought her a couple of acres of land and presented her with the deed. She's converting it to an orchard, I believe. She misses her parents' estate." Rick noted his friend's disinterest and supplied an alternative. "I heard clocks are the modern course to go."

"I gave her a new watch for her birthday," Pierce sighed. He picked up his shovel and looked at the wood chips.

"Why don't you ask her?" Rick said, uncomfortable with the other's labor.

"There's an idea," Pierce stated. He looked at his friend and held the shovel out to him. "Why don't you stay and help?"

Rick wrinkled his nose in disgust. "No, thank you. I don't how Elizabeth gets you to do all this stuff, Pierce. Beneath a Chaiseworth, I think." Rick turned away to leave but added over his shoulder, "She must be good in bed."

Pierce dug into the wood chips and dumped them on the area that surrounded an artificial pool. He smiled as he thought silently at the retreating figure, *You'd drop dead if you knew, pal.*

He had just stepped out of the shower and into the bedroom when the door opened and she returned. A quick glance at the clock assured him that she was early. He stood perfectly still as she walked around him. She paused behind him, pressing against his bare body. Her arms slipped under his arms, her hands caressed his nipples still firm from the hot and relaxing shower.

She moved around to face him, one part of her body at all times touching him. "I thought I would surprise you," she said. Stepping away, she took a few moments to look with approval over his body.

He parted his lips to speak but closed them so as not to disturb her gaze.

"What?" she said, tossing her jacket on the floor. "Speak to me."

"It is almost a year since you agreed to accept me as a husband," he said, his voice quaking as he spoke. "I would like to give you a gift to show my gratitude, Mistress." He paused and took a deep breath, "Do you have a suggestion?"

She reached up and touched his cheek, feeling him flinch slightly. "Am I so terribly cruel that you fear even asking a question out of love?"

"No. Never cruel," he replied, his chest filling with sorrow at the obvious pain his question had caused her. "I...I'm not very good at picking out gifts," he offered.

"Something simple," she said. She stepped away and fixed her eyes upon him in a more commanding gaze. "Remove my shoes." He knelt on one knee, then the other. He slipped each shoe off as she offered it to him.

"Now the hose," she instructed, standing over him. He reached under her skirt and released the hose from the garters. Slowly he rolled them down her firm legs.

"The shirt," she ordered softly, her eyes sparkling. He stood up, his height only inches above hers. Taking his time, but gauging the speed by her breathing, he unbuttoned each pearl button. He slipped the silk shirt from her body, his breathing now audible. He touched her white bra strap in hope.

"No," she stated. A smile touched her lips as he let his hands fall to his sides. "The skirt."

Kneeling again, he loosened her belt and laid it by her

bare feet. Next he unbuttoned the skirt and slipped it down her heels to reveal the white garter belt and white bikini briefs. He looked up anxiously.

She walked behind him and ran her fingers through his hair. "Stand up," she ordered. As soon as he stood, she pressed her now-naked form against him. She kneaded his buttocks with her hands and her hips. Teasingly, she moved her fingers slowly around his hips until they caressed his pubic area, occasionally venturing to touch his now-hard cock and balls. His legs shook beneath her touch so she removed her hands and backed away a step. "Turn around," she whispered. He turned, his body flushed and ready for her. "You know what I want," she said, her voice sounding husky as she pushed him to his knees by his shoulders.

He didn't need further instructions. His tongue flicked out and teased her nipples. He caressed her breasts as he circled them with tiny kisses. His lips and tongue followed the curves of her body down her stomach and pubic mound. Her thighs opened to his gentle, hot, probing tongue. When her fingers grasped his hair, he scooped her up into his arms and carried her to the bed.

"Aren't you glad I came home?" she asked as he paused in his attentions to make sure she was comfortable.

He smiled, his blue eyes almost black from desire. "Yes, Mistress," he croaked, then dove between her legs with his hungry tongue. He could feel her glans swell in response to his attention. His hands caressed her thighs and moved up to her breasts so he could feel her breathing better.

Her fingers intertwined in the bedspread as she felt his mouth suck up the lubrication that now flowed freely from her. She moaned and clenched her thighs around his head as she felt her pelvis flood with blood. "Go!" she ordered, her fingers now wrapped around his brown locks of hair. The room whirled and she heard her own breath gasping then stopping, gasping then stopping. She screamed as the pressure exploded from her.

The orgasm increased her strength and she rolled them over, pinning his arms beneath him. Her eyes burned into his as she crashed onto his shaft. Her muscles still clenched, and within seconds he was rolling his eyes back in ecstasy. Their hips ground together as she pushed, forcing him in further and further. "Wait!" she demanded when she noticed him opening his mouth to beg.

He opened his eyes a crack and moaned in desire, but kept his lips sealed. He gasped as she stopped moving. He opened his eyes wider as she grasped him by the chin.

"Eyes on me!" She smiled as she began to move, enjoying the great internal struggle he fought just to obey her. "On the count of ten we come together," she mandated their pleasure.

His vision blurred even though he managed to keep his eyes open. The room seemed to dim and spin as she counted higher. He felt his cock trapped inside her, her muscles doing all the work. At her word, he heard himself scream as she milked him dry.

She shuddered, the second climax not being as strong as her first. She let him relax inside her, enjoying the feeling of her contractions. Then she climbed off him and lay next to him. "Come to the shower with me," she whispered, biting his earlobe.

Later that evening, while they sat at their favorite table in one of the city's finest Italian restaurants, he ventured to clarify her answer. "May I ask what you meant by 'something simple,' Mistress?" He said the word very softly. She prized discretion in public, but he wished to show her his full respect.

Elizabeth frowned slightly. "You don't have to get me anything, Pierce."

He bowed his head and leaned across the table. "Please," he begged, "let me give you things. Let me worship you that way as well." He was sure that this brought a blush to her cheeks.

"Just something simple," she replied.

She licked her lips and sat back in her chair. "Your heart on a silver platter," she joked.

"You already have it," he replied with a sad look.

She quickly grabbed his hand and kissed it. "Then what more do I need?"

"Hey, Pierce!"

He looked up to see a dark-haired woman in a pink linen suit walking toward him. He leaned on his shovel. "Hey, Marcy!" His heart had that same sinking feeling he had experienced during the last month they had dated.

"Hey, it looks nice," Marcy commented as she looked around at the landscaping he had completed. "I like the gazebo especially," she complimented him as she stopped only a foot or two from him.

"Hi, Marcy. Rick's not here if you're looking for him," he added, hoping she'd leave at the news.

"Oh, I know. He's on the phone for the charity auction." She took a step toward him. "You've done a lot in three months," she said, glancing back at the gazebo.

"So, what do you want, Marcy?" He heard the harshness in his voice and was pleasantly surprised.

Marcy batted her blue eyes and pouted. "Ah, come on, Pierce. It's been three years already. Give me a break."

He glanced away and noticed the curtains in the mansion move. "What do you want, Marcy?"

"To invite you, and your wife," she said with a sneer, "to our celebrity auction this weekend."

Pierce looked at her in interest. "What's that?"

"Well, it's a benefit for the construction of a new research facility for STDs," she explained. "Some of the biggest names in show biz will be auctioning off a day of their lives. They'll do anything," she whispered, moving closer to him. "Bet Elizabeth would get a kick out of that; bet you would, too."

"Stop screwing with my head, Marcy." He tried to sound firm but found his mind jerked back to their year together.

Honesty might be the best approach, Pierce had told himself when he had met the brunette at a local singles bar. So he had introduced himself and said he liked to be tied up by women. The woman hadn't blinked an eye but had simply taken him to her home, where she had tied him to her bed with scarves. In the morning she had said her name was Marcy.

For eleven months, he had told himself over and over that he was in heaven. A woman who tied him up whenever he asked, one who went into porn shops with him and even watched movies with him. He could ignore the little comments she made about how sick and dirty it all was. He had to, because he just knew he'd never find another woman from his same social class who'd do these things to him.

Finally, he had convinced her to go to an SM club in the city for the anniversary of their first encounter. She didn't say anything as they drove to the club, nor when he handed her a black bag with the toys they had collected over the year. But when he sank to his knees outside the club door and waited for his collar, she exploded.

"You're doing this in public!" she screamed, throwing the bag to her feet. "Why can't you be a man, for Christ's sake? I think, sure he's my class and he's nice, I'll go along with his little games, but fuck, you get off on this, don't you?"

Pierce looked up at his girlfriend in surprise. "Marcy, I've always been honest with you. If you weren't ready to come to a club…" He paused and stood up. "I'll take you home."

"Get your perverted hands off me!" she screamed and pushed him away.

Pierce just stood there dumbfounded as he watched the best thing in his life walk away and hail a cab. Giggles behind him made him look toward the club. There in the doorway stood three women in full leather. The two blondes laughed the loudest while the redhead simply smiled. With effort, Pierce crouched and picked up his toy bag and returned to his car.

"Let's screw something, then," Marcy said, her hand slipping inside of his jeans and jolting him back to the present.

"Well, Pierce, darling," his wife suddenly called from the house. "I didn't know you had company."

"Great timing," the brunette muttered, stepping away.

"Why, what a surprise to see you here, Marcy," Elizabeth said as she joined them. "Care for a cookie?" she offered, shoving the platter she carried between her husband and his ex.

"You bake?" Marcy asked with a snort of laughter.

"Yes, I just made them." Elizabeth narrowed her eyes and glanced at her husband.

"I didn't encourage her," Pierce said, almost sinking to his knees right there, but her glare stopped him.

The women exchanged challenging stares before the brunette chuckled and glanced at her shoes. "I came by to invite you both to the charity celebrity auction this weekend."

"Oh, that sounds interesting," Elizabeth said. "Do you have any literature on it?"

"As a matter of fact, I was just about to give it to Pierce when you joined us," Marcy replied, opening the purse she carried over one shoulder. "Here, it describes the cause and the celebrities who have agreed to participate." She glanced at the man as she continued, "I thought it might be something you two would be interested in."

"Well, anything for charity," Elizabeth said. She stared down the other woman until the brunette glanced at her watch and excused herself. "Please tell Rick that we'll see you both at the auction!" Elizabeth called after her. "Bitch," she muttered under her breath. Without a word, she turned on her heel and walked back to the mansion.

He dropped the shovel and followed close behind. As soon as the door was closed, he prostrated himself at her feet.

"Get up." Her voiced sounded tired.

Pierce followed her to the kitchen and silently watched her remove the last batch of cookies.

"That bitch made me burn these!" she exclaimed, dumping them into the trash can. She brushed her hair back from her face and finally turned to him.

Immediately, he dropped to his knees. "I told her to leave, Mistress," he pleaded.

Elizabeth lifted her hand, noted his flinch, and simply tucked one auburn curl behind an ear. "I know. She's still got the hots for you, though."

"I don't understand it," he said, taking her offered hand and standing up. "She tops me for a year, fucks my mind up bad, then leaves me, saying I'm a sick pervert." He followed her to the kitchen table and sat down across from her. "Then, as soon as I meet you, she starts making a pass at me, and she's married to my best friend, too!"

Elizabeth handed him a cookie. "She's confused because she wants to be a dom, but she thinks it's sick. Goddess knows, Rick won't let her." Sticking a cookie in her mouth, she walked to the fridge and got the milk jug. "Be careful at that auction," she warned, returning to the table.

"I'll stick to you like glue, Mistress," he promised, pouring milk into the two glasses she had earlier placed on the table.

"No," she corrected him, "I can't go."

He set his glass back on the table. "You can't go?"

"I have a business trip this weekend," she stated.

Pierce looked blankly at the table. "Are you commanding me to go?" he asked slowly.

"Yes, it might be fun and you need to spend a little time around your peers," she added. She handed him the brochure. "You might find someone to help you landscape."

He sat and watched her leave the kitchen. He wanted to run after her and remind her: *Our anniversary is on Monday. You can't leave me for the whole weekend.* Instead, he waited for a few minutes, then found her in the front room, about to watch one of her favorite movies. He knelt next to her seat. "Will you be home by Monday, Mistress?"

"Yeah, I should be home by Sunday evening, but not in time for supper," she added as the name of her favorite star appeared. After it vanished, she managed a smile at her husband. "Don't worry, I won't forget our anniversary. I have something special planned for you."

"Thank you, Mistress." He blushed and bowed his head. "I have to put away the landscaping materials and take a shower before dinner." When she didn't reply but only stared at the black-haired, almond-eyed actor, he added, "May I be excused?"

She nodded and waved her hand in dismissal.

Pierce frowned as he left the living room. He fought the desire to glare at that actor. Seeing the auction bulletin, he muttered, "Are you in here, stud?" The names were in alphabetical order, so it took a few pages to find it. A smile crept onto his face. "Something simple, huh?"

Pierce looked around the auditorium. Hundreds of his financial peers had come, along with hundreds of spectators. He turned when he heard his name.

"Pierce!" Marcy called as she approached him with outstretched arms. "I'm so glad you came!"

He allowed her to hug him briefly, then pushed her away. "Elizabeth sends her regrets," he said, then immediately regretted it when his ex cooed in interest. "I'm here for the charity, Marcy."

"Sure you are," the woman said as she took his arm and started walking around the room with him.

"Marcy?" He had decided that she was the person to ask. "Are any of the guys, you know, like me?"

Marcy rolled her eyes. "Perverts? Subs? Yeah, there are quite a few. That's why they came."

"Could you tell who they are?" he asked casually.

Marcy stopped moving and looked up at him. "Why? You want to compare notes?"

"What does it matter, Marcy? I'm willing to pay a lot," he said, looking at her without fear and with his mind solidly focused. Elizabeth had given him that strength, the strength that Marcy and society had taken.

After a moment of thinking, his ex held out her hand. "Give me your bulletin and I'll mark them for you."

Fifteen minutes later, he had been saved from her presence by Rick and was thumbing through the bulletin. He smiled as his hopes were confirmed.

Bidding started in the next hour. Prices were high, especially for the superstars. That's why he wasn't surprised to find his own bid up to five thousand. It was between him and a woman he recognized as a member of his country club. She kept throwing him dirty looks. Pierce simply shrugged and upped the bid.

The auctioneer looked at the woman, who shook her head and walked away. "Sold for seven thousand, five hundred dollars to Mr. Pierce Chaiseworth!"

Pierce went to the clerk and wrote out the check. Soon his purchase joined him. "So, you're Kurt?"

"Yup, that's what my mother tells me," the young man, actually his age peer, replied casually.

"Okay if we hang out a bit?" Pierce asked.

"Whatever you want, Sir," the actor said with a bow and a twinkle in his eyes.

The two men walked to one of the cafes that had sprung up around the auditorium. After ordering two coffees, Pierce tried to smile at the actor. "So, what made you agree to this humiliating auction?"

The actor's eyes twinkled again. "Hey, it's a good charity cause and it's fun, you know?"

Pierce shook his head. "Fulfill a fantasy or something for you?"

The actor chuckled. "What makes you think that?"

"You seemed to be enjoying yourself up there," Pierce said, then leaned back in his chair. "Plus I saw you in that collar a few years back in that street hustler movie. Very nice," he whispered.

The almond-shaped eyes focused on their buyer as the actor leaned back in his chair with a frown. "You into that, Sir?" he asked, his voice holding a challenge.

Pierce felt his cheeks redden as he remembered the last test that Elizabeth had put him through before agreeing to marry him. He tapped the table in nervousness but forced his eyes to look back at the actor. "You mean men or SM?"

Kurt leaned forward and placed his arms on the table. "Both?"

"Only been with one man," Pierce replied uneasily. "You?"

"A few, but I usually don't do men," the actor added. "I bottom on occasion. Helps relieve the stress of acting," he said.

"I'm a lifestylist," Pierce said, finally feeling more at ease. He sipped at his coffee while the other man looked at him, trying not to appear nonplussed by the comment.

"I don't get it," Kurt said. "If you got someone steady, why do you want me?"

"For my mistress," Pierce explained. "See, it's our anniversary, and I want to prove to her that I'm not..." He paused, searching for the right words.

"Possessive?" the actor suggested, taking a sip of coffee.

"Yeah, possessive. See, she owns me, but I don't own her." Pierce frowned. "Sounds crazy, huh?"

The actor shrugged. "I've seen weirder stuff at discos in Hollywood." He finished his coffee and leaned across the table. "So what do I do, Sir?"

"Come back to our place, I'll fill you in on the plan. She should be home late tonight." Pierce stood up, as did the actor. "You got a car here?"

"Nope, didn't think I'd be needing it," Kurt replied with a grin.

After dinner, Pierce took the actor to the guest room.

"Nice house," Kurt said again, as he sat down on the bed. He picked up the card fastened to a pink ribbon which lay on the bed. "So I wear this and nothing else?"

"Unless you have a problem with that?" Pierce said. "If you don't want to do this, just tell me and you can help me with the landscaping," he reminded the actor.

"Nah." The actor stood up and looked into the bathroom. He turned to his host with a smile. "She looks very pretty," he said, referring to the picture he had been shown earlier. "And you said she honors safewords and there are condoms?"

"Yeah." Pierce had to swallow before he could reply. "Well, I'll get you in the morning. Good night." Pierce left the room and hurried to the main bedroom. Shutting the door, he finally allowed himself to sigh deeply.

He went to the bathroom and took a thorough shower, making sure he was closely shaved and completely cleaned. *Please come home soon*, he thought silently as he closed his eyes and let the water fall upon him.

As soon as he could make his skin squeak, he turned off the shower and stepped out onto the bathmat. He rubbed his skin dry quickly, his body chilling. He ran into the bedroom and turned the heater on low. After the goose bumps vanished, he cleaned up the bathroom, pausing to glance in the mirror. *Am I as handsome as he? You're the best you can be*, he assured himself. He crawled into bed, making sure he was on his side.

Pierce opened his eyes as soon as he felt something sliding up his inner thigh. He swallowed once and spoke as loudly as he could, "Who are you?"

A giggle and a push onto his stomach was his answer.

Recognizing the sound of his mistress's voice, he relaxed and opened his legs as her hand continued to travel up his inner thigh. He felt the bed move as she crawled up next to him, laying her body along side him. Her other hand stroked his hair and the fingers on her first hand now traced around his anus. As she poked her finger in to the first joint, he clenched his legs shut in shame.

Immediately, the finger was withdrawn and he felt her get out of bed. "I'm sorry," he whispered as he heard her return. Instead of a vocal answer, he felt something cool and hard touch his anus. He relaxed his muscles and let the plug in easily to where it just brushed his prostate gland. The plug was pulled out and pushed in with an increasing tempo. His cock poked into the mattress in response.

As the tempo of her thrusting increased, his fingers wrapped themselves in the sheet as he tried to be patient. A particularly strong thrust pushed his gland sharply and he sucked in his breath loudly. A drop of sweat fell into his eye. "Please?" he begged quietly. The thrusting stopped, the plug in. He glanced over his shoulder, only to have her hand grip his hair and shove his face into the pillow. He didn't struggle and within seconds he was released and could breathe again.

That hand now rested on his bare back and she patted in time to the thrusting of the plug. Pierce's fingers dug into the sheets and he bit his lip as the pressure built up inside. His breath came in loud gasps as he desperately fought his voice. *Please, please, please,* he silently yelled.

"Scream!" she commanded, shoving the plug in as deep as she could.

Pierce arched his back as he screamed in pleasure. He propped himself up above the growing hot wet spot on the bed. The plug was slowly pulled out and he felt her get off the bed. He turned his head just enough to see her disappear into the bathroom. He hopped off the bed and pulled the sheets off before his ejaculate stained the mattress. He stuffed the sheets into the laundry chute.

"I'm home," she said, standing naked in the doorway separating the bathroom from the bedroom. "Shower?" she asked, stepping aside.

Pierce couldn't meet her eyes as he slid past and into the shower. Quickly he washed the already drying come from his stomach and crotch. He dried himself off quickly and grabbed new sheets from the linen closet in the bathroom. He didn't say a word as he replaced the sheets and she stalked him closely, making sure her body bumped his. As soon as the sheets and blanket were in place, he turned to face her and found himself flat on his back with her on top of him.

"I missed you, baby," she whispered as she nipped his earlobe. "Talk to me," she said.

"I missed you so much, Mistress," he repeated over and over as he hugged her close.

The alarm rang and he opened his eyes. He watched her glance at the clock, then angrily at him. "It's early," she muttered and pulled the sheets over her head.

Silently but quickly Pierce scrambled from bed. He hit the shower and quickly pulled on his work clothes, sighing in relief to see her still under the covers. He sneaked out of the bedroom and knocked on the guest room door.

"I'm ready." The actor answered the door in nothing but the anniversary card tied around his neck by a pink ribbon.

"I'll get breakfast ready and bring it up to you," Pierce reminded them both. In less than twenty minutes he returned carrying a tray of hot coffee, an English muffin with jelly, an omelet, and two strips of bacon. "You sure you want to do this?" he asked as he handed the actor the tray.

Almond eyes twinkling, Kurt nodded. "Just open the door and trust her," he added.

Pierce nodded and opened the bedroom door. He couldn't look in, so he simply ran downstairs and out to the backyard. *Calm down, you don't have the right to feel this way,* he chastised himself. He paced under the bedroom window, wondering what course of action she would take. As soon as she appeared at the window, he froze.

She looked down at him, her face expressionless at first, then breaking into a grin. She simply shut the curtains, signaling that she was accepting his anniversary gift.

Pierce nodded, wiped the tears from his eyes and went to the tool shed to get his equipment.

A glance at his watch when he paused for lunch told him it had been over four hours. Pierce cleaned the countertop off and took his sandwich outside where he couldn't hear the cries from the main bedroom. He sat on the ground next to his shovel and looked up at the bedroom window, where an occasional silhouette would appear. With a determined sigh he turned away from the window and concentrated on the sculptured backyard. Elizabeth was always telling him that he sold himself short. With a chuckle, he remembered their three years together.

It had started back at the club, that same night, in fact, that Marcy had left him. After driving around for an hour, he had decided that the only way to deal with this was to do just what he had intended to do. He froze when he found himself in the parking lot. *Except she won't be there to buy me,* he thought in horror. With a deep breath, he got out of the car, locked the door behind him, and walked as calmly as he could into the club.

Pierce felt his legs shaking as he walked onto the auction block set up at the center of the club. He had his black leather collar on, his black jeans torn in strategic places, plain white T-shirt, and white sneakers. *Why am I doing this?* he wondered miserably as he waited for his eyes to adjust to the light.

"Oh, no, it's the loser from the parking lot!" a woman's voice yelled out and was immediately followed with a roar of laughter from the crowd.

"Yeah, bring on something worth our money!" a man's voice ordered.

"Hey, like you lack club credits," someone from the back of the room sneered.

Pierce glanced at the auctioneer, who winked at him, then spoke. "Come on, folks! Everyone has a right to be auctioned off if they want! So, this is Pierce, swears it's his real name, and he has wandered around our club for several years but finally got the nerve to be put up for sale."

"Who's putting him up?" a man's voice near the stage asked.

"He is putting himself up!" the auctioneer replied.

"Total newbie," the man replied.

"Should be your speed then, John!" someone heckled from the back of the room.

"Gentlemen, please!" the auctioneer pleaded. "The auction, please!"

"Yeah, let's hurry and get some first-class material up there!" a woman's voice ordered. This was one of the women who'd seen him outside, Pierce decided when she spoke and his eyes found her and her two friends.

"Yes, so." The auctioneer wiped the sweat from his brow and looked at the information sheet Pierce had filled out when he had entered the auction. "Says that he has had one owner but has only experienced a little bondage and humiliation! Says he wants to learn more!"

"I got something he can learn," the man in front jeered again. Pierce swallowed and swore *If that's the only action I can get, then, hell, it must be better than nothing.*

The auctioneer saved him with a quick comment, "Says he's hetero, John! Now can we have serious bids, please?"

It seemed to take forever, but Pierce knew it was one of the quickest sales of the night and one of the lowest prices. He found himself led over to the group of three women who had witnessed Marcy's dumping him, and his heart fell into his stomach. The redhead took out a thin leather leash and attached it to the D-ring at the front of his collar.

"Why did you waste your money on that?" one of the

blondes commented. "His kind crawl to our doors every-day."

"He's never been at my door," the redhead replied; her voice was feminine but firm. She led him over to a small table. She nodded when he pulled out her chair for her. "Get me a ginger ale," she ordered, looping the leash around one of his wrists.

Pierce went to the bar and got the drink. When he returned, he paused, wondering how he should offer it to her. The books said one thing, Marcy wanted another, and the computer chat group said something completely differ-ent. He decided simply to stand still, just within her line of vision, until she spoke to him.

The redhead appeared to nod slightly, then spoke softly, "On your knees and hold the drink up to me."

Pierce obeyed, then waited until she motioned for him to sit in the other chair. He removed the leash from his wrist and laid it on the table so she could take it.

They sat for almost an hour, watching the auction in silence. He never turned his head to see the auction directly, but kept his eyes on her even when she turned her attention to the block. One man on the stage was looking pathetically at the redhead as his bidding rose. At one point, the bidding slowed so the redhead raised her hand and spoke, telling the room that he was one of her clients. His price was the highest male bottom bid of the night.

When she finished her ginger ale, the redhead put her little black purse up on the table. "How much was the drink?"

Pierce blinked a couple of times, then found his voice. "Three dollars, but don't worry about it, ma'am."

The redhead smiled and took out the money. As she placed it into his hand, he noticed that her eyes were green. "I bought you, you didn't hire me."

"You're a pro, then?" he asked, his hopes dashed for a real relationship but seeing an opportunity to move into the pro scene, where at least he had the money to get what he wanted, what he needed.

"What makes you think so?" She seemed amused with her question.

"Well," he glanced around and noticed with a touch of envy that her two friends were working over the men they had bought. "Well, you said you trained that one guy and his price went way up, so I figured you must be good enough to be a pro."

She laughed out loud then, and Pierce felt like sinking into the floor. Then her hand was on top of his and her voice spoke gently, "You sell yourself short."

"Huh?" he asked, his heart skipping a beat as she took the leash in hand again.

"Up there, your stance was why your price was so low. You need to be more comfortable with yourself." She stood up and led him to the coat check. "I prefer to play in private, unless you'd be more comfortable here."

Pierce glanced back into the main room. *Never be alone with a play partner you just met.* "Wherever you want to go," he assured her.

"Good." They got their coats and left the club. Instead of catching a taxi immediately, she led him along the sidewalk. He moved as close to her as he could, growing more uncomfortable as they moved further from the club. She stopped at one corner and raised her hand. Soon a taxi stopped. Ignoring the driver's comment, they got into the back seat.

Pierce sat next to his owner for the evening, his breath jagged as he worried more and more whether he was being foolish. *If I had to, I could take her out.* He followed her in a daze out of the cab and upstairs to the penthouse of one of the best buildings in the city. The door was answered by a young woman in a rubber maid's uniform, her hands cuffed in front of her. Pierce blinked in confusion as his coat was taken and the maid led him into what appeared to be an ordinary living room.

"Would you like a drink, sir?" the maid asked.

Pierce ran one of his hands through his hair and shook his head. He stood up when the pro returned, this time wearing a handsome cream-colored robe. She sat down in a chair and motioned for him to return to the couch. The maid presented her mistress with a steaming cup. "You may retire for the night, Amy," the redhead stated.

"Yes, Mistress." The maid rose, then sank back to her knees. "Mistress, may I please?"

The redhead looked directly at her and clicked her tongue in disapproval.

The maid rose with a sob, but managed to leave the room gracefully.

Pierce turned his full attention back to this strange woman whose home he had obviously entered.

"May I look at your toy bag?" she asked as she sat her cup down on the coffee table.

"Yes, of course." He picked up the bag he had put on the couch next to him and stood. Following the maid's example, he offered her the small bag.

"You learn quickly," the woman complimented him. "Stay there," she ordered softly when he started to move. She held up each item and asked him about it. She rewarded each blush this examination caused him with a smile. "What's your name again?" she asked when she handed the bag back to him.

"Pierce," he replied. "What's yours? Sorry," he said when she frowned at the question.

"You have potential but you are very raw," she replied as

she stood up. She unclipped the leash from his collar. "Follow me," she instructed him and led him back to the door.

Pierce was clearly disappointed but tried to redeem himself by kissing her hand when she offered it to him.

"Here," the woman said, dropping a card into his palm. With a parting smile, she shut the door on him.

Pierce stood outside the door for a moment and looked at the card. MISTRESS ELIZABETH: PROFESSIONAL DOMINATRIX AND EDITOR. OWNER OF CINDERELLA'S OTHER FANTASIES, a store in the city he and Marcy had visited. He said the name out loud, tasting the sound, "Elizabeth."

"Hey, Sir." Kurt tapped the other man on the shoulder again.

Pierce looked up and quickly stood.

"She wants you upstairs with her lunch," the movie star stated again.

Pierce nodded and went into the house. As he prepared the tray, he noticed that the man was shoving the wood chips into the carefully marked areas. He went to the door and called out to him, "Hey, you don't have to do that!"

"She said I should," Kurt replied. He smiled and paused to take off his shirt.

Pierce bit his lip as he saw the welts already turning a nice black-and-blue color. He picked up the tray and slowly went up the steps, determined not to ruin this day for her with any jealousy he might still have.

The door was open and he found her sitting up in bed waiting for him. "Come in," she said with a wave of her hand. He came to her and laid the tray across her lap. "Stay," she whispered as he turned to leave.

He stopped in his tracks and looked down at her. At her subtle signal, he pulled off his shirt, stepped out of his shoes, and unbuttoned his jeans. The socks were next, then he slid the jeans down to reveal his bare body. "Close your eyes and stay perfectly still," she ordered.

His legs felt numb, his back ached, and he had an increasing itch on his neck. It had been hours for certain since he had delivered her lunch. During her shower he remained in position and he felt her move around him as she dressed. Then he heard another set of feet in the room and stiffened. A blindfold was placed over his eyes and earplugs placed in his ears. His arms were strapped back and his hands cuffed. Legcuffs were also attached and a blanket tossed around him and straps tightened over it. Then the room tilted as he was hoisted up and carried.

He recognized the trunk of the car when he was placed in it from the familiar scent and feel of the steel on his feet. *A trip. The special evening she talked about?* He relaxed and tried to stay awake as the car moved. It stopped once for more than a mere traffic signal, then drove on further.

When it stopped again, the engine was turned off. A few seconds later, the trunk opened and several pairs of hands lifted him out and carried him. His feet were set down on something slick but soft. The blanket was removed, and his arms and legs released, only to be spread-eagled against a frame behind him. Then the earplugs were removed and he could hear several soft female voices and gentle classical music. He didn't open his eyes when the blindfold was removed.

"Open your eyes, Pierce," Elizabeth commanded.

After a few seconds, he could see her in the brightly lit room. She was in her full working leathers, and almost all of her top friends were in the room as well, along with a few of their bottoms. He swallowed as a gentleman he recognized and dreaded held a needle up in front of him.

"It's been one year, Pierce." Elizabeth placed her hands on her hips. "Are you mine completely?"

"Yes, Mistress," he replied automatically. His eyes followed the needle as it was wiped with a cloth. *Not this, not this.* He looked at his wife with pleading eyes.

"Your gift to me was wonderful," she told him softly, licking her lips in the professionally seductive manner that he had seen with floor men who claimed to be tops or gay. "My gift to you is to accept your final limit being crossed."

He rolled his eyes up and moaned slightly. *I've had a tattoo, a brand, been fucked by a man but not this, please.* He met her eyes and focused on the emerald depths entirely. His fear decreased, his mouth spoke, "Do it."

"Look at me, directly in the eyes, and don't look away," Elizabeth said as she moved closer until the piercer's hand rested on her thigh, telling her that was as close as she could get. "Stay focused no matter what," she whispered.

The room narrowed to her eyes and her voice. The pain felt like mere pricks with a sewing needle in his right ear, his nipples, and the skin around the head of his cock. Sounds slipped into silence and the world turned green as she stepped right up to him and embraced him carefully.

"Happy anniversary, darling," she whispered in his ear.

ROSEBUD BOOKS

THE ROSEBUD READER

Rosebud has contributed greatly to the burgeoning genre of lesbian erotica—to the point that authors like Lindsay Welsh, Aarona Griffin and Valentina Cilescu are among the hottest and most closely watched names in lesbian and gay publishing. Here are the finest moments from **Rosebud**'s contemporary classics. $5.95/319-8

K. T. BUTLER

TOOLS OF THE TRADE

A sparkling mix of lesbian erotica and humor. A sizzling encounter with ice cream, cappuccino and chocolate cake; an affair with a complete stranger; a pair of faulty handcuffs; and love on a drafting table. Seventeen delightful tales. $5.95/420-8

LOVECHILD

GAG

From New York's thriving poetry scene comes this explosive volume of work from one of the bravest, most cutting young writers you'll ever encounter. The poems in *Gag* take on American hypocrisy with uncommon energy, and announce Lovechild as a writer of unique and unforgettable rage. $5.95/369-4

ALISON TYLER

DIAL "L" FOR LOVELESS

Meet Katrina Loveless—a private eye talented enough to give Sam Spade a run for his money. In her first solo case, Katrina investigates a murder implicating a host of society's darlings—including Tessa and Baxter Saint Claire (heirs to an unimaginable fortune), and the lovely, tantalizing, infamous Geneva twins. Loveless is just the investigator to untangle the ugly mess—even while working herself into a variety of highly compromising knots with the many lovelies who cross her path! $5.95/386-4

THE VIRGIN

Does he satisfy you? Is something missing? Maybe you don't need a man at all—maybe you need me. Veronica answers a personal ad in the "Women Seeking Women" category—and discovers a whole sensual world she never knew existed! And she never dreamed she'd be prized as a virgin all over again, by someone who would deflower her with a passion no man could ever show.... $5.95/379-1

THE BLUE ROSE

The tale of a modern sorority—fashioned after a Victorian girls' school. Ignited to the heights of passion by erotic tales of the Victorian age, a group of lusty young women are encouraged to act out their forbidden fantasies—all under the tutelage of Mistresses Emily and Justine, two avid practitioners of hard-core discipline! $5.95/335-X

ELIZABETH OLIVER

THE SM MURDER: Murder at Roman Hill

Intrepid lesbian P.I.s Leslie Patrick and Robin Penny take on a really hot case: the murder of the notorious Felicia Roman. The circumstances of the crime lead the pair on an excursion through the leatherdyke underground, where motives—and desires—run deep. But as Leslie and Robin soon find, every woman harbors her own closely guarded secret.... $5.95/353-8

PAGAN DREAMS

Cassidy and Samantha plan a vacation at a secluded bed-and-breakfast, hoping for a little personal time alone. Their hostess, however, has different plans. The lovers are plunged into a world of dungeons and pagan rites, as the merciless Anastasia steals Samantha for her own. B&B—B&D-style! $5.95/295-7

ROSEBUD BOOKS

SUSAN ANDERS

CITY OF WOMEN

A collection of stories dedicated to women and the passions that draw them together. Designed strictly for the sensual pleasure of women, Anders' tales are set to ignite flames of passion from coast to coast. The residents of *City of Women* hold the key to even the most forbidden fantasies. $5.95/375-9

PINK CHAMPAGNE

Tasty, torrid tales of butch/femme couplings—from a writer more than capable of describing the special fire ignited when opposites collide. Tough as nails or soft as silk, these women seek out their antitheses, intent on working out the details of their own personal theory of difference. $5.95/282-5

LAVENDER ROSE

Anonymous

A classic collection of lesbian literature. From the writings of Sappho, Queen of the island Lesbos, to the turn-of-the-century *Black Book of Lesbianism*; from *Tips to Maidens* to *Crimson Hairs*, a recent lesbian saga—here are the great but little-known lesbian writings and revelations. A one volume survey of hot lesbian writing. $4.95/208-6

LAURA ANTONIOU, EDITOR

LEATHERWOMEN II

A follow-up volume to the popular and controversial *Leatherwomen*. Laura Antoniou turns an editor's discerning eye to the writings of women on the edge—resulting in a collection sure to ignite libidinal flames. Leave taboos behind, because these Leatherwomen know no limits.... $4.95/229-9

LEATHERWOMEN

These fantasies, from the pens of new or emerging authors, break every rule imposed on women's fantasies. The hottest stories from some of today's newest and most outrageous writers make this an unforgettable exploration of the female libido. $4.95/3095-4

LESLIE CAMERON

THE WHISPER OF FANS

"Just looking into her eyes, she felt that she knew a lot about this woman. She could see strength, boldness, a fresh sense of aliveness that rocked her to the core. In turn, she felt open, revealed under the woman's gaze—all her secrets already told. No need of shame or artifice...." $5.95/259-0

AARONA GRIFFIN

PASSAGE AND OTHER STORIES

An S/M romance. Lovely Nina is frightened by her lesbian passions, until she finds herself infatuated with a woman she spots at a local café. One night Nina follows her, and finds herself enmeshed in an endless maze leading to a world where women test the edges of sexuality and power. A wildly popular title. $4.95/3057-1

VALENTINA CILESCU

MISTRESS WITH A MAID I: MY LADY'S PLEASURE

Dr. Claudia Dungarrow, a lovely, powerful, but mysterious figure at St. Matilda's College, comes face to face with desires that might prove the undoing of an ordinary woman. For when her hungers lead her to attempt seducing the virginal Elizabeth Stanbridge, she sets off a chain of events that eventually cost her her job. But Claudia vows revenge—and has it in her power to make her foes pay deliciously.... $5.95/412-7

ROSEBUD BOOKS

THE ROSEBUD SUTRA

"Women are hardly ever known in their true light, though they may love others, or become indifferent towards them, may give them delight, or abandon them, or may extract from them all the wealth that they possess." So says *The Rosebud Sutra*—a volume promising women's inner secrets. One woman learns to use these secrets in a quest for pleasure with a succession of lady loves.... Scalding heat from one of lesbian erotica's biggest names. $4.95/242-6

THE HAVEN

J craves domination, and her perverse appetites lead her to the Haven: the isolated sanctuary Ros and Annie call home. Soon J forces her way into the couple's world, bringing unspeakable lust and cruelty into their lives. $4.95/165-9

MISTRESS MINE

Sophia Cranleigh sits in prison, accused of authoring the "obscene" *Mistress Mine*. For Sophia has led no ordinary life, but has slaved and suffered—deliciously—under the hand of the notorious Mistress Malin. How long had she languished under the dominance of this incredible beauty? $5.95/445-3

LINDSAY WELSH

MILITARY SECRETS

Colonel Candice Sproule heads a highly specialized boot camp. Assisted by three dominatrix sergeants, Col. Sproule takes on the talented submissives sent to her by secret military contacts. Then comes Jesse Robbins—whose pleasure in being served matches the Colonel's own. This new recruit sets off fireworks in the barracks—and beyond.... $5.95/397-X

ROMANTIC ENCOUNTERS

Beautiful Julie, the most powerful editor of romance novels in the industry, spends her days igniting women's passions through books—and her nights fulfilling those needs with a variety of lovers. Julie's two worlds come together in the type of bodice-ripping Harlequin could never imagine! $5.95/359-7

THE BEST OF LINDSAY WELSH

A collection of this popular writer's best work. This author was one of Rosebud's early bestsellers, and remains highly popular. A sampler set to introduce some of the hottest lesbian erotica to a wider audience. $5.95/368-6

PROVINCETOWN SUMMER

This completely original collection is devoted exclusively to white-hot desire between women. From the casual encounters of women on the prowl to the enduring erotic bonds between old lovers, the women of *Provincetown Summer* will set your senses on fire! A national bestseller. $5.95/362-7

NECESSARY EVIL

What's a girl to do? When her Mistress proves too systematic, too by-the-book, one lovely submissive takes the ultimate chance—choosing and creating a Mistress who'll fulfill her heart's desire. Little did she know how difficult it would be—and, in the end, rewarding.... $5.95/277-9

A VICTORIAN ROMANCE

Lust-letters from the road. A young Englishwoman realizes her dream—a trip abroad under the guidance of her eccentric maiden aunt. Soon, the young but blossoming Elaine comes to discover her own sexual talents, as a hot-blooded Parisian named Madelaine takes her Sapphic education in hand. $5.95/365-1

A CIRCLE OF FRIENDS

The author of the nationally best-selling *Provincetown Summer* returns with the story of a remarkable group of women. Slowly, the women pair off to explore all the possibilities of lesbian passion, until finally it seems that there is nothing—and no one—they have not dabbled in. $4.95/250-7

ROSEBUD BOOKS

PRIVATE LESSONS

A high voltage tale of life at The Whitfield Academy for Young Women—where cruel headmistress Devon Whitfield presides over the in-depth education of only the most talented and delicious of maidens. Elizabeth Dunn arrives at the Academy, where it becomes clear that she has much to learn—to the delight of Devon Whitfield and her randy staff of Mistresses! $4.95/116-0

BAD HABITS

What does one do with a poorly trained slave? Break her of her bad habits, of course! The story of the ultimate finishing school, *Bad Habits* was an immediate favorite with women nationwide. "Talk about passing the wet test!... If you like hot, lesbian erotica, run—don't walk—and pick up a copy of *Bad Habits*."—*Lambda Book Report* $5.95/446-1

ANNABELLE BARKER

MOROCCO

A luscious young woman stands to inherit a fortune—if she can only withstand the ministrations of her cruel guardian until her twentieth birthday. With two months left, Lila makes a bold bid for freedom, only to find that liberty has its own excruciating and delicious price.... $4.95/148-9

A.L. REINE

DISTANT LOVE & OTHER STORIES

A book of seductive tales. In the title story, Leah Michaels and her lover, Ranelle, have had four years of blissful, smoldering passion together. One night, when Ranelle is out of town, Leah records an audio "Valentine:" a cassette filled with erotic reminiscences.... $4.95/3056-3

RHINOCEROS BOOKS

TRISTAN TAORMINO & DAVID AARON CLARK, EDITORS

RITUAL SEX

A volume of literary explorations of the many intersections of sex and religion. While many people believe the body and soul to occupy almost completely independent realms, the many contributors to *Ritual Sex* know—and demonstrate—that the two share more common ground than society feels comfortable acknowledging. From personal memoirs of ecstatic revelation, to fictional quests to reconcile sex and spirit, to historical overviews of religion's obsession with regulating the libido, *Ritual Sex* delves into forbidden areas with gusto, providing an unprecedented look at private life. $6.95/391-0

TAMMY JO ECKHART

PUNISHMENT FOR THE CRIME

Five scalding tales of power, pleasure and pain from an uncompromising writer. Peopled by characters of rare depth, the stories in *Punishment for the Crime* explore the true meaning of dominance and submission, and offer some surprising revelations. From an encounter between two of society's most despised individuals, to the explorations of longtime friends, these tales take you where few others have ever dared.... $6.95/427-5

THOMAS S. ROCHE, EDITOR

NOIROTICA: An Anthology of Erotic Crime Stories

A collection of darkly sexy tales, taking place at the crossroads of the crime and erotic genres. Thomas S. Roche has gathered together some of today's finest writers of sexual fiction, all of whom explore the murky terrain where desire runs irrevocably afoul of the law. $6.95/390-2

RHINOCEROS BOOKS

DAVID MELTZER

UNDER

Under is the story of a sex professional whose life at the bottom of the social heap is, nevertheless, filled with incident. Other than numerous surgeries designed to increase his physical allure, he is faced with an establishment intent on using any body for genetic experiments. These forces drive the cyber-gigolo underground—where even more bizarre cultures await.... A mind-blowing journey with one of alterna-lit's longtime masters. $6.95/290-6

ORF

He is the ultimate musician-hero—the idol of thousands, the fevered dream of many more. And like many musicians before him, he is misunderstood, misused—and totally out of control. Every last drop of feeling is squeezed from a modern-day troubadour and his lady love. $6.95/110-1

AMARANTHA KNIGHT, EDITOR

FLESH FANTASTIC

Humans have long toyed with the idea of "playing God": creating life from nothingness, bringing life to the inanimate. Now Amarantha Knight, author of the "Darker Passions" series of erotic horror novels, collects stories exploring not only the allure of Creation, but the lust that follows.... $6.95/352-X

RENE MAIZEROY

FLESHLY ATTRACTIONS

Lucien Hardanges was the son of the wantonly beautiful actress, Marie-Rose Hardanges. When she decides to let a "friend" introduce her son to the pleasures of love, Marie-Rose could not have foretold the erotic excesses that would lead to her own ruin and that of her cherished son. $6.95/299-X

LAURA ANTONIOU, EDITOR

NO OTHER TRIBUTE

A collection of stories sure to challenge Political Correctness in a way few have before, with tales of women kept in bondage to their lovers by their deepest passions. Love pushes these women beyond acceptable limits, rendering them helpless to deny the men and women they adore. $6.95/294-9

SOME WOMEN

Over forty essays written by women actively involved in consensual dominance and submission. Professional mistresses, lifestyle leatherdykes, whipmakers, titleholders—women from every conceivable walk of life lay bare their true feelings about issues as explosive as feminism, abuse, pleasures and public image. $6.95/300-7

BY HER SUBDUED

Stories of women who get what they want. The tales in this collection all involve women in control—of their lives, their loves, their men. So much in control, in fact, that they can remorselessly break rules to become powerful goddesses of the men who sacrifice all to worship at their feet. $6.95/281-7

JEAN STINE

THRILL CITY

It is a place of hundred pleasures, the place of a thousand pains. Thrill City is the seat of the world's increasing depravity, and Jean Stine's classic novel transports you there with a vivid style you'd be hard pressed to ignore. No writer is better suited to describe the unspeakable extremes of this modern Babylon, and no generation more likely to see itself reflected in the sharp, glittering surfaces of Thrill City.... $6.95/411-9

RHINOCEROS BOOKS

SEASON OF THE WITCH

"A future in which it is technically possible to transfer the total mind...of a rapist killer into the brain dead but physically living body of his female victim. Remarkable for intense psychological technique. There is eroticism but it is necessary to mark the differences between the sexes and the subtle altering of a man into a woman."　　　　　　　　　*—The Science Fiction Critic*　$6.95/268-X

JOHN WARREN

THE TORQUEMADA KILLER

Detective Eva Hernandez has finally gotten her first "big case": a string of vicious murders taking place within New York's SM community. Piece by piece, Eva assembles the evidence, revealing a picture of a world misunderstood and under attack—and gradually comes to understand her own place within it. A hot, edge-of-the-seat thriller.　　　　　　　　$6.95/367-8

THE LOVING DOMINANT

Everything you need to know about an infamous sexual variation—and an unspoken type of love. Mentor—a longtime player in the dominance/submission scene—guides readers through this world and reveals the too-often hidden basis of the D/S relationship: care, trust and love.　　　　$6.95/218-3

GARY BOWEN

DIARY OF A VAMPIRE

"Gifted with a darkly sensual vision and a fresh voice, [Bowen] is a writer to watch out for."　　　　　　　　　　　　　*—Cecilia Tan*

The chilling, arousing, and ultimately moving memoirs of an undead—but all too human—soul. Bowen's Rafael, a red-blooded male with an insatiable hunger for the same, is the perfect antidote to the effete malcontents haunting bookstores today. *Diary of a Vampire* marks the emergence of a bold and brilliant vision, firmly rooted in past *and* present.　　　　$6.95/331-7

GRANT ANTREWS

SUBMISSIONS

Once again, Antrews portrays the very special elements of the dominant/submissive relationship with restraint—this time with the story of a lonely man, a winning lottery ticket, and a demanding dominatrix. One of erotica's most discerning writers.　　　　　　　　　　　　　　　　$6.95/207-8

MY DARLING DOMINATRIX

When a man and a woman fall in love, it's supposed to be simple, uncomplicated, easy—unless that woman happens to be a dominatrix. Curiosity gives way to unblushing desire in this story of one man's awakening to the joys to be experienced as the willing slave of a powerful woman.　　$6.95/447-X

LAURA ANTONIOU WRITING AS "SARA ADAMSON"

THE TRAINER

The long-awaited conclusion of Adamson's stunning Marketplace Trilogy! The ultimate underground sexual realm includes not only willing slaves, but the exquisite trainers who take submissives firmly in hand. And it is now the time for these mentors to divulge their own secrets—the desires that led them to become the ultimate figures of authority.　　　　　$6.95/249-3

THE SLAVE

The second volume in the "Marketplace" trilogy. *The Slave* covers the experience of one talented submissive who longs to join the ranks of those who have proven themselves worthy of entry into the Marketplace. But the price, while delicious, is staggeringly high....　　　　　　　　　$6.95/173-X

RHINOCEROS BOOKS

THE MARKETPLACE

"Merchandise does not come easily to the Marketplace.... They haunt the clubs and the organizations.... Some are so ripe that they intimidate the poseurs, the weekend sadists and the furtive dilettantes who are so endemic to that world. And they never stop asking where we may be found...." $6.95/3096-2

THE CATALYST

After viewing a controversial, explicitly kinky film full of images of bondage and submission, several audience members find themselves deeply moved by the erotic suggestions they've seen on the screen. "Sara Adamson's" sensational debut volume! $5.95/328-7

DAVID AARON CLARK

SISTER RADIANCE

A chronicle of a most desperate obsession—rife with Clark's trademark vivisections of contemporary desires, sacred and profane. The vicissitudes of lust and romance are examined against a backdrop of urban decay and shallow fashionability in this testament to the allure—and inevitability—of the forbidden. $6.95/215-9

THE WET FOREVER

The story of Janus and Madchen—a small-time hood and a beautiful sex worker on the run from one of the most dangerous men they have ever known—*The Wet Forever* examines themes of loyalty, sacrifice, redemption and obsession amidst Manhattan's sex parlors and underground S/M clubs. Its combination of sex and suspense led Terence Sellers to proclaim it "evocative and poetic." $6.95/117-9

ALICE JOANOU

BLACK TONGUE

"Joanou has created a series of sumptuous, brooding, dark visions of sexual obsession, and is undoubtedly a name to look out for in the future."
—*Redeemer*
Another seductive book of dreams from the author of the acclaimed *Tourniquet*. Exploring lust at its most florid and unsparing, *Black Tongue* is a trove of baroque fantasies—each redolent of the forbidden. Joanou creates some of erotica's most mesmerizing and unforgettable characters. $6.95/258-2

TOURNIQUET

A heady collection of stories and effusions from the pen of one our most dazzling young writers. Strange tales abound, from the story of the mysterious and cruel Cybele, to an encounter with the sadistic entertainment of a bizarre after-hours cafe. A sumptuous feast for all the senses. $6.95/3060-1

CANNIBAL FLOWER

"She is waiting in her darkened bedroom, as she has waited throughout history, to seduce the men who are foolish enough to be blinded by her irresistible charms.... She is the goddess of sexuality, and *Cannibal Flower* is her haunting siren song."—Michael Perkins $4.95/72-6

MICHAEL PERKINS

EVIL COMPANIONS

Set in New York City during the tumultuous waning years of the Sixties, *Evil Companions* has been hailed as "a frightening classic." A young couple explores the nether reaches of the erotic unconscious in a shocking confrontation with the extremes of passion. With a new introduction by science fiction legend Samuel R. Delany. $6.95/3067-9

THE MARKETPLACE

SARA ADAMSON

$6.95 (CANADA $7.95) • RHINOCEROS BOOKS

"Compelling, charged with electricity,
pleasurable as leather rain."

---Kitty Tsui

RHINOCEROS BOOKS

AN ANTHOLOGY OF CLASSIC ANONYMOUS EROTIC WRITING

Michael Perkins, acclaimed authority on erotic literature, has collected the very best passages from the world's erotic writing—especially for Rhino*ceros* readers. "Anonymous" is one of the most infamous bylines in publishing history—and these steamy excerpts show why! An incredible smorgasbord of forbidden delights. **$6.95/140-3**

THE SECRET RECORD: Modern Erotic Literature

Michael Perkins surveys the field with authority and unique insight. Updated and revised to include the latest trends, tastes, and developments in this misunderstood and maligned genre. **$6.95/3039-3**

HELEN HENLEY

ENTER WITH TRUMPETS

Helen Henley was told that women just don't write about sex—much less the taboos she was so interested in exploring. So Henley did it alone, flying in the face of "tradition," by producing *Enter With Trumpets*, a touching tale of arousal and devotion in one couple's kinky relationship. A mature—and decidedly "adult"—romance. **$6.95/197-7**

PHILIP JOSE FARMER

FLESH

Space Commander Stagg explored the galaxies for 800 years. Upon his return, the hero Stagg is made the centerpiece of an incredible public ritual—one that will repeatedly take him to the heights of ecstasy, and inexorably drag him toward the depths of hell. **$6.95/303-1**

A FEAST UNKNOWN

"Sprawling, brawling, shocking, suspenseful, hilarious..."
—Theodore Sturgeon

Farmer's supreme anti-hero returns. "I was conceived and born in 1888." Slowly, Lord Grandrith—armed with the belief that he is the son of Jack the Ripper—tells the story of his remarkable and unbridled life. His story begins with his discovery of the secret of immortality.... **$6.95/276-0**

THE IMAGE OF THE BEAST

Herald Childe has seen Hell, glimpsed its horror in an act of sexual mutilation. Childe must now find and destroy an inhuman predator through the streets of a polluted and decadent Los Angeles of the future. One clue after another leads Childe to an inescapable realization about the nature of sex and evil.... **$6.95/166-7**

LEOPOLD VON SACHER-MASOCH

VENUS IN FURS

This classic 19th century novel is the first uncompromising exploration of the dominant/submissive relationship in literature. The alliance of Severin and Wanda epitomizes Sacher-Masoch's dark obsession with a cruel, controlling goddess and the urges that drive the man held in her thrall. Includes the letters exchanged between Sacher-Masoch and Emilie Mataja, an aspiring writer he sought as the avatar of his forbidden desires. **$6.95/3089-X**

SOPHIE GALLEYMORE BIRD

MANEATER

Through a bizarre act of creation, a man attains the "perfect" lover—by all appearances a beautiful, sensuous woman, but in reality something far darker. Once brought to life she will accept no mate, seeking instead the prey that will sate her hunger for vengeance. A biting take on the war of the sexes, this debut goes for the jugular of the "perfect woman" myth. **$6.95/103-9**

RHINOCEROS BOOKS

LIESEL KULIG

LOVE IN WARTIME
An uncompromising look at the politics, perils and pleasures of sexual power. Madeleine knew that the handsome SS officer was a dangerous man, but she was just a cabaret singer in Nazi-occupied Paris, trying to survive in a perilous time. When Josef fell in love with her, he discovered that a beautiful and amoral woman can sometimes be more dangerous than a highly skilled soldier.
$6.95/3044-X

MASQUERADE BOOKS

TARNSMAN OF GOR
John Norman

This legendary—and controversial—series returns! *Tarnsman* finds Tarl Cabot transported to Counter-Earth, better known as Gor. He must quickly accustom himself to the ways of this world, including the caste system which exalts some as Priest-Kings or Warriors, and debases others as slaves. A spectacular world unfolds in this first volume of John Norman's million-selling Gorean series.
$6.95/486-0

KISS ME, KATHERINE
Chet Rothwell

Husband—or slave? Beautiful Katherine can hardly believe her luck. Not only is she married to the charming and oh-so-agreeable Nelson, she's free to live out all her erotic fantasies with other men as well. Katherine has discovered Nelson to be far more devoted than the average spouse—and the duo soon begin exploring a relationship that could prove more demanding than marriage!
$5.95/410-0

THE STONED APOCALYPSE
Marco Vassi
"Marco Vassi is our champion sexual energist."
—*VLS*

During his lifetime, Marco Vassi was hailed as America's premier erotic writer and most worthy successor to Henry Miller. His work was praised by writers as diverse as Gore Vidal and Norman Mailer, and his reputation was worldwide. *The Stoned Apocalypse* is Vassi's autobiography, financed by the other groundbreaking erotic writing that made him a cult sensation. Chronicling a crosscountry trip on America's erotic byways, it offers a rare glimpse of a generation's sexual imagination.
$5.95/401-1

TABITHA'S TEASE
Robin Wilde

The Valentine Academy: an ultra-exclusive, all-girl institution, soon to receive its first male charge. When poor Robin arrives, he finds himself subject to the tortuous teasing of Tabitha—the Academy's most notoriously domineering coed. What Robin doesn't realize—but soon learns—is that Tabitha is pledgemistress of a secret sorority dedicated to enslaving young men. Soon he finds himself the utterly helpless (and wildly excited) captive of Tabitha & Company's weird desires!
$5.95/387-2

HELLFIRE
Charles G. Wood

A vicious murderer is running amok in New York's sexual underground—and Nick O'Shay, a virile detective with the NYPD, plunges deep into the case. He soon becomes embroiled in an elusive world of fleshly extremes, hunting a madman seeking to purge America with fire and blood sacrifices. An incredible, edge-of-the-seat thriller.
"[Wood] betrays a photographer's eye for tableau and telling detail in his evocation of the larger-than-life figures of the late-'70s to mid-'80s sexual demimonde." —*David Aaron Clark, author of The Wet Forever*
$5.95/358-9

MASQUERADE BOOKS

PIRATE'S SLAVE *Erica Bronte*
Lovely young Erica is stranded in a country where lust knows no bounds. Desperate to escape, she finds herself trading her firm, luscious body to any and all men willing and able to help her. Her adventure has its ups and downs, ins and outs—all to the undeniable pleasure of lusty Erica! $5.95/376-7

THE MISTRESS OF CASTLE ROHMENSTADT
Olivia M. Ravensworth
Lovely Katherine inherits a secluded European castle from a mysterious relative. Upon arrival she discovers, much to her delight, that the castle is a haven of sensual pleasure. Katherine learns to shed her inhibitions and enjoy her new home's many delights. $5.95/372-4

COMPLIANCE *N. Whallen*
Fourteen stories exploring the pleasures of release. Characters from many walks of life learn to trust in the skills of others, only to experience the thrilling liberation of submission. Here are the real joys to be found in some of the most forbidden sexual practices around.... $5.95/356-2

LA DOMME: A DOMINATRIX ANTHOLOGY *Edited by Claire Baeder*
A steamy smorgasbord of female domination! Erotic literature has long been filled with heartstopping portraits of domineering women, and now the most memorable come together in one beautifully brutal volume. $5.95/366-X

THE GEEK *Tiny Alice*
"An adventure novel told by a sex-bent male mini-pygmy. This is an accomplishment of which anybody may be proud."—Philip José Farmer

The Geek is told from the point of view of, well, a chicken, who reports on the various perversities he witnesses as part of a traveling carnival. When a gang of renegade lesbians kidnaps Chicken and his geek, all hell breaks loose. A strange tale, filled with outrageous erotic oddities. $5.95/341-4

SEX ON THE NET *Charisse van der Lyn*
Electrifying erotica from one of the Internet's hottest and most widely read authors. Encounters of all kinds—straight, lesbian, dominant/submissive and all sorts of extreme passions—are explored in thrilling detail. Discover what's turning on hackers from coast to coast! $5.95/399-6

BEAUTY OF THE BEAST *Carole Remy*
A shocking tell-all, written from the point-of-view of a prize-winning reporter. And what reporting she does! All the secrets of an uninhibited life are revealed, and each lusty tableau is painted in glowing colors. Join in—and reap the rewards of her extensive background in Erotic Affairs! $5.95/332-5

NAUGHTY MESSAGE *Stanley Carten*
Wesley Arthur, a withdrawn computer engineer, discovers a lascivious message on his answering machine. Aroused beyond his wildest dreams by the unmentionable acts described, Wesley becomes obsessed with tracking down the woman behind the seductive voice. His search takes him through strip clubs and no-tell motels—and finally to his randy reward.... $5.95/333-3

The Marquis de Sade's JULIETTE *David Aaron Clark*
The Marquis de Sade's infamous Juliette returns—and emerges as the most perverse and destructive nightstalker modern New York will ever know. Under this domina's tutelage, two women come to know torture's bizarre attractions as they grapple with the price of Juliette's promise of immortality.
Praise for Dave Clark:
"David Aaron Clark has delved into one of the most sensationalistically taboo aspects of eros, sadomasochism, and produced a novel of unmistakable literary imagination and artistic value." —Carlo McCormick, *Paper*
$5.95/240-X

MASQUERADE BOOKS

BLUE TANGO   *Hilary Manning*

Ripe and tempting Julie is haunted by the sounds of extraordinary passion beyond her bedroom wall. Alone, she fantasizes about taking part in the amorous dramas of her hosts, Claire and Edward. When she finds a way to watch the nightly debauch, her curiosity turns to full-blown lust! $4.95/3037-7

LOUISE BELHAVEL

FRAGRANT ABUSES

The saga of Clara and Iris continues as the now-experienced girls enjoy themselves with a new circle of worldly friends whose imaginations match their own. Perversity follows the lusty ladies around the globe! $4.95/88-2

DEPRAVED ANGELS

The final installment in the incredible adventures of Clara and Iris. Together with their friends, lovers, and worldly acquaintances, Clara and Iris explore the frontiers of depravity at home and abroad. $4.95/92-0

TITIAN BERESFORD

THE WICKED HAND

With a special Introduction by *Leg Show*'s Dian Hanson. A collection of fanciful fetishistic tales featuring the absolute subjugation of men by lovely, domineering women. From Japan and Germany to the American heartland—these stories uncover the other side of the "weaker sex." $5.95/343-0

CINDERELLA

Beresford triumphs again with this intoxicating tale, filled with castle dungeons and tightly corseted ladies-in-waiting, naughty viscounts and impossibly cruel masturbatrices—nearly every conceivable method of erotic torture is explored and described in lush, vivid detail. $4.95/305-8

JUDITH BOSTON

Young Edward would have been lucky to get the stodgy old companion he thought his parents had hired for him. Instead, an exquisite woman arrives at his door, and Edward finds his compulsively lewd behavior never goes unpunished by the unflinchingly severe Judith Boston! $4.95/273-6

NINA FOXTON

An aristocrat finds herself bored by run-of-the-mill amusements for "ladies of good breeding." Instead of taking tea with proper gentlemen, naughty Nina "milks" them of their most private essences. No man ever says "No" to Nina! $5.95/443-7

A TITIAN BERESFORD READER

Wild dominatrixes, perverse masochists, and mesmerizing detail are the hallmarks of the Beresford tale—and encountered here in abundance. The very best scenarios from all of Beresford's bestsellers make this a must-have for the Compleat Fetishist. $4.95/114-4

CHINA BLUE

KUNG FU NUNS

"When I could stand the pleasure no longer, she lifted me out of the chair and sat me down on top of the table. She then lifted her skirt. The sight of her perfect legs clad in white stockings and a petite garter belt further mesmerized me. I lean particularly towards white garter belts." China Blue returns! $4.95/3031-8

HARRIET DAIMLER

DARLING • INNOCENCE

In *Darling*, a virgin is raped by a mugger. Driven by her urge for revenge, she searches New York in a furious sexual hunt that leads to rape and murder. In *Innocence*, a young invalid determines to experience sex through her voluptuous nurse. Two critically acclaimed novels. $4.95/3047-4

MASQUERADE BOOKS

LYN DAVENPORT

DOVER ISLAND

Off the coast of Oregon, Dr. David Kelly has planted the seeds of his dream—a Corporal Punishment Resort. Soon, many people from varied walks of life descend upon this isolated retreat, intent on fulfilling their every desire. Included in this elite gathering is Marcy Harris, who will prove the perfect partner for the lonely but lustful Doctor.... $5.95/384-8

TESSA'S HOLIDAYS

Tessa's lusty lover, Grant, makes sure that each of her holidays is filled with the type of sensual adventure most young women only dream about. What will her insatiable man dream up next? Only he knows—and he keeps his secrets until the lovely Tessa is ready to explode with desire! $5.95/377-5

THE GUARDIAN

Felicia grew up under the tutelage of the lash—and she learned her lessons well. Sir Rodney Wentworth has long searched for a woman capable of fulfilling his cruel desires, and after learning of Felicia's talents, sends for her. Upon arrival in his home, Felicia discovers that the "position" offered her is delightfully different than anything she could have expected! $5.95/371-6

P. N. DEDEAUX

THE NOTHING THINGS

More classic sorority sexcapades! Beta Beta Rho—highly exclusive and widely honored—has taken on a new group of pledges. The five women will be put through the most grueling of ordeals, and punished severely for any shortcomings—much to everyone's delight! $5.95/404-6

TENDER BUNS

Meet Marc Merlin, the wizard of discipline! In a fashionable Canadian suburb, Merlin indulges his yen for punishment with an assortment of the town's most desirable and willing women. Things come to a rousing climax at a party planned to cater to just those whims Marc is most able to satisfy.... $5.95/396-1

AKBAR DEL PIOMBO

SKIRTS

Randy Mr. Edward Champdick enters high society—and a whole lot more—in his quest for ultimate satisfaction. For it seems that once Mr. Champdick rises to the occasion, nothing can bring him down. $4.95/115-2

DUKE COSIMO

A kinky romp played out against the boudoirs, bathrooms and ballrooms of the European nobility, who seem to do nothing all day except each other. The lifestyles of the rich and licentious are revealed in all their glory. $4.95/3052-0

A CRUMBLING FAÇADE

The return of that incorrigible rogue, Henry Pike, who continues his pursuit of sex, fair or otherwise, in the most elegant homes of the most debauched aristocrats. No one can resist the irrepressible Pike! $4.95/3043-1

PAULA

This canny seductress tests the mettle of every man who comes under her spell—and every man does! $4.95/3036-9

ROBERT DESMOND

PROFESSIONAL CHARMER

A gigolo lives a life of luxury by providing his sexual services to the rich and bored. Traveling in exclusive circles, this gun-for-hire will gratify the lewdest sexual cravings! This pro leaves no one unsatisfied. $4.95/3003-2

TOP
SHELF
FOR ADULTS ONLY

TESSA'S
HOLIDAYS

LYN
DAVENPORT

MASQUERADE BOOKS

THE SWEETEST FRUIT

Connie is determined to seduce and destroy the devoted Father Chadcroft. She corrupts the unsuspecting priest into forsaking all that he holds sacred, destroys his parish, and slyly manipulates him with her smoldering looks and hypnotic aura. This Magdalene drags her unsuspecting prey into a hell of unbridled lust.

$4.95/95-5

MICHAEL DRAX

SILK AND STEEL

"He let his robe fall to the floor. She could offer no resistance as the shadowy figure knelt before her, gazing down upon her. Why would she resist? This was what she wanted all along...." $4.95/3032-6

OBSESSIONS

Victoria is determined to become a model by sexually ensnaring the powerful people who control the fashion industry: Paige, who finds herself compelled to watch Victoria's conquests; and Pietro and Alex, who take turns and then join in for a sizzling threesome. $4.95/3012-1

LIZBETH DUSSEAU

TRINKETS

"Her bottom danced on the air, pert and fully round. It would take punishment well, he thought." A luscious woman submits to an artist's every whim—becoming the sexual trinket he had always desired. $5.95/246-9

THE APPLICANT

"Adventuresome young woman who enjoys being submissive sought by married couple in early forties. Expect no limits." Hilary answers an ad, hoping to find someone who can meet her needs. Beautiful Liza turns out to be a flawless mistress; with her husband Oliver, she trains Hilary to be submissive. $4.95/306-6

SPANISH HOLIDAY

She didn't know what to make of Sam Jacobs. He was undoubtedly the most remarkable man she'd ever met.... Lauren didn't mean to fall in love with the enigmatic Sam, but a once-in-a-lifetime European vacation gives her all the evidence she needs that this hot man might be the one for her.... $4.95/185-3

CAROLINE'S CONTRACT

After a life of repression, Caroline goes out on a limb. On the advice of a friend, she meets with the alluring Max Burton—a man more than willing to indulge her fantasies of domination and discipline. Caroline soon learns to love his ministrations—and agrees to a very *special* arrangement.... $4.95/122-5

MEMBER OF THE CLUB

"Deep down inside, I had the most submissive thoughts: I imagined myself under the grip of men I hardly knew. If there were a club to join, it could take my deepest dreams and make them real. My only question was how far I'd really go?" A woman finally goes all the way in a quest to satisfy her most secret hungers, joining a club where she *really* pays her dues—with any one of the many men who desire her! $4.95/3079-2

SARA H. FRENCH

MASTER OF TIMBERLAND

"Welcome to Timberland Resort," he began. "We are delighted that you have come to serve us. And...be assured that we will require service of you in the strictest sense. Our discipline is the most demanding in the world...." A tale of sexual slavery at the ultimate paradise resort. One of our bestselling titles, this trek to Timberland has ignited passions the world over—and stands poised to become one of modern erotica's legendary tales. $5.95/327-9

MASQUERADE BOOKS

RETURN TO TIMBERLAND

It's time for a trip back to Timberland, the world's most frenzied sexual resort! Prepare for a vacation filled with delicious decadence, as each and every visitor is serviced by unimaginably talented submissives. These nubile maidens are determined to make this the raunchiest camp-out ever—and succeed with the help of their rampant campers! $5.95/257-4

SARAH JACKSON

SANCTUARY

Tales from the Middle Ages. *Sanctuary* explores both the unspeakable debauchery of court life and the unimaginable privations of monastic solitude, leading the voracious and the virtuous on a collision course that brings history to throbbing life. $5.95/318-X

HELOISE

A panoply of sensual tales harkening back to the golden age of Victorian erotica. Desire is examined in all its intricacy, as fantasies are explored and urges explode. Innocence meets experience time and again. $4.95/3073-3

JOCELYN JOYCE

PRIVATE LIVES

The lecherous habits of the illustrious make for a sizzling tale of French erotic life. A widow has a craving for a young busboy; he's sleeping with a rich businessman's wife; her husband is minding his sex business elsewhere! Mind boggling sexual entanglements run throughout this tale of upper crust lust!

$4.95/309-0

CANDY LIPS

The world of publishing serves as the backdrop for one woman's pursuit of sexual satisfaction. From a fiery femme fatale to a voracious Valentino, she takes her pleasure where she can find it. Luckily for her, it's most often found between the legs of the most licentious lovers! $4.95/182-9

KIM'S PASSION

The life of a beautiful English seductress. Kim leaves India for London, where she quickly takes upon herself the task of bedding every woman in sight! $4.95/162-4

CAROUSEL

A young American woman leaves her husband when she discovers he is having an affair with their maid. She then becomes the sexual plaything of various Parisian voluptuaries. Wild sex, low morals! $4.95/3051-2

SABINE

There is no one who can refuse her once she casts her spell; no lover can do anything less than give up his whole life for her. Great men and empires fall at her feet; but she is haughty, distracted, impervious. It is the eve of WWII, and Sabine must find a new lover equal to her talents. $4.95/3046-6

THE WILD HEART

A luxury hotel is the setting for this artful web of sex, desire, and love. A newlywed sees sex as a duty, while her hungry husband tries to awaken her to its tender joys. A Parisian entertains wealthy guests for the love of money. Each episode provides a new variation in this lusty Grand Hotel! $4.95/3007-5

JADE EAST

Laura, passive and passionate, follows her husband Emilio to Hong Kong. He gives her to Wu Li, a connoisseur of sexual perversions, who passes her on to Madeleine, a flamboyant lesbian. Madeleine's friends make Laura the centerpiece in Hong Kong's infamous underground orgies. Steamy sluts for sale!

$4.95/60-2

MASQUERADE BOOKS

RAWHIDE LUST

Diana Beaumont, the young wife of a U.S. Marshal, is kidnapped as an act of vengeance against her husband. Jack Beaumont sets out on a long journey to get his wife back, but finally catches up with her trail only to learn that she's been sold into white slavery in Mexico. $4.95/55-6

THE JAZZ AGE

The time: the Roaring Twenties. A young attorney becomes suspicious of his mistress, while his wife has a fling with a lesbian lover. *The Jazz Age* is a romp of erotic realism from the heyday of the speakeasy—when all pleasures were taken in private. $4.95/48-3

AMARANTHA KNIGHT

THE DARKER PASSIONS:
THE FALL OF THE HOUSE OF USHER

The Master and Mistress of the house of Usher indulge in every form of decadence, and are intent on initiating their guests into the many pleasures to be found in utter submission. But something is not quite right in the House of Usher, and the foundation of its dynasty begins to crack.... $5.95/313-9

THE DARKER PASSIONS: *FRANKENSTEIN*

What if you could create a living, breathing human? What shocking acts could it be taught to perform, to desire, to love? Find out what pleasures await those who play God.... $5.95/248-5

THE DARKER PASSIONS: *DR. JEKYLL AND MR. HYDE*

It is an old story, one of incredible, frightening transformations achieved through mysterious experiments. Now, Amarantha Knight explores the steamy possibilities of a tale where no one is quite who—or what—they seem. Victorian bedrooms explode with hidden demons. $4.95/227-2

THE DARKER PASSIONS: *DRACULA*

The infamous erotic retelling of the Vampire legend.
"Well-written and imaginative, Amarantha Knight gives fresh impetus to this myth, taking us through the sexual and sadistic scenes with details that keep us reading....This author shows superb control. A classic in itself has been added to the shelves." —*Divinity* $5.95/326-0

ALIZARIN LAKE

SEX ON DOCTOR'S ORDERS

A chronicle of selfless devotion to mankind! Beth, a nubile young nurse, uses her considerable skills to further medical science by offering incomparable and insatiable assistance in the gathering of important specimens. No man leaves naughty Nurse Beth's station without surrendering exactly what she needs! A guaranteed cure for all types of fever, Beth single-handedly redfines "bedside manner" for all time! $5.95/402-X

THE EROTIC ADVENTURES OF HARRY TEMPLE

Harry Temple's memoirs chronicle his amorous adventures from his initiation at the hands of insatiable sirens, through his stay at a house of hot repute, to his encounters with a chastity-belted nympho! Here's one hot stud who's always in demand. $4.95/127-6

MORE EROTIC ADVENTURES OF HARRY TEMPLE

Harry Temple's lustful adventures continue. This time he begins his amorous pursuits by deflowering the ample and eager Aurora. Harry soon discovers that his little protégée is more than able to match him at every lascivious game and very willing to display her own talents. An education in sensuality that only Harry Temple can provide! $4.95/67-X

MASQUERADE BOOKS

CLARA

The mysterious death of a beautiful, aristocratic woman leads her old boyfriend on a harrowing journey of discovery. His search uncovers a woman on a quest for deeper and more unusual sensations, each more shocking than the one before. $4.95/80-7

DIARY OF AN ANGEL

A long-forgotten diary tells the story of angelic Victoria, lured into a secret life of unimaginable depravity. "I am like a fly caught in a spider's web, a helpless and voiceless victim of their every whim." $4.95/71-8

EROTOMANIA

The bible of female sexual perversion! It's all here, everything you ever wanted to know about kinky women past and present. From simple nymphomania to the most outrageous fetishism, all secrets are revealed in this look into the forbidden rooms of feminine desire. $4.95/128-4

AN ALIZARIN LAKE READER

A selection of wicked musings from the pen of Masquerade's perennially popular author. It's all here: *Business as Usual, The Erotic Adventures of Harry Temple, Festival of Venus*, the mysterious *Instruments of the Passion*, the devilish *Miss High Heels*—and more. $4.95/106-3

MISS HIGH HEELS

It was a delightful punishment few men dared to dream of. Who could have predicted how far it would go? Forced by his sisters to dress and behave like a proper lady, Dennis finds he enjoys life as Denise much more! $4.95/3066-0

THE INSTRUMENTS OF THE PASSION

All that remains is the diary of a young initiate, detailing the twisted rituals of a mysterious cult institution known only as "Rossiter." Behind sinister walls, a beautiful young woman performs an unending drama of pain and humiliation. Will she ever have her fill of utter degradation? $4.95/3010-5

FESTIVAL OF VENUS

Brigeen Mooney fled her home in the west of Ireland to avoid being forced into a nunnery. But the refuge she found in the city turned out to be dedicated to a very different religion. The women she met there belonged to the Old Religion, devoted to the ways of sex and sacrifices. $4.95/37-8

PAUL LITTLE

THE DISCIPLINE OF ODETTE

Odette's family was harsh, but not even public humiliation could keep her from Jacques. She was sure marriage would rescue her from her family's "corrections." To her horror, she discovers that Jacques, too, has been raised on discipline. A shocking erotic coupling! $5.95/334-1

THE PRISONER

Judge Black has built a secret room below a penitentiary, where he sentences the prisoners to hours of exhibition and torment while his friends watch. Judge Black's House of Corrections is equipped with one purpose in mind: to administer his own brand of rough justice! $5.95/330-9

TUTORED IN LUST

This tale of the initiation and instruction of a carnal college co-ed and her fellow students unlocks the sex secrets of the classroom. Books take a back seat to secret societies and their bizarre ceremonies in this story of students with an unquenchable thirst for knowledge! $4.95/78-5

DANGEROUS LESSONS

Incredibly arousing morsels of Paul Little classics: *Tears of the Inquisition, Lust of the Cossacks, Poor Darlings, Captive Maidens, Slave Island*, even the scandalous *The Metamorphosis of Lisette Joyaux*. $4.95/32-7

MASQUERADE BOOKS

ALEXANDER TROCCHI

THONGS

"...In Spain, life is cheap, from that glittering tragedy in the bullring to the quick thrust of the stiletto in a narrow street in a Barcelona slum. No, this death would not have called for further comment had it not been for one striking fact. The naked woman had met her end in a way he had never seen before—a way that had enormous sexual significance. My God, she had been..." **$4.95/217-5**

HELEN AND DESIRE

Helen Seferis' flight from the oppressive village of her birth became a sexual tour of a harsh world. From brothels in Sydney to harems in Algiers, Helen chronicles her adventures fully in her diary. Each encounter is examined in the scorching and uncensored diary of the sensual Helen! **$4.95/3093-8**

THE CARNAL DAYS OF HELEN SEFERIS

P.I. Anthony Harvest is assigned to save Helen Seferis, a beautiful Australian who has been abducted. Following clues in her explicit diary of adventures, he pursues the lovely, doomed Helen—the ultimate sexual prize. **$4.95/3086-5**

WHITE THIGHS

A fantasy of obsession from a modern erotic master. This is the story of Saul and his sexual fixation on the beautiful, tormented Anna. Their scorching passion leads to murder and madness every time. **$4.95/3009-1**

SCHOOL FOR SIN

When Peggy leaves her country home behind for the bright lights of Dublin, her sensuous nature leads to her seduction by a stranger. He recruits her into a training school where no one knows what awaits them at graduation, but each student is sure to be well schooled in sex! **$4.95/ 89-0**

MY LIFE AND LOVES (THE 'LOST' VOLUME)

What happens when you try to fake a sequel to the most scandalous autobiography of the 20th century? If the "forgers" are two of the most important figures in modern erotica, you get a masterpiece, and THIS IS IT! One of the most thrilling forgeries in literature. **$4.95/52-1**

MARCUS VAN HELLER

TERROR

Another shocking exploration of lust by the author of the ever-popular *Adam & Eve*. Set in Paris during the Algerian War, *Terror* explores the place of sexual passion in a world drunk on violence. **$5.95/247-7**

KIDNAP

Private Investigator Harding is called in to investigate a mysterious kidnapping case involving the rich and powerful. Along the way he has the pleasure of "interrogating" an exotic dancer named Jeanne and a beautiful English reporter, as he finds himself enmeshed in the crime underworld. **$4.95/90-4**

LUSCIDIA WALLACE

KATY'S AWAKENING

Katy thinks she's been rescued after a terrible car wreck. Little does she suspect that she's been ensnared by a ring of swingers, whose tastes run to domination and unimaginably depraved sex parties. With no means of escape, Katy becomes the newest initiate in this sick private club—much to her pleasure! **$4.95/308-2**

FOR SALE BY OWNER

Susie was overwhelmed by the lavishness of the yacht, the glamour of the guests. But she didn't know the plans they had for her: sexual torture, training and sale into slavery! How many maids had been lured onto this floating prison? And how many gave as much pleasure as the newly wicked Susie? **$4.95/3064-4**

MASQUERADE BOOKS

THE ICE MAIDEN

Edward Canton has ruthlessly seized everything he wants in life, with one exception: Rebecca Esterbrook. Frustrated by his inability to seduce her with money, he kidnaps her and whisks her away to his remote island compound, where she emerges as a writhing, red-hot love slave! $4.95/3001-6

DON WINSLOW

KATERINA IN CHARGE

Two incorrigible vixens find themselves intrigued with a handsome millionaire and his stunning, imperious mistress. When invited to a country retreat by this mysterious couple, the two randy young ladies can hardly resist! But do they have any idea what they're in for? Whatever the case, Katerina will make her strange desires known very soon—and demand that they be fulfilled.... $5.95/409-7

THE MANY PLEASURES OF IRONWOOD

Seven lovely young women are employed by The Ironwood Sportsmen's club for the entertainment of gentlemen. A small and exclusive club with seven carefully selected sexual connoisseurs, Ironwood is dedicated to the relentless pursuit of sensual pleasure. $5.95/310-4

CLAIRE'S GIRLS

You knew when she walked by that she was something special. She was one of Claire's girls, a woman carefully dressed and groomed to fill a role, to capture a look, to fit an image crafted by the sophisticated proprietress of an exclusive escort agency. High-class whores blow the roof off! $5.95/440-2

GLORIA'S INDISCRETION

"He looked up at her. Gloria stood passively, her hands loosely at her sides, her eyes still closed, a dreamy expression on her face... She sensed his hungry eyes on her, could almost feel his burning gaze on her body...." $4.95/3094-6

THE MASQUERADE READERS

THE COMPLETE EROTIC READER

The very best in erotic writing together in a wicked collection sure to stimulate even the most jaded and "sophisticated" palates. $4.95/3063-6

INTIMATE PLEASURES

Forbidden liaisons, bizarre public displays of carnality and insatiable cravings abound in these excerpts from six bestsellers. $4.95/38-6

THE VELVET TONGUE

An orgy of oral gratification! *The Velvet Tongue* celebrates the most mouth-watering, lip-smacking, tongue-twisting action. A feast of fellatio and *soixante-neuf* awaits readers of excellent taste at this steamy suck-fest. $4.95/3029-6

A MASQUERADE READER

A sizzling sampler Strict lessons are learned at the hand of *The English Governess*. Scandalous confessions are found in *The Diary of an Angel*, and the story of a woman whose desires drove her to the ultimate sacrifice in *Thongs* completes the collection. $4.95/84-X

THE CLASSIC COLLECTION

PROTESTS, PLEASURES AND RAPTURES

Invited for an allegedly quiet weekend at a country vicarage, a young woman is stunned to find herself surrounded by shocking acts of sexual sadism. Soon, her curiosity is piqued, and she begins to explore her own capacities for cruelty —leading to an all-out search for an appropriately punishable partner. Latent depravity explodes in this tale of long-hidden desires unleashed! Soon, no one is safe from the ravages of this licentious crew. $5.95/400-3

MASQUERADE

The Yellow Room

ANONYMOUS

MASQUERADE BOOKS

SACRED PASSIONS

Young Augustus comes into the heavenly sanctuary seeking protection from the enemies of his debt-ridden father. Within these walls he learns lessons he could never have imagined and soon concludes that the joys of the body far surpass those of the spirit. $4.95/21-1

CLASSIC EROTIC BIOGRAPHIES

JENNIFER III

The further adventures of erotica's most daring heroine. Jennifer, the quintessential beautiful blonde, has a photographer's eye for detail—particularly details of the masculine variety! A raging nymphomaniac! $5.95/292-2

JENNIFER AGAIN

One of contemporary erotica's hottest characters returns, in a sequel sure to blow you away. Once again, the insatiable Jennifer seizes the day—and extracts from it every last drop of sensual pleasure! $4.95/220-5

JENNIFER

From the bedroom of an internationally famous—and notoriously insatiable—dancer to an uninhibited ashram, *Jennifer* traces the exploits of one thoroughly modern woman. $4.95/107-1

ROSEMARY LANE *J.D. Hall*

The ups, downs, ins and outs of Rosemary Lane. Raised as the ward of Lord and Lady D'Arcy, after coming of age she discovers that her guardians' generosity is boundless—as they contribute to her carnal education! $4.95/3078-4

THE ROMANCES OF BLANCHE LA MARE

When Blanche loses her husband, it becomes clear she'll need a job. She sets her sights on the stage—and soon encounters a cast of lecherous characters intent on making her path to sucksess as hot and hard as possible! $4.95/101-2

THE FURTHER ADVENTURES OF MADELEINE

Join Madeleine as she explores Paris' sexual underground. She discovers that the finest clothes may cover the most twisted personalities of all—and sexual desires that match even those of the wicked Madeleine! $4.95/04-1

KATE PERCIVAL

Kate, the "Belle of Delaware," divulges the secrets of her scandalous life, from her earliest sexual experiments to the deviations she learns to love. Nothing is secret, and no holes barred in this titillating tell-all. $4.95/3072-5

THE AMERICAN COLLECTION

LUST *Palmiro Vicarion*

A wealthy and powerful man of leisure recounts his rise up the corporate ladder and his corresponding descent into debauchery. A tale of a classic scoundrel with an uncurbed appetite for sexual power! $4.95/82-3

WAYWARD *Peter Jason*

A mysterious countess hires a tour bus for an unusual vacation. Traveling through Europe's most notorious cities, she picks up friends, lovers, and acquaintances from every walk of life in pursuit of pleasure. $4.95/3004-0

LOVE'S ILLUSION

Elizabeth Renard yearned for the body of Dan Harrington. Then she discovers Harrington's secret weakness: a need to be humiliated and punished. She makes him her slave, and together they commence a journey into depravity that leaves nothing to the imagination—*nothing!* $4.95/100-4

DANCE HALL GIRLS

The dance hall in Modesto was a ruthless trap for women of all ages. They learned to dance under the tutelage of sexual professionals. So grateful were they for the attention, they opened their hearts and their legs! $4.95/44-0

THE RELUCTANT CAPTIVE

Kidnapped by ruthless outlaws who kill her husband and burn their prosperous ranch, Sarah's journey takes her from the bordellos of the Wild West to the bedrooms of Boston, where she's bought by a stranger from her past. The ultimate erotic road novel! $4.95/3022-9

CHARLES HENRI FORD & PARKER TYLER

THE YOUNG AND EVIL

"The Young and Evil *creates [its] generation as* This Side of Paradise *by Fitzgerald created his generation.*" —Gertrude Stein

"*The first candid, gloves-off account of more or less professional young homosexuals.*" —Louis Kronenberger, *New Republic*

An infamous novel returns. Originally published in 1933, *The Young and Evil* was an immediate sensation due to its unprecedented portrayal of young gay artists living in New York's notorious Greenwich Village. From flamboyant drag balls to squalid bohemian flats, Ford & Tyler's characters followed love and art wherever it led them—with a frankness that had the novel banned for many years. $12.95/431-3

SHAR REDNOUR, EDITOR

VIRGIN TERRITORY

An anthology of writing by women about their first-time erotic experiences with other women. From the longings and ecstasies of awakening dykes to the sometimes awkward pleasures of sexual experimentation on the edge, each of these true stories reveals a different, radical perspective on one of the most traditional subjects around: virginity. $12.95/457-7

HEATHER FINDLAY, EDITOR

A MOVEMENT OF EROS: 25 Years of Lesbian Erotica

One of the most scintillating overviews of lesbian erotic writing ever published. Heather Findlay has assembled a roster of stellar talents, each represented by their best work. Tracing the course of the genre from its pre-Stonewall roots to its current renaissance, Findlay examines such diverse talents as Jewelle Gomez, Chrystos, Pat Califia and Linda Smukler, placing them within the context of lesbian community and politics. $12.95/421-6

MICHAEL BRONSKI, EDITOR

FLASHPOINT: The Best Gay Male Sexual Writing

A collection of the most compelling, provocative testaments to gay eros. Longtime cultural critic Michael Bronski (*Culture Clash: The Making of Gay Sensibility*) presents over twenty of the genre's best writers, exploring areas such as Enlightenment, Violence, True Life Adventures and more. Sure to be one of the most talked about and influential volumes ever dedicated to the exploration of gay sex and sexuality. $12.95/424-0

LARRY TOWNSEND

ASK LARRY

Starting just before the onslaught of AIDS, Townsend wrote the "Leather Notebook" column for *Drummer* magazine. Now, readers can avail themselves of Townsend's collected wisdom, as well as the author's contemporary commentary—a careful consideration of the way life has changed in the AIDS era. Don't miss this ultimate reference volume. $12.95/289-2

A RICHARD KASAK BOOK

CECILIA TAN, EDITOR

SM VISIONS: The Best of Circlet Press

"Fabulous books! There's nothing else like them."

         —Susie Bright, *Best American Erotica* and *Herotica 3*

A volume of the very best speculative erotica available today. Circlet Press, the first publishing house to devote itself exclusively to the erotic science fiction and fantasy genre, is now represented by the best of its very best: *SM Visions*—sure to be one of the most thrilling and eye-opening rides through the erotic imagination ever published.   **$10.95/339-2**

FELICE PICANO

DRYLAND'S END

Set five thousand years in the future, *Dryland's End* takes place in a fabulous techno-empire ruled by intelligent, powerful women. While the Matriarchy has ruled for over two thousand years and altered human language, thought and society, it is now unraveling. Military rivalries, religious fanaticism and economic competition threaten to destroy the empire from within—just as a rebellion also threatens human existence throughout the galaxy. **$12.95/279-5**

RANDY TUROFF, EDITOR

LESBIAN WORDS: State of the Art

One of the widest assortments of lesbian nonfiction writing in one revealing volume. Dorothy Allison, Jewelle Gomez, Judy Grahn, Eileen Myles, Robin Podolsky and many others are represented by some of their best work, looking at not only the current fashionability the media has brought to the lesbian "image," but important considerations of the lesbian past via historical inquiry and personal recollections. A fascinating, provocative volume.   **$10.95/340-6**

MICHAEL ROWE

WRITING BELOW THE BELT: Conversations with Erotic Authors

Journalist Michael Rowe interviewed the best erotic writers—both those well-known for their work in the field and those just starting out—and presents the collected wisdom in *Writing Below the Belt*. Rowe speaks frankly with cult favorites such as Pat Califia, crossover success stories like John Preston, and up-and-comers Michael Lowenthal and Will Leber.   **$19.95/363-5**

EURYDICE

f/32

"It's wonderful to see a woman…celebrating her body and her sexuality by creating a fabulous and funny tale."

         —Kathy Acker

With the story of Ela (whose name is a pseudonym for orgasm), Eurydice won the National Fiction competition sponsored by Fiction Collective Two and Illinois State University. A funny, disturbing quest for unity, *f/32* prompted Frederic Tuten to proclaim "almost any page…redeems us from the anemic writing and banalities we have endured in the past decade…"   **$10.95/350-3**

RUSS KICK

OUTPOSTS:
A Catalog of Rare and Disturbing Alternative Information

A huge, authoritative guide to some of the most bizarre publications available today! Rather than simply summarize the plethora of opinions crowding the American scene, Kick has tracked down and compiled reviews of work penned by political extremists, conspiracy theorists, hallucinogenic pathfinders, sexual explorers, and others. Each review is followed by ordering information for the many readers sure to want these publications for themselves.   **$18.95/0202-8**

A RICHARD KASAK BOOK

LUCY TAYLOR

UNNATURAL ACTS

"A topnotch collection..." —*Science Fiction Chronicle*

A remarkable debut volume from an acclaimed writer. *Unnatural Acts* plunges deep into the dark side of the psyche, far past all pleasantries and prohibitions, and brings to life a disturbing vision of erotic horror. Unrelenting angels and hungry gods play with souls and bodies in Taylor's murky cosmos: where heaven and hell are merely differences of perspective; where redemption and damnation lie behind the same shocking acts. A frightening look at human desire. $12.95/181-0

SAMUEL R. DELANY

THE MOTION OF LIGHT IN WATER

"A very moving, intensely fascinating literary biography from an extraordinary writer. Thoroughly admirable candor and luminous stylistic precision; the artist as a young man and a memorable picture of an age."

—William Gibson

Award-winning author Samuel R. Delany's riveting autobiography covers the early years of one of science fiction's most important voices. Delany paints a vivid and compelling picture of New York's East Village in the early '60s—a time of unprecedented social transformation. *The Motion of Light in Water* traces the roots of one of America's most innovative writers. $12.95/133-0

THE MAD MAN

For his thesis, graduate student John Marr researches the life and work of the brilliant Timothy Hasler: a philosopher whose career was cut tragically short over a decade earlier. Marr soon begins to believe that Hasler's death might hold some key to his own life as a gay man in the age of AIDS.

What Delany has done here is take the ideas of the Marquis de Sade one step further, by filtering extreme and obsessive sexual behavior through the sieve of post-modern experience....   —*Lambda Book Report*

Delany develops an insightful dichotomy between [his protagonist]'s two worlds: the one of cerebral philosophy and dry academia, the other of heedless, 'impersonal' obsessive sexual extremism. When these worlds finally collide ... the novel achieves a surprisingly satisfying resolution....   —*Publishers Weekly* $23.95/193-4/hardcover

KATHLEEN K.

SWEET TALKERS

Kathleen K., a highly successful businesswoman, opens up her diary for a rare peek at her day-to-day life. What makes Kathleen's story unusual is the nature of her business. Kathleen K. is a popular phone sex operator—and she now reveals a number of secrets and surprises. Far from being a sleazy, underground scam, the service Kathleen provides often speaks to the lives of its customers with a compassion they receive nowhere else. $12.95/192-6

ROBERT PATRICK

TEMPLE SLAVE

You must read this book.   —Quentin Crisp

This is nothing less than the secret history of the most theatrical of theaters, the most bohemian of Americans and the most knowing of queens. Patrick writes with a lush and witty abandon, as if this departure from the crafting of plays has energized him. Temple Slave is also one of the best ways to learn what it was like to be fabulous, gay, theatrical and loved in a time at once more and less dangerous to gay life than our own. —*Genre*

$12.95/191-8

A RICHARD KASAK BOOK

PAT CALIFIA

SENSUOUS MAGIC

A new classic, destined to grace the shelves of anyone interested in contemporary sexuality—as well as all those interested in owning the ultimate SM "how-to" volume.

Sensuous Magic is clear, succinct and engaging even for the reader for whom S/M isn't the sexual behavior of choice.... Califia's prose is soothing, informative and non-judgmental—she both instructs her reader and explores the territory for them.... When she is writing about the dynamics of sex and the technical aspects of it, Califia is the Dr. Ruth of the alternative sexuality set.... —*Lambda Book Report*

Don't take a dangerous trip into the unknown—buy this book and know where you're going! —*SKIN TWO* $12.95/**424-0**

CARO SOLES

MELTDOWN!

An Anthology of Erotic Science Fiction and Dark Fantasy for Gay Men

Editor Caro Soles has put together one of the most explosive collections of gay erotic writing ever published. *Meltdown!* contains the very best examples of this increasingly popular sub-genre: stories meant to shock and delight, to send a shiver down the spine and start a fire down below. $12.95/**203-5**

LARS EIGHNER

ELEMENTS OF AROUSAL

Acclaimed writer Lars Eighner develops a guideline for success with one of publishing's best kept secrets: the novice-friendly field of gay erotic writing. Eighner details his craft, providing the reader with sure advice. Because that's what *Elements of Arousal* is all about: the application and honing of the writer's craft, which brought Eighner fame with not only the steamy *Bayou Boy*, but the illuminating *Travels with Lizbeth*. $12.95/**230-2**

MICHAEL PERKINS

COMING UP: THE WORLD'S BEST EROTIC WRITING

Author and critic Michael Perkins has scoured the field of erotic writing to produce this anthology sure to challenge the limits of even the most seasoned reader. Using the same sharp eye and transgressive instinct that have established him as America's leading commentator on sexually explicit fiction, Perkins here presents the cream of the current crop. $12.95/**370-8**

THE GOOD PARTS: An Uncensored Guide to Literary Sexuality

Michael Perkins, one of America's only critics to regularly scrutinize sexual literature, presents sex as seen in the pages of over 100 major volumes from the past twenty years. *The Good Parts* takes an uncensored look at the complex issues of sexuality investigated by so much modern literature. $12.95/**186-1**

MARCO VASSI

THE STONED APOCALYPSE

" ...Marco Vassi is our champion sexual energist."—*VLS*

During his lifetime, Marco Vassi was hailed as America's premier erotic writer. His reputation was worldwide. *The Stoned Apocalypse* is Vassi's autobiography, financed by his other groundbreaking erotic writing. $12.95/**132-2**

A DRIVING PASSION

While the late Marco Vassi was primarily known and respected as a novelist, he was also an effective and compelling speaker. *A Driving Passion* collects the wit and insight Vassi brought to his lectures, and distills the philosophy—including the concept of Metasex—that made him an underground sensation. $12.95/**134-9**

BADBOY BOOKS

CLAY CALDWELL

ASK OL' BUDDY

Set in the underground SM world, Caldwell takes you on a journey of discovery—where men initiate one another into the secrets of the rawest sex of all. And when each stud's initiation is complete, he takes his places among the masters—eager to take part in the training of another hungry soul.... $5.95/346-5

SERVICE, STUD

The setting is the Los Angeles of a distant future. Here the all-male populace is divided between the served and the servants—an arrangement guaranteeing the erotic satisfaction of all involved.. $5.95/336-8

STUD SHORTS

"If anything, Caldwell's charm is more powerful, his nostalgia more poignant, the horniness he captures more sweetly, achingly acute than ever."
—Aaron Travis

A new collection of this legendary writer's latest sex-fiction. With his customary candor, Caldwell tells all about cops, cadets, truckers, farmboys (and many more) in these dirty jewels. $5.95/320-1

QUEERS LIKE US

A very special delivery. For years, the name Clay Caldwell has been synonymous with the hottest, most finely crafted gay tales available. *Queers Like Us* is one of his best: the story of a randy mailman's trek through a landscape of willing, available studs. $4.95/262-0

CLAY CALDWELL/LARS EIGHNER

QSFx2

A volume of the wickedest, wildest, other-worldliest yarns from two master storytellers. Caldwell and Eighner take a trip to the furthest reaches of the sexual imagination, sending back stories proving that as much as things change, one thing will always remain the same.... $5.95/278-7

LARS EIGHNER

WHISPERED IN THE DARK

Hailed by critics, Eighner continues to produce gay fiction whose quality rivals the best in the genre. *Whispered in the Dark* demonstrates Eighner's unique combination of strengths: poetic descriptive power, an unfailing ear for dialogue, and a finely tuned feeling for the nuances of male passion. $5.95/286-8

AMERICAN PRELUDE

Praised by the *New York Times*, Eighner is widely recognized as one of our best, most exciting gay writers. What the *Times* won't admit, however, is that he is also one of gay erotica's true masters. Scalding heat blends with wry emotion in this red-blooded bedside volume. $4.95/170-5

DAVID LAURENTS, EDITOR

WANDERLUST: HOMOEROTIC TALES OF TRAVEL

A volume dedicated to the special pleasures of faraway places. Gay men have always had a special interest in travel—and not only for the scenic vistas. *Wanderlust* celebrates the freedom of the open road, and the allure of men who stray from the path.... $5.95/395-3

THE BADBOY BOOK OF EROTIC POETRY

Over fifty of gay literature's biggest talents are here represented by their hottest verse. Erotic poetry has long been considered the *enfant terrible* of serious literature. *The Badboy Book of Erotic Poetry* aims at rectifying this situation,restoring eros to its rightful place in contemporary gay writing.$5.95/382-1

Lars Eighner

American Prelude

AUTHOR OF
TRAVELS* with *LIZBETH

BADBOY BOOKS

LARRY TOWNSEND

LEATHER AD: S

The second half of Larry Townsend's acclaimed tale of lust through the personals. This time around, the story's told from a Top's perspective. A simple ad generates responses from the eccentric to the exceptional, and one lucky man finds himself in the enviable position of putting his studly applicants through their paces..... $5.95/407-0

LEATHER AD: M

John's curious about what goes on between the leatherclad men he's seen and fantasized about. After receiving little encouragement from friends, he takes out a personal ad—and starts a journey of self-discovery that will leave no part of his life unchanged.... $5.95/380-5

BEWARE THE GOD WHO SMILES

Two lusty young Americans are transported to ancient Egypt—where they are taken as slaves by marauding barbarians. Soon, it seems that their own rampant libidos hold the key to freedom. $5.95/321-X

RUN, LITTLE LEATHER BOY

The classic story of one man's sexual awakening. A chronic underachiever, Wayne seems to be going nowhere. When he is sent abroad, Wayne soon finds himself bored with the everyday and increasingly drawn to the masculine intensity of a dark sexual underground. $4.95/143-8

SEXUAL ADV. OF SHERLOCK HOLMES

Holmes's most satisfying adventures, from the unexpurgated memoirs of the faithful Mr. Watson. "A Study in Scarlet" is transformed to expose Mrs. Hudson as a man in drag, the Diogenes Club as an S/M arena, and clues only Sherlock Holmes could piece together. $4.95/3097-0

AARON TRAVIS

BIG SHOTS

Two fierce tales in one electrifying volume. In *Beirut,* Travis tells the story of ultimate military power and erotic subjugation; *Kip,* Travis' hypersexed and sinister take on film noir, appears in unexpurgated form for the first time. $5.95/448-8

SLAVES OF THE EMPIRE

"[A] wonderful mythic tale. Set against the backdrop of the exotic and powerful Roman Empire, this wonderfully written novel explores the timeless questions of light and dark in male sexuality. Travis has shown himself expert in manipulating the most primal themes and images. The locale may be the ancient world, but these are the slaves and masters of our time...."
—John Preston $4.95/3054-7

MAX EXANDER

DEEDS OF THE NIGHT: Tales of Eros and Passion

From the man behind *Mansex* and *Leathersex*—two whirlwind tours of the masculine libido—comes another unrestrained volume of fantasies.$5.95/348-1

JOHN PRESTON

TALES FROM THE DARK LORD

Twelve stunning works from the man called "the Dark Lord of gay erotica." The ritual of lust and surrender is explored in all its manifestations in this triumph of authority and vision from the Dark Lord! $5.95/323-6

MR. BENSON

A classic novel from a time when there was no limit to what a man could dream of doing. Jamie is led down the path of erotic enlightenment by the magnificent Mr. Benson, learning to accept cruelty as love, anguish as affection, and this man as his master. $4.95/3041-5

HARD CANDY

PATRICK MOORE
IOWA

"Patrick Moore has...taken the classic story of the Midwest American boyhood that Hemingway, Sinclair Lewis and Sherwood Anderson made classic and he's done it fresh and shiny and relevant to our time. *Iowa* is full of terrific characters etched in acid-sharp prose, soaked through with just enough ambivalence to make it thoroughly romantic." —Felice Picano

"Moore is the Tennessee Williams of the nineties—profound intimacy freed in a compelling narrative." —Karen Finley

$6.95/423-2

RED JORDAN AROBATEAU
DIRTY PICTURES

"Red Jordan Arobateau is the Thomas Wolfe of lesbian literature...Like Wolfe's fiction, Arobateau's work overflows with vitality and pulsing life. She's a natural—raw talent that is seething, passionate, hard, remarkable." —Lillian Faderman, editor of *Chloe Plus Olivia: An Anthology of Lesbian Literature from the 17th Century to the Present*

Another red-hot tale from Red Jordan Arobateau. *Dirty Pictures* tells the story of a lonely butch tending bar—and the femme she finally calls her own. With the same precision that made *Lucy and Mickey* a breakout debut, Arobateau tells a love story that's the flip-side of "lesbian chic." $5.95/345-7

LUCY AND MICKEY

"*Lucy and Mickey*...is both deeply philosophical and powerfully erotic. A necessary reminder to all who blissfully—some may say ignorantly—ride the wave of lesbian chic into the mainstream." —Heather Findlay, editor-in-chief of *Girlfriends*

$6.95/311-2

STAN LEVENTHAL
BARBIE IN BONDAGE

A volume of probing stories from the acclaimed author of *Mountain Climbing in Sheridan Square*. Widely regarded as one of the most refreshing, clear-eyed interpreters of big city gay male life, Leventhal here provides a series of explorations of love and desire between men. *Barbie in Bondage* is a fitting tribute to the late author's unique talents. $6.95/415-1

SKYDIVING ON CHRISTOPHER STREET

"Positively addictive." —Dennis Cooper

Aside from a hateful job, a hateful apartment, a hateful world and an increasingly hateful lover, life seems, well, *all right* for the protagonist of Stan Leventhal's latest novel, *Skydiving on Christopher Street*. Having already lost most of his friends to AIDS, how could things get any worse? But things soon do, and he's forced to endure much more.... A touching and eloquent tribute to the human spirit. $6.95/287-6

THE GAUDY IMAGE *William Talsman*

"To read *The Gaudy Image* now is not simply to enjoy a great novel or an artifact of gay history—it is to see first-hand the very issues of identity and positionality with which gay men and gay culture were struggling in the decades before Stonewall. For what Talsman is dealing with...is the very question of how we conceive ourselves gay."—from the introduction by Michael Bronski $6.95/263-9

GAY COSMOS *Lars Eighner*

A title sure to appeal not only to Eighner's gay fans, but the many converts who first encountered his moving nonfiction work. Praised by the press, *Gay Cosmos* is an important contribution to the burgeoning area of Gay and Lesbian Studies—and sure to provoke many readers. $6.95/236-1

HARD CANDY

FELICE PICANO

THE LURE

"Picano does for New York gay life what Arthur Hailey did for airports and hotels. He plays out the novel's secrets brilliantly, one deliberate card at a time.... The subject matter, plus the authenticity of Picano's research are, combined, explosive. Felice Picano is one hell of a writer." —Stephen King

Noel Cummings is about to change—irrevocably. After witnessing a brutal murder, he is recruited by the police—to assist as a lure for the killer-at-large. Undercover, Noel moves deep into the freneticism of Manhattan's gay high-life—where he gradually becomes aware of the darker forces at work in his once-placid life. In addition to the mystery behind his mission, he begins to recognize changes: in his relationships with the men around him, in himself... $6.95/398-8

AMBI*DEXTROUS*

"Deftly evokes those placid Eisenhower years of bicycles, boners, and book reports. Makes us remember what it feels like to be a child..." —The Advocate

Ambi*dextrous* tells the story of Picano's youth in the suburbs of New York during the '50s. Picano's "memoir in the form of a novel" tells all: home life, school face-offs, the ingenuous sophistications of his first sexual steps. In three years' time, he's had his first gay fling—and is on his way to becoming the widely praised writer he is today. $6.95/275-2

MEN WHO LOVED ME

"Zesty...spiked with adventure and romance...a distinguished and humorous portrait of a vanished age." —Publishers Weekly

In 1966, at the tender-but-bored age of twenty-two, Felice Picano abandoned New York, determined to find true love in Europe. When the older (slightly) and wiser (vastly) Picano returns to New York at last, he plunges into the city's thriving gay community—experiencing the frenzy and heartbreak that came to define Greenwich Village society in the 1970s. Lush and warm, *Men Who Loved Me* is a matchless portrait of an unforgettable decade. $6.95/274-4

ORDERING IS EASY!

MC/VISA orders can be placed by calling our toll-free number

PHONE 800-375-2356 / FAX 212 986-7355

or mail this coupon to:

MASQUERADE DIRECT
DEPT. BMRH46, 801 2ND AVE., NY, NY 10017

BUY ANY FOUR BOOKS AND CHOOSE ONE ADDITIONAL BOOK, OF EQUAL OR LESSER VALUE, AS YOUR FREE GIFT.

QTY.	TITLE	NO.	PRICE
			FREE
			FREE

BMRH46

SUBTOTAL

We Never Sell, Give or Trade Any Customer's Name.

POSTAGE and HANDLING

TOTAL

In the U.S., please add $1.50 for the first book and 75¢ for each additional book; in Canada, add $2.00 for the first book and $1.25 for each additional book. Foreign countries: add $4.00 for the first book and $2.00 for each additional book. No C.O.D. orders. Please make all checks payable to Masquerade Books. Payable in U.S. currency only. New York state residents add 8.25% sales tax. Please allow 4-6 weeks for delivery.

NAME

ADDRESS

CITY _____ STATE _____ ZIP _____

TEL ( )

PAYMENT: ☐ CHECK ☐ MONEY ORDER ☐ VISA ☐ MC

CARD NO. _____ EXP. DATE _____